Praise for JESSICA SPEART's Rachel Porter Mysteries

"Fresh and close to the bone. [Speart's]
characters breathe with the endlessly fascinating
idiosyncrasies of living people."

Nevada Barr

"The author portrays the stark atmosphere . . .
vividly. . . . There are plenty of appealing characters,
not the least of which is Rachel herself."

Publishers Weekly

"[Speart's] mysteries take readers to all sorts of
interesting places. . . . She has a real flair for bringing
colorful characters to life on the page."

Connecticut Post

"Rachel's take-no-prisoners attitude is fun and exciting.
Plan to stay up all night!"

Glynco Observer (GA)

Other Rachel Porter Mysteries by
Jessica Speart
from Avon Books

GATOR AIDE
TORTOISE SOUP
BIRD BRAINED
BORDER PREY

JESSICA SPEART

A RACHEL PORTER MYSTERY
BLACK DELTA NIGHT

AVON BOOKS
An Imprint of HarperCollins*Publishers*

AVON BOOKS
An Imprint of HarperCollins*Publishers*
10 East 53rd Street
New York, New York 10022-5299

Copyright © 2001 by Jessica Speart
ISBN: 0-380-81041-7
www.avonbooks.com

First Avon Books paperback printing: June 2001

Avon Trademark Reg. U.S. Pat. Off. and in Other Countries, Marca Registrada, Hecho en U.S.A.
HarperCollins ® is a trademark of HarperCollins Publishers Inc.

Printed in the U.S.A.

10 9 8 7 6 5 4 3 2 1

Acknowledgments

Thanks go to USFWS Deputy Assistant Regional Director Mike Elkins, who helped open those all important research doors; to Special Agent Zach Green, for trudging through kudzu and showing me the Delta; and to Special Agent Dave Cartwright, who so generously shared his knowledge and Beanie Weenies.

I am also grateful to Adair and Jim Schippers for their Southern hospitality. And lastly, to Jayne and Kyle Creson, who not only took me into their home, but made certain that I experienced the real Memphis, from Beale Street, to Graceland, to Al Green's Full Gospel Tabernacle.

One

"**M**y daddy says this picture is worth a hundred thousand dollars!"

The snapshot was waved like a red flag in front of my face by the underage tartlet sitting next to me, who clutched a fried bologna sandwich in her other hand. The stench of greasy, seared meat filled the interior of my Ford SUV and I held my breath, trying to fight off the memory of having eaten one too many barbecued ribs last night. Oh no! Too late! She bit into the meat, causing a wave of nausea to roll from my stomach into my throat. I quickly lowered my window, despite the cold.

"But I'm gonna let you have it for just fifty thousand bucks." Wynona Hardy bargained like a seasoned pro.

I took the photo as I drove and glanced at fifty pairs of beady, camera-flashed red eyes that swam in a blackness as impenetrable as the Tennessee woods on a moonless night.

"Do you want to explain exactly what I'm looking at that's so valuable?"

"For chrissakes! They're coons, of course!" Wynona's full lips formed a well-practiced pout, her dark lashes

fluttering like a professional "virgin" whose innocence had been questioned.

"Okay, so what makes this Quik Pik photo worth
fifty thousand dollars?"

We passed a Piggly Wiggly supermarket held captive by a series of rough-and-tumble pawnshops on either side, all proudly advertising an arsenal of guns for
sale. I turned onto a narrow street where dilapidated
houses were the norm, their front yards littered with
junked cars and flat tires. Either I'd stumbled onto the
set of the old *Jeff Foxworthy Show,* or I was once again
in redneck country.

"Daddy bought those coons for next to nothing
from a holding station in Ohio." Wynona smiled slyly.
"Is that a big enough clue for you?"

It was slowly coming together. A former trapper,
Woody Hardy had turned to training and selling coon
dogs to hunters after the bottom fell out of the fur
trade. He must have decided to tip the scales in his favor during the most recent field trial, by dumping
coons in the area where his dogs would be hunting.
And to save a few bucks, he'd apparently purchased
an illegal haul of rabid critters from a greedy em-
ployee at a quarantine station. Woody probably figured they were going to be destroyed anyway, so what
did it matter how they met their Maker?

It was easy to imagine Woody releasing feverish
coons the night before the trial. They wouldn't get
very far as they stumbled along, bumping into obsta-
cles in their path. By the time morning rolled around,
any five-dollar, biscuit-eating mutt from off a front
porch could have treed the coons in no time flat. The

scam was as rank as the sandwich Wynona had just polished off.

She snatched the photo back, adding a grease stain to its surface. Then extracting a cube of bubble gum from her jeans, Wynona peeled off the worn wrapper and popped it into her mouth.

"I was gonna blackmail him, but the old bastard would probably just whack me. So you're it. Whadda ya say? Have we got a deal?"

As I hit a bump, the handcuffs dangling from the shift on my steering column caught the sun's beams, causing light to glimmer and dance on the dashboard. It proved too much for Wynona. Her fingers twitched, irresistibly drawn toward them.

"Hey! Leave those alone!" I warned, but I might as well have been Wile E. Coyote trying to fend off a speeding train. She swiped the cuffs as I swerved to stay on the road.

"Put those back!"

Wynona hooked the steel bracelets firmly around her wrists, and her manacled hands began to prance like two high-kicking Rockettes. "You know how many guys would pay good money to get hold of me like this? It's that 'women in prison' fantasy they get off on." She giggled.

I had the feeling she knew only too well what she was talking about. "What else have you got besides the snapshot?" I asked, with a sigh of resignation.

"What do you mean, what else? Isn't that enough?" She scowled.

Yeah—enough to get me laughed right out of the Memphis district attorney's office. Still, I was itching to grab Woody on something. He was a good ol' boy who believed God's creatures had been placed on this earth for only two possible reasons—to fill his belly or to bring in money to line his pockets. I'd been after him since my arrival in west Tennessee five months ago, and had yet to catch him red-handed.

"The photo alone won't do. Would you be willing to testify against him in court?"

She indignantly popped a bubble in my direction. Even her gum held the faint whiff of bologna.

"Whadda ya, crazy? Didn't you hear what I said? He'd off me without giving it a second thought!" Wynona tried to wriggle out of the handcuffs, only to discover that her wrists were stuck. "Hey! What's going on? I used to be able to get out of these things real easy!"

Wynona had spent the majority of her youth in and out of drug rehab, which was where she'd learned to become a female Houdini. It also explained the tee-shirt she now wore—a lovely little number declaring, *Rehab Is for Quitters!*

I pulled over, fished the key from my pocket, and unlocked the handcuffs. Wynona rubbed her wrists, as if embarrassed that her flight skills had become so rusty.

"So, am I getting the money or what?" she groused.

It looked like a visit to Woody Hardy was in order, and this seemed as good a time as any to drop in on him up at Reelfoot Lake. The day begged me to stay outside and play—especially since a massive pile of paperwork was waiting back at the office.

"Why do you want to turn your father in, anyway?"

Wynona grimaced in distaste. "It's that new wife of his. She musta been a contortionist in the circus, the way she's got him all twisted around her little finger. Seems her and her brats are in his will and I'm out."

She grabbed an edge of her bubble gum and stretched it as thin as a string of dental floss. "Daddy ain't cutting me outta my rightful share of money. We'll just see who wins this game!" Wynona flashed a vindictive smile.

Ah! Family discord! It often turned out to be a federal agent's best friend. I dropped Wynona at her latest boyfriend's digs and hit the road to pay Woody a visit.

Two

The top brass in the U.S. Fish and Wildlife Service seemed to have given up all hope of obedience training with me. The cold, hard fact was that I'd been hired as a token woman to fill their federal quota; they hadn't counted on my doing my job so vigorously.

There was little chance I'd ever work my way up the Service's career ladder, but I was more than happy to stay far away from headquarters, with its wing-clipping rules and regulations. Whenever there was a choice to be made between obeying the rules or protecting wildlife, I always followed my personal mantra: Damn the bureaucracy and full speed ahead.

The Service had responded by dumping me back in the South to play with the rattlers—both reptile and redneck, equally venomous. The post I was now stationed at had been vacant for the past thirteen years, and rumor said the area was too damn dangerous for a Fish and Wildlife agent—especially a female Yankee.

My new territory consisted of west Tennessee and parts of Mississippi and Kentucky. It's an area ruled by tight-knit locals whose attitude toward federal officials was, *Turn your back and you might get something in it.*

I headed for Highway 51 and shot onto the four-lane road that follows the Mississippi. The river lay to my west, and the land to my east looked as if it had been beaten by nature's rolling pin. Flat fields lay fallow, patiently waiting to be planted with soybean and cotton. Likewise idle were the fireworks stands that flew by.

The landscape gradually mutated into crosswork patches of piney woods, interrupted by occasional outposts of civilization. Bumpers Drive-In offered "5 Burgers For $5," while You All's country store attempted to lure in stray tourists with statues of obsequiously smiling black jockeys. The scenery soon degenerated into nothing but car junkyards, proof that I was in auto theft country.

I spotted a sign peppered by gunshot and swung left onto a narrow country road. Out here Confederate flags hung off Chevy pick-ups, with vehicles and drivers alike decked out in eye-catching camouflage.

Reelfoot Lake, in the northwest corner of Tennessee, has thousands of submerged cypress stumps poking up through its liquid roof. Legend has it the area was formed when an Indian chief, Reelfoot, kidnapped and married an Indian maiden against her father's wishes. In retaliation the Great Spirit angrily stamped his foot, causing the Mighty Mississippi to flow backward, the earth to shake, and the thundering sky to roar. The river swallowed up Reelfoot, his bride, and all of his people. The cypress stumps stand as memorials marking their watery graves.

Local law enforcement agents refer to the area as the Lake of a Thousand Arsonists, since the locals tend to torch the property of those they don't want around. Many evenings, flames can be seen fiercely licking a striated sky.

Reelfoot is merely eerie during the day. At night, it's absolutely ominous.

Hardy's cabin leaned alongside the road like a tuckered-out hound after a lifetime of hunting. I parked near a wire pen filled with flea-bitten mongrels who announced my arrival with welcoming howls. Just past their cage sat a broken-down trailer bearing the logo COON DOG EXPRESS. I was about to wander over when two young boys appeared to see what all the commotion was about.

Though the weather was brisk, they were perspiring hard from the game they were playing—attacking each other with tin cans held together with twine.

The younger boy dropped his weapon and idly kicked it about. "You here to buy one of Pawpaw's dawgs?" he questioned.

The other boy took advantage of the moment to bash his little brother across the head. A sharp metal edge found its mark, nicking its victim above the brow. The younger boy screamed and began pummeling his sibling into the ground, and they quickly became a blurred cloud of motion. Just as quickly, the battling stopped.

"This one here's a good dawg." The injured boy pointed to a mutt, while rubbing a dirt-covered hand across his cut.

The elder brother amused himself by swinging his tin cans at the pen, prompting the coon dogs to howl again.

"I'm not here for a dog. I just stopped by to say hello. Maybe you should get that cut cleaned up," I suggested, wondering if all little boys were walking petri dishes of bacteria.

"He'll live," scoffed his churlish sibling.

Having determined I was of little interest, both boys took off around the back of the house. I waited until they were out of sight, then opened the door of the Coon Dog Express. A musky aroma wafted out. I climbed inside and found droppings and clumps of fur littering the metal floor. While it confirmed Woody had indeed used the trailer for hauling raccoons, there was no evidence of any wrongdoing. Nothing useful like a sworn statement admitting, *"The critters inside here were rabid."*

Exiting the trailer, I made my way to the cabin and up a rickety set of steps. An old easy chair sat on the porch, its flowered upholstery faded and torn. I knocked hard on the door to be heard above the ruckus going on inside. The third knock proved to be the charm. It was answered by Woody Hardy's latest here-today, gone-tomorrow spouse.

Wife number five's dyed blond hair hung limp as a dishrag, its dark roots creeping south. A thick layer of foundation lay caked on her face, as if she never bothered to wash it off. Her hands flew to check that her dingy shirt was closed, revealing skin roughened by manual labor and chipped nails, as a screaming baby clung to her ankle, intermittently trying to scale her leg.

The girl had clearly been through her share of bad relationships. Whatever fire had once been in her eyes was now gone; the corners of her mouth turned down in a permanent state of dissatisfaction. The next thing I noticed was the prominent bulge of her tummy: Woody Hardy's young wife was pregnant again.

"Sorry to disturb you, but is your husband at home?" I asked, trying to be heard above the baby's bawling.

The girl rolled her eyes and pointed toward a room. Then she walked away, the baby dragging behind her like a dust mop. I interpreted this as an invitation to enter and walked inside, where I found Woody sprawled on a couch.

He was dressed in bib overalls, sans shirt, with a chest full of wiry hair curling over the top. Protruding out the open sides were thick rolls of flesh that undulated like two well-fed seals. His shoes had been kicked off, and his socks emitted an odious stench. They probably could have stood up and walked on their own, except for the missing toes and heels.

The decor consisted mainly of three dilapidated black-and-white TVs, each with tinfoil balls atop their rabbit-ear antennas. Hmm. Perhaps Woody was attempting to contact a higher form of intelligence. Only one set showed any sign of life, producing the squawk of a sick parrot. It apparently didn't bother Woody, who dozed, lulled by what appeared to be a nature documentary. One of his own loud snores woke him, and he caught sight of me and jumped. Then he rubbed his back on the sofa like a bear scratching against the wall of his lair.

"Hey, Porter! Whatchoo doin' in these parts?" he

asked. "Lookee there at those birdies on that animal
show. You ever seen anything so pretty in all your
damn life?" Hardy pointed his foot at the blizzard on
his TV, and then began to pick his toes. "Hell, instead
of standing here trying to scare the living daylights
out of me, you should be policing all of them critters."

Woody clearly needed a bath. Even a billy goat
wouldn't have shared a bed with him. A visible layer
of dirt and grime had formed a protective coating over
his skin. Throw a handful of grass seed on the man,
and he'd have turned into an overweight Chia Pet.

The room wasn't in much better condition. Woody
reached down for one of the Mountain Dew cans littering the floor, found one not yet empty, and took a sip.

"I'd be careful if I were you. I hear that stuff lowers
your sperm count," I dryly informed him.

"Sheeet! Don't you believe those God awful rumors. Why, you just take a look at my Tammy. She's
got one on the floor and another bun in her oven."

Maybe his wife wasn't buying the right kind of
Dew.

Woody grinned, displaying a prominent gap where
his two front teeth should have been. He could have
passed as the poster boy for a local saying: "The far-
ther south you go, the less teeth you grow."

"Southern men can drink Dew and make babies,
too!" Woody guffawed, with a slap of his knee.

I suspected too much of the stuff had gone to his
brain.

"Wasn't Tammy the name of your last wife also?" I
inquired.

Woody nodded and threw me a wink. "I call all my wives Tammy. That way I don't screw up their names when I'm all hot and in the throes of passion."

He was apparently feeling a little frisky right now; spittle had formed at the corner of his lips.

"Why Woody, you're frothing at the mouth. I hope it's not anything contagious."

Woody's smirk collapsed into an uncertain scowl. "What is that nasty-ass remark supposed to mean?"

"I heard a bunch of rabid coons were trucked into the area, and you know how I worry about you. I'd hate to think one had snuck up and given you a love bite. Then I'd have to decide whether to get you some shots or just shoot you."

"Very funny, Porter. I'm about to bust a gut," Woody sourly retorted. "I ain't heard about no coons; it's got nothing to do with me."

"Word has it *you're* the one who bought and re-leased them. That wasn't very smart, Woody. Now I'm going to have to watch every move you make." I fig-ured the least I could do was to give him the begin-nings of an ulcer.

"Let me guess who started that vicious rumor. It couldn't have been that darling little daughter of mine, now, could it?" Hardy spat. "She's just pissy 'cause she's trying to get money outta me that I ain't got, the ungrateful little bitch."

I only hoped Tammy V didn't nourish the same fi-nancial delusions. Though I couldn't imagine what Woody might possibly offer that would be worth en-during another day in his paradise.

Woody rolled off the couch and waddled to the TV,

where he switched off one set and turned on another. Bending over, he fiddled with its antennas, swiveling each the slightest bit. One quick glimpse was enough to confirm that a shirt wasn't the only item of apparel Woody was lacking. He was obviously into embracing his inner caveman these days. I just wished he'd kept the family jewels under wraps.

Woody delicately twirled the rabbit ears back and forth until the semblance of a picture appeared. Mission accomplished, he turned back to face me. "Besides, how'm I supposed to take care of my family? Why don't you tell me *that,* Miss Smarty Pants?"

The bristles on his chin angrily erupted in a quivering wave, like a throng of hostile porcupine quills.

"I ain't had no decent money since those goddamn bunny huggers slowed the fur trade to a crawl. And now there's gonna be another mouth to feed, on top of it. Meanwhile, Wynona's jerking me around for a car and Tammy's demanding a new refrigerator. Dammit to hell! I'm already working day and night doing what a man's gotta do. All I ask is gimme a market!"

He looked like he was about to pound on his chest like an angry gorilla.

"I got me a freezer full of coon, beaver, and muskrat skins outside. I got bundles of mink and fox pelts waiting to be shipped to a buyer. I can show you thousands of furs wrapped in plastic, going to waste. Hell, the only thing we're living offa are the coon dogs I'm able to sell, and now you're even trying to screw me outta that!"

I was tempted to remind Hardy of the monthly disability check he collected from his bogus claim of having a bad back, but getting kicked out of his house would only curtail my snooping.

"Free enterprise doesn't give you the right to create a rabies epidemic," I warned. "Besides, you don't want your kids to get infected, do you?"

Woody laid back down on the couch, picked up his remote, and flicked through the channels.

"I ain't done nothing wrong," he obstinately declared. "But since you know it all, why don't you take a look at my dogs and tell me if you spot the slightest sign of rabies? By the time you're through, I bet you'll end up wanting to buy one of 'em for yourself. Tell you what! I'll sell you my champion dog dirt cheap: you can have him for just twenty-thousand dollars."

Gee, like father, like daughter.

Annoyed, I gave the TV antennas a whirl, bringing a curse to Woody's lips, and then headed outside.

The sound of screams drifted from the back of the house, accompanied by the clatter of tin can weapons. I wondered if Woody's kids regularly received tetanus shots—or if Tammy V secretly hoped they'd contract lockjaw just to give her a few weeks of peace.

As I approached, the coon dogs broke into joyful song, wagging their tails and pressing against the cage. I gave each mutt a scratch, noticing that none was foaming at the mouth. The dogs began barking once more as the two boys again came hurtling toward me. This time it was the unpleasant elder sibling—Prince Charming—who'd been nailed by his brother. A trickle of blood dripped from his nose.

"Shouldn't you boys be in school?" I inquired.

"Nah. Pawpaw says he can teach us everything we need to know," answered the scrappy younger one.

Oh brother. Were these kids ever in trouble.

"So, what else do you do for fun besides beat each other up?"

"We play with Pa's traps. They're real cool! You wanna see them?" Prince Charming gallantly offered.

Who was I to turn down such an invitation? I followed the two dynamos into a wooden shack, where they headed straight for three large freezer chests.

"Pawpaw's got over a thousand traps in here!" little Spunky bragged, throwing open one of the lids.

I took a peek inside. He was right; it was filled with deadly steel contraptions.

Prince Charming roughly shoved his brother aside and removed a few of the traps from the defective freezer. "This is a double-spring coil. And this here is a one-and-a-half-long Victor."

I began to understand Hardy's homeschooling curriculum as son number one proceeded to educate me on the ways of trapping and killing God's little creatures.

"They'll catch an animal, but they won't snuff it. For that, you gotta have something Pa calls Sudden Death. It's a 130 Conibear and a real killer!" the boy explained, holding one up. "This thing's so strong, you gotta set it with tongs. Then you put it in a box with some food and wait for the action."

"Yeah! When the critter crawls inside, the trap goes *Snap! Bam! Boom!*" Spunky added, with a karate kick. "Sometimes they die with their eyes wide open, like they don't know what hit 'em, and then they look like this." The kid's eyes glazed over and his tongue lolled out of his mouth.

So much for instilling a healthy respect for all living things.

"This other freezer is where Pa stores his animal skins. He says they're worth a hundred million dollars," Prince Charming boasted.

No wonder Wynona and Tammy V thought Woody was rich.

"And this last one is filled with deer meat," the kid added, hoisting himself on to the third freezer's lid.

"What's in there?" I asked, pointing to a large refrigerator that stood by itself in the corner.

Prince Charming began to fidget. "Pa keeps his fishing bait in there."

"That's not true! Pawpaw has it filled with deer meat. We got so much there's no more room for it in the freezer," Spunky crowed.

Prince Charming shot his younger brother a dirty look. That could mean only one thing: Woody was having a very successful poaching season.

"My Pawpaw's killed *sooo* many deer that Ma has to think of a hundred different ways to cook it," Spunky bragged. "She makes deer hamburgers, deer meatloaf, and deer spaghetti. Then there's deer chops, deer steak, and deer barbecue. Tonight we're having deer Sloppy Joes for dinner."

"Shut up!" Prince Charming ordered, giving his brother a sharp rap to the head.

The little boy burst into loud tears.

I didn't want Woody to come out just when I was

making some headway. "Behave yourselves, and you can each have one of these," I bribed, holding out a couple of Snickers.

Both boys grabbed the candy as if they were snatching it out of a trap. As they stuffed the chocolate in their mouths, I opened the refrigerator and began to rummage around.

The boys hadn't exaggerated, and I began to wonder if Woody was working as the neighborhood meat market. Then my gaze fell on a large white plastic container. It peeked out from behind a partial haunch of venison, stuck in the rear of the fridge.

Sometimes you can't be sure why something strikes you as funny. God knows, my own refrigerator is chock full of things I'd just as soon forget. All I knew was that the container probably didn't hold deer meat, and was using up valuable space. That alone made me curious.

"Hey! Why are you taking all the meat out of the fridge? Pa isn't going to like that!" Prince Charming protested.

His tone plainly revealed there was something I wasn't supposed to find, and I continued to clear a path. Prince Charming bolted toward the house as Spunky jumped up and down like a hyperactive kangaroo by my side.

"Stop that! Pawpaw never lets us play in there!" the child vehemently objected. He picked up his tin can weapon and twirled it with a threatening air.

Great. I was being held captive by a maniacal munchkin.

"Put your weapon down and I'll give you the very last candy bar."

Spunky pulled on his lip while mulling the offer over. "What kind is it?"

"It's a special Mars bar with extra creamy caramel inside," I blatantly lied.

Spunky went for the bribe, and I turned back to the task at hand. I removed the last chunks of meat and pulled the bucket toward me.

It was the type of three-pound deli container in which my grandmother used to store chicken soup. I popped open the lid, half-expecting to find matzo balls and chicken grease. Instead, I discovered something of far greater value. Gleaming up at me was what could have passed for glistening black pearls, but I knew the contents were Delta Gold—more properly known as highly prized paddlefish eggs. And the last thing Woody would be using them for was bait.

An ancient species, the paddlefish dates back almost 400 million years, inhabiting the earth long before dinosaurs. Its appearance is highly unusual due to an elongated, paddle-shaped snout. Slate-gray in color, the fish once grew over six feet in length and weighed up to two hundred pounds. But that was when the species was plentiful along its migration route—the Mississippi River and its tributaries. Today they've been wiped out in four states, with only remnant populations in others, due to overexploitation from commercial fishing and habitat destruction. I felt like Mary Leakey, having stumbled upon a lead.

A toss of the genetic dice is responsible for why the paddlefish is now in more trouble than ever. Talk about having bad luck when it comes to getting stuck with the wrong relatives: paddlefish are the North

American cousin to the Russian sturgeon. In other words, they're free-floating caviar on the fin, and therefore very lucrative. While most Southern states won't allow paddlefish to be caught, Tennessee does. Still, the trade is highly regulated and seasonal, requiring a commercial fishing license along with an official permit to sell their eggs. Neither of which Hardy had, I was sure. What I did know was that this was the best time of year for poaching them. February is when female paddlefish are ripe with large, luscious eggs.

I dipped my finger in and tasted the briny roe. One of this planet's greatest survivors was near extinction, just to satisfy the feeding frenzy of connoisseurs who demand caviar spread upon their toast.

"See, Pa? I told you she was doing something bad!" Prince Charming yelled.

I was tempted to grab the kid and shake him until I got my Snickers bar back.

"I stayed to keep an eye on her, Pawpaw. Just in case she tried to get away," Spunky chimed in.

So much for loyalty. My only consolation was that the Mars bar I'd given him was stale.

Hardy ignored his miniature informants and turned to me. "I can give you some of those eggs, if you gotta hankering for them," he offered, in an innocent tone.

I finally had the opportunity to nail him!

"Why, Woody, what a wonderful surprise! I didn't know you'd become a commercial fisherman. How about letting me see your license?" I suggested pleasantly.

Woody broke into a nervous shuffle. "Hell, Porter.

You know I ain't got one of those things. It was a friend of mine who brought those eggs here. Tammy's developed a craving for salty stuff—you know, what with her condition and all."

"Sure, I understand. Just give me the name of your friend so I can pass on your regards," I countered.

Woody hitched his thumbs in his overalls and slyly grinned at me. "Okay, you got me. I've been a *baaaad* boy. But, hell, I gotta do something 'sides lay around all day eating crackers!"

I pointedly looked at the scars on his hands. They'd been created by the kickback from a double-barrel rifle. I suspected most of his time was spent poaching critters, stopping only when he ran out of shells.

"Besides, it was just one itty-bitty little paddlefish that got stuck in my net. It seemed okay to take the eggs, being that it was already dead. I figured my brother Virgil could use 'em for happy hour at his bar."

The Sho Nuf was a local dive hidden away in the backwoods, where rednecks regularly gathered to drink moonshine. Not the kind of place that catered to your caviar clientele.

"Save the tap dancing, Woody. I'm not in the mood for your crap," I warned. "If you're not dealing in paddlefish eggs, how do you know how to process them?"

Woody's mouth flew open in surprise.

Fresh roe will begin to spoil unless processed within a couple of hours. Though not a complicated procedure, it requires the use of a wire mesh screen. The eggs are gently pushed back and forth over this sieve to remove all fatty tissue and membranes, after which they're lightly salted. Only someone involved in the caviar business would have any reason to know the steps.

"While we're at it, I also have proof that you transported rabid coons over state lines," I bluffed, beginning to feel lucky.

"Bullshit!" Woody shot back, finally finding his voice. "There's no way in hell you got any proof of that!"

"Oh no? Just take a look at this." I produced a piece of coon fur with a flourish. "I found it on the floor of your trailer."

Woody began to laugh. "Well, ain't that just dandy. Pick yourself up enough of that shit and maybe you can make yourself a coonskin jacket!"

"I plan to send it off to our forensics lab. Obviously you don't realize it, but coons from Ohio have much thicker fur than their southern cousins." I stared him down.

"Dammit!" Woody mumbled, falling for my ploy.

"I figure between this piece of fur and trafficking in the eggs of a protected species, you won't have to worry about how to spend your time anymore. You'll be busy picking up litter as part of a prison gang for years."

"Is she really gonna send you to jail, Pawpaw?" Spunky began to bawl.

"Don't be such a wuss!" Prince Charming reproached, giving his brother a knuckle punch on the arm. "It'll be just like on TV, where Pa escapes and is on the run. We can even help him plan the breakout!"

"Get the hell out of here now!" Woody bellowed.

Both boys scurried through the shed door. Then Hardy turned toward me with a surly expression.

"Well, you must be feeling pretty high and mighty right about now, Porter."

Actually, I *was* feeling pretty darned good.

Woody took a pack of Redman tobacco from his pocket and bit off a plug. A bulge the size of a large tumor formed in the side of his cheek.

"I mean, especially for a low-level government lackey like yourself, who makes nothing but chump change," Hardy began to needle.

"What's the matter, Woody? Have you got something against an honest day's work?"

"Come on, Porter, we both know what your bosses think of you. From what I hear, they'd gladly send you to Siberia if they could find a cubbyhole there to put you in."

"What's your point, Woody?" I asked in annoyance, wondering where he was getting his information.

"My point is that you've been in trouble with the Service since the day you joined." Hardy chuckled. "Don't look so surprised. You'd be impressed with the sources I got. What I do know is that you ain't never going to be their golden girl. Do you really think they sent a woman down here, expecting her to handle the situation? They're probably hoping someone like me will bash your brains in with a shovel, drag your body into the delta, and make all their troubles disappear."

My heart began to beat faster as I caught sight of the metal shovel standing in the corner of the shed.

Hardy noted my glance and his smile grew even more cocky. "Don't worry, Porter. I'm not gonna knock you off. But it should make you realize that Fish and Wildlife ain't never gonna reward anything you do. Maybe it's time to reevaluate things and start planning for your future."

I was still trying to figure out where he was going with all this, when Hardy headed for the back of the shed. He pushed pieces of plywood out of the way until a foot locker sat uncovered on the floor. Woody threw the lid wide open and began to reach inside. My hand flew for the .38 I kept tucked in the waistband of my pants.

"Don't even think about trying anything funny!" I warned.

Hardy slowly turned around holding a smell metal box. Then he began to walk toward me.

"Put it down, Woody," I cautioned.

Hardy placed the receptacle on a wooden table between us.

"Now open it very slowly." I had every intention of nailing his ass to the wall should there be a handgun inside.

Woody raised the cover, allowing me a glimpse of its contents. A stash of hundred-dollar bills filled the container.

I stared at Woody in amazement, wondering what

bank he had robbed. It took a moment before the realization hit me: the caviar trade was one of the last big money markets left to be drained. I also knew there was no way in hell I could ever prove where he'd gotten the cash.

He pulled out a thick wad of moolah and pushed the pile toward me.

"Just think about it, Porter. What's gonna happen if the Service finds a way to dump your ass in the next coupla years? It'll take time to find a new job. And God knows, you don't have a husband to fall back on. Hell! Even if you stay, I'm sure you could use a little extra cash to pay some bills. If nothing else, this would make it easier to deal with that pain-in-the-ass boss of yours. You can daydream about how to spend the extra ten grand while he's chewing your ass up one side and down the other for not keeping up with your paperwork."

Woody grinned confidently—and I realized the best way to catch the man was to convince him that I was just as bad as he was.

There was no time to get permission for what I was planning. Not only that, but the chance it would ever be granted was slim. I'd pursued every other case by the seat of my pants; why should this one be any different?

If I didn't act now, the opportunity might never present itself again. I could spend the next ten years playing cat and mouse with Woody while the paddlefish disappeared—or grab the shot I was being given. Besides, I wanted to pay Woody back for his crack about my not having a husband to fall back on.

Still, I wavered, aware that I was about to take a step that could plunge me into a career abyss. My pulse raced as my hand began to inch forward. Then my fingers slowly wrapped around the money.

Three

"**Y**ou did what?! Are you out of your ever-lovin', cotton-pickin', friggin' mind? If you think you've pissed off the big boys before, they're gonna chew your ass to grass but good, this time!"

Charlie Hickok's words reverberated around the room like Hurricane Andrew. I could feel the heat rising within him; he was a human thermometer whose mercury was about to burst. I wouldn't have been surprised if his railroad cap had blasted off his head and soared into orbit.

"Didn't it ever cross your mind for just *one* nanosecond that *maybe* you should have checked with me first?" he roared.

I gave a noncommittal shrug, worried that if I said no, he'd explode into a million pieces.

Not only had I been transferred back to the South, but guess who'd been sent up from New Orleans via special express, and put in charge of me? Only one other agent had ever been in more trouble with the Service's top brass than me. But then, Charlie Hickok had a good fifteen years more experience. Given the same amount of time, I had no doubt that I could easily surpass him. The question was whether I'd still be around.

Someone in Fish and Wildlife's bureaucracy must have had one hell of a quirky sense of humor. Either that, or the powers-that-be figured if they threw us back together, we'd most likely self-destruct, knocking off two troublesome birds with one well-aimed stone. How better to get rid of two hardheaded, strong-willed agents than to let them duke it out in the Land of Dixie? Any way you cut it, it was clear they were out to get me.

Hickok continued to glower. "Are you purposely trying to kamikaze the itty-bitty pathetic scrap of a career that you still got left? I know New Yorkers have a screw or two loose, but you take the whole damn cake! I bet you never even bothered to consider what this will do to my standing in Fish and Wildlife. Did you, Bronx?"

As far as I could tell, neither of us had much of that left.

"I have no intention of blowing my pension sky-high to cover your ass on this little caper. For chrissakes! I only got another eighteen months to go!" Hickok fumed. "Goddammit, the minute they mentioned your name, I knew it meant nothing but trouble. If I had any brains, I would have put in for early retirement right then and there!"

I'd asked to be transferred from New Orleans to begin with because Charlie Hickok and I spent most of our time butting heads.

"And what was I supposed to do?" I said, launching into my defense. "Would you rather I'd simply taken the fish eggs and slapped him with a twenty-five-dollar fine? That's not how the Charlie Hickok I *used* to know would have worked it," I asserted, beginning to limber up and get off the ropes.

"He'd be ordering me back into the field right now, demanding that I ferret out the next link in the chain of command. *That* Charlie Hickok would continue to raise Cain until I learned exactly who Woody's employers were, and what they were doing with all those eggs. *That's* the man I remember working for in New Orleans. *That's* the legend I looked up to, and *that's* the type of agent I wanted to be when I joined the Service!"

Yep. My touch was coming back just fine.

Charlie narrowed his eyes, as if aware of what I was up to. "So let me get this straight. You think that passing yourself off as some sorta flimflam agent is gonna make Woody Hardy go all soft and mushy, and tell you everything you wanna know?"

If there had been a set of rattlers attached to the man's rear end, they'd have started vibrating right about now.

"Well, I got a news flash for you, Bronx. Hardy's just another bubba out there trying to catch enough paddlefish to buy his next six-pack, while dreaming about a muffler for his pick-up. All you succeeded in doing is making every poacher in the area believe you're corrupt. You just green-lighted a whole bunch of them to blast away at whatever they want. They'll figure nobody's watching, with only two of us to hold down the fort and one of us bought off. And you know what? They're absolutely right. There ain't enough of us to do the job!"

Charlie morosely hunkered his two-hundred-pound frame down into his chair.

This seemed the right moment to cheer him up. Hickok had been dragged kicking and screaming to Memphis—reason enough to make him cantankerous as a grizzly. Added to that were years of trying to do his job while juggling policy with a bunch of nitpicking government bureaucrats. A little less paperwork and a good dose of adventure might be exactly what the man needed to brighten his day. Besides, I had to confess just how far I'd gone—whether I liked it or not.

"You're wrong, Charlie. Woody's no ordinary bubba out in a fishing boat. I snagged my hook into something much bigger this time. Just take a gander at how much he paid me not to talk: this kind of money can buy an entire warehouse full of mufflers."

I pulled the stack of bills out of my bag and slapped the greenbacks down on the desk in front of him.

Hickok let loose with a low whistle as his hand went in search of his coffee cup. He nearly knocked over an enormous pile of papers, and I deftly shifted my hip to the left just in time to keep the leaning tower of files from falling down. Charlie's trembling hand latched on to his mug and he took a deep gulp.

It must have been one hell of a cup of joe; calm literally engulfed the man. My guess was that a larger than usual splash of Jack Daniels had been added to the brew.

"If Woody forked over ten grand just to buy my silence, then imagine the amount he must be raking in!" I cajoled.

Hickok opened a desk drawer and pulled out two large candy bars. He threw one my way and I gratefully caught it. Snickers always helped clear our thought processes. I was especially appreciative since Woody's ungrateful kids had cleaned out my own stash.

"Hell, money like that goes a long way toward explaining how Hardy keeps getting all those young wives." Charlie finally chuckled. "It sure ain't that ol' beer gut of his, or the value he places on personal hygiene."

A vision of Woody minus his skivvies flashed through my mind. The sight could have made me swear off men permanently, if I weren't already practically celibate.

"Man, what a sweet deal that cracker's got going," Hickok exclaimed, continuing to savor his coffee. "It don't even require much of an investment. All you need is a bubba in a boat and a gill net, and the profit return is unbelievable."

"That's right. But I think we need to aim higher than just Woody," I delicately added. "You've always said an agent has to set his sights on going after the snake's head. Only when that's been lopped off can we expect to bring an end to the trade." I took a deep breath, hoping he'd be impressed that I remembered one of his sayings. "Well, Hardy is my stepping-stone to the top. By pretending to be corrupt, I plan to find out who's pulling his strings and paying him to supply paddlefish eggs!"

I waited for Hickok to enthusiastically join in my

war cry. Instead, he continued to munch away on his candy.

"Come on, Charlie! I've heard you say it yourself: we're the thin green line out there that has to keep fighting to protect wildlife. We're the only voice they've got!"

Hickok turned a critical eye my way. "First off, you're feeling way too damn high and mighty, reminding me of my own words. I ain't lost my memory yet. Second, I never said nothing about snakes. If you're gonna spout off, Bronx, at least get your comparisons straight: it's fish. You knock out the big suckers, and all the itty-bitty fish will fall into place. And third, this ain't no kid's game you're talking about playing. Working undercover will screw with your head. It can be as addictive as narcotics, but you always feel as if you're walking on glass. It gets so that you're tiptoeing around, trying to keep your feet from getting cut. Paranoia comes with the territory. It's an occupational hazard."

He could have told me that I'd be confronted by the mother of all tarantulas, and I'd still have been determined to do it.

"You keep forgetting that I was an actress before I joined Fish and Wildlife," I reminded him.

"Yeah. And look how well *that* turned out," he sourly retorted. "This ain't no soap opera, Bronx. This is real life that we're talking about here."

I ignored the low blow.

"For God sakes, Charlie, just me give a chance! I swear that I'm a natural at this! Besides, I've already taken the first step. Why waste it? And you can always pull the plug whenever you want." I wasn't beyond begging when necessary.

"You really have enough damn ego to believe that something you do is gonna help save the paddlefish?" Hickok angrily demanded.

"Absolutely!" I responded between clenched teeth.

"Hell. Wouldn't you just know—I've gone and created another damn version of me," he muttered. "Listen here, Bronx. It don't make no difference what I think anyway. You know the top brass ain't never gonna approve this thing."

But I saw his mouth begin to twitch as he fought to hold in a grin, and I knew the rebel in him had been won over.

"Then what do you say we just forget to tell them about it for a while?" I suggested.

I received my reply as a belly laugh burst from Hickok's lips and filled the room.

Four

Having achieved a temporary victory, I plunked my laurels down on the driver's seat of my Ford Excursion and headed west for home. There was no trouble with traffic, since the upwardly mobile Beamers, Range Rovers, and Saabs were eagerly scrambling back east to the shelter of their suburban abodes.

Named after Egypt's ancient capital, Memphis sits high above the banks of the "American Nile," atop the fourth Chickasaw Bluff. A thirty-two-story stainless-steel pyramid rises over the Big Muddy like a prophetic Egyptian ghost. Its entrance is guarded by Ramses, but no entombed pharaohs lay sleeping within its womb. Instead, the structure hosts sporting events and rock concerts.

But more than anything, Memphis is a state of mind. It's here that the blues were spawned, and rock and roll exploded into rowdy, raucous being. Today, Memphis remains a crossroads where music, cultures, and people collide. Steeped in a restless and violent history, its soul drips with seduction and mystery, all wrapped up in the honeyed veneer of the Old South.

I turned onto Monroe Avenue, rolled down my window, and took a deep breath. I already knew where I wanted my ashes scattered when I left this life, so that I could equally enjoy the next: around the grounds of the Wonderbread Factory on the corner of Monroe and Lauderdale. The addictive scent of yeast filled my vehicle, and I thanked the gods of Hostess cupcakes, Pecan Swirls, Honey Buns, and Twinkies. I was so grateful that I even promised to give their wheat bread a whirl.

I passed Main Street and hit Front, where the Hernando de Soto bridge came into view. Its silver span connects Memphis to the banks of Arkansas with elongated steel limbs like those of a prima ballerina. A carnival of bright lights hung gaily from it arches, turning the bridge into a sparkling diva and transforming the muddy Mississippi into liquid shimmers of gold. Suspended above was a fiery setting sun that permeated the Southern belle of a sky with radiant beams of burnt orange, vermilion, and fuchsia.

I veered on to South Front, formerly known as Cotton Row. It was in the 1880s that Memphis emerged as the world's largest inland cotton market. The Civil War was over, Reconstruction had taken place, and cotton was crowned king. I caught up to a barge leisurely gliding down to New Orleans. These days its cargo was more likely to be petrochemicals rather than bales of cotton.

I heard the sound of historic Beale Street before I even arrived, throbbing and oozing the blues.

Oooh, my man left me and now I'm so all alone!

I slowed to pay my respects as I passed by the crown jewel of Memphis's soul, then continued on home.

I passed the community of South Bluff, its abodes flaunting lace curtains. One *oh-so-chic* townhouse fashionably displayed a shocking pink toilet, being used as a planter, out on its stoop. Another residence sported a classic orange-and-white '64 Corvette parked in its drive, looking as luscious as a Cream-sicle.

I kept driving south, beyond the hip enclaves where wealthy yuppies had begun to move in, until I arrived in the land of seedy storefronts and abandoned flop-houses—the last bastion of truly affordable rents. Parking near Big Daddy's Tattoo Parlor, I locked my vehicle and entered a red brick warehouse.

Even now I could smell the faint scent of produce that the building had once housed. I imagined piles of apples, bananas, and oranges as I began my climb up the stairs. By the time I reached the third floor, I felt sure I'd worked off my daily dose of chocolate. Not only was the hike good exercise, but it also meant I could feel totally guilt-free as I ate dessert tonight. As I began the ritual of unfastening the three locks on my door it was pulled open by my old pal Terri Tune, dressed in a bright red kimono decorated with minia-ture dancing Sumo wrestlers. Two large piña coladas were ready and waiting on a tray in his hand, each topped with a festive purple umbrella.

"*Oy gevalt,* what a day!" He handed me a frosted glass. "I was on the phone talking business with So-phie for hours. First thing tomorrow, I'm going out and getting a computer. It's time you caught up with the rest of civilization and learned the joy of using e-mail, Rach."

Terri was my best friend in the world. He was also the girl I most wanted to be. We'd first met when I was a rookie agent posted in New Orleans. He'd owned a building in the Quarter, and I'd needed a cheap place to live. After a five-minute interview, he'd declared we were soul mates forever and knocked the rent down to what I could afford. It had nothing to do with astrological signs, or anything of that nature; it was because we both knew every line from *A Streetcar Named Desire* by heart.

Terri had instantly taken me under his wing, providing facials, makeup tricks, and advice on the latest in fashion. Who else would be more knowledgeable on "the most important things a woman should know to look her very best," than a top-notch female impersonator? I'd seen his act, and it was great. Not only did he sing and dance as well as Cher and Madonna and Liza, but he could have given them tips on how to improve *their* makeup.

Terri left his club, the Boy Toy, and the French Quarter behind after a particularly nasty breakup. By that time I was stationed in Miami. So, guess who decided to change his life and was now living there permanently? These days he was in business with Sophie and Lucinda, my two former Miami landlords, designing "must have" yarmulkes for the jet set's hot-to-trot pets.

"Besides, I need to see what Sophie's doing with our Web page. You know how schmaltzy she can get," Terri confided, adding a little more rum to our drinks.

The Internet turned out to be the defining factor that

transformed the trio of "designing women" into a virtual business powerhouse. Ralph Lauren, Calvin Klein, and Versace were passé compared to Yarmulke Schlemmer's new Web site.

"And I had an absolute brainstorm today! I've decided to add a new tropical design to the line: little white dogs all lifting their legs and peeing on palm trees. You just know every macho man out there is going to love it. I'm feeling more creative than ever, lately. Memphis must be good for me!"

Terri had come to see me in Memphis for a short weekend visit. That was over two months ago. It wasn't that I didn't enjoy his company; it was the fact that he was beginning to redecorate that had me worried.

"I was going to make something for us to nosh on, but decided against it when I saw what Vincent is whipping up for dinner tonight. God! One more month of your landlord's cooking, and I'm going to have to take the three of us off to some wonderfully decadent spa," Terri moaned.

"Are you sure Sophie and Lucinda don't mind your being away for so long?" I asked, taking a sip of my piña colada. Mmm, was this good! Maybe my place *could* use a little sprucing up.

"Of course they don't mind. That's what computers and fax machines are for," he scoffed. "Not that you have either, but I plan to remedy that."

Terri reached into my glass for one of my two maraschino cherries. He was just about to take a bite, when he stopped and shot a reproachful glance my way. "Unless that was a subtle hint. You wouldn't be trying to get rid of me by any chance, would you?" He looked as pathetic as an unwanted puppy in a pet store window.

"Absolutely not," I assured him, and added my other cherry to his glass as undeniable proof. "After all, you still have the bedroom to decorate."

"That room is *definitely* going to take a lot of time. I'll have to give it some thought while I'm working on Yarmulke Schlemmer's new fall line. But right now, I'm going to get dressed for dinner," he announced, with a flounce of his wig's long blond curls.

I knew it couldn't be the allure of barbecued ribs that was keeping him here. And while Terri had plenty of soul, it veered more toward Diana Ross and sequined dresses than the plaintive wail of B. B. King or John Lee Hooker.

As the sun gave a last existential gasp and began to sink beneath the murky depths of the Mississippi, I stood by the living room window and basked in the final light of day. This was the hour I always loved best. It was when magic happened. The dwindling rays bounced off the water in a suicidal splatter, transforming my dingy walls into a radiant opus to Sunset Boulevard. *Lights! Camera! Action! Miss Norma Desmond is ready for her final close-up!*

The warehouse district is where the trolley car ends and the train station resides. It's also the midway stop for the legendary City of New Orleans railroad. The ever-punctual train had become my alarm clock, helping me to keep track of my life. It tells me when it's eleven P.M. and time to douse the lights, as it departs for Chicago. The morning whistle gets me up each day as it races toward New Orleans. I love the transient feel of the area. It's a home for restless souls who long to be on the move, yet still need a place to lay their heads late at night.

My rented loft was home for now, but it would never beckon for me to permanently stay. High ceilings and tall windows not only gave it an open feeling, but provided fertile space in which a labyrinth of cobwebs gleefully played. Their gossamer network created an elaborate design on the plaster canopy, crawling in spiderlike fashion down along the windowpane. I liked to imagine the delicate filaments were lace curtains, in a nod to the tony dwellings a few blocks away.

The radiator hissed, not happy with the heat it was forced to provide, and the cold wooden floor creaked as it expanded. I walked to the kitchen and placed my glass in the sink. When I looked back up, the last vestige of light had been doused, its departure as silent as a life that's been taken away. I shrugged off the shiver that goosebumped my skin, and headed into the bathroom to shower and change.

Terri was dressed and waiting when I came back out, and I was surprised to find that his long blond curls were gone, replaced by a sleekly chic new wig. I did a double take, astonished at the transformation.

Terri preened and turned, showing off his new do. "Farrah Fawcett's staying home tonight. I've decided to up the charm factor and go more Sharon Stone. So, what do you think?"

"You look absolutely stunning," I answered truthfully.

He was dressed in an elegant, tapered shirt and the finest of soft wool pants.

"You know, you might want to consider losing the Goldilocks look yourself," Terri suggested, lightly pulling back my red hair.

"No way!" If I gave up my badge of youth, who knew what would go next? First my waist would thicken. Then my rear end would sag. I didn't even want to imagine what else might start drooping!

"Okay." Terri sighed. "But you don't see Sharon Stone running around with that long mop anymore. And just think about how Farrah looks."

"Yeah, but then there's Cindy Crawford. She hasn't cut *her* hair yet," I countered.

Terri gave me a disdainful glance. "I have only one word for you, Rach. *Younger.*"

Neither my pride nor I answered as we headed for the door.

"You know perfectly well you look gorgeous, Rach. For God sakes, I've been doing your makeup myself! All I'm suggesting is that we lop a few inches off the bottom and do a little shaping. It'll give that mop of yours more style. It's not as if I'm trying to drag you down to Rio for some nips or tucks—though when it's time, you can be sure that I'll tell you!"

Wynona's impenetrable jungle of hair popped into my mind. My fingers wandered up into my own primeval forest of curls, and got tangled in the undergrowth. Hmm, Terri just might be right.

"I'll think about it," I agreed, secretly appeased to know I didn't yet need to be carted off to a plastic surgeon.

We walked down a flight to Vincent's floor and rang
the bell. Six feet, five inches of rock-solid muscle
opened the door and bade us enter.

Terri flitted beguilingly by the man who could have
passed as half human, half sequoia. I followed behind,
hoping to pick up some pointers on how to ooze
charisma and yet act natural, but my thoughts were
abruptly interrupted as I was attacked from the rear.

Two thick arms wrapped themselves around my
chest, pinning my arms to my sides. I instantly placed
my left leg behind Vincent's right leg. Then, dropping
down, I wrapped my hands under his knee and quickly
lifted his foot off the ground. The action caused Vincent to lose his balance and he fell to the floor with a
crash. The room shook with the resounding thud.

"Very good. But you still should have been more
prepared for the unexpected," Vincent lectured from
where he lay on his back.

A former wrestler, Vincent had taken me on as a
tenant under one condition: if I was going to live in
the isolated warehouse district, I'd have to allow him
to teach me some wrestling moves. The fact that I was
a wildlife agent had made him all the more adamant.

"What happens if you can't get to your gun in
time?" he'd demanded. "You gonna *charm* some thug
into crying uncle while he lets you slip the cuffs on
him?"

His point had been well-taken.

Vincent picked himself up and brushed a few
specks of dust off his burgundy velour jumpsuit. "By
the way, Ter, you look like a million bucks. Do I detect
a hint of Sharon Stone?"

Terri nodded, and his near-perfect complexion blushed beneath its light cover of Chanel oil-free foundation.

"Nice touch," Vincent's ringside baritone approvingly rumbled.

Enough talk of fashion. The aroma wafting from the kitchen had my attention.

"Mmm. What smells so good?" My latest diet scheme was to skip one meal a day, but so far, its sole effect was to make me absolutely ravenous.

"I thought we'd start with a little antipasto while we wait for Gena to join us." Vincent waved toward the platter of food that sat artistically arranged on his coffee table. "After that, we'll have homemade ravioli stuffed with ricotta and spinach, along with a Caesar salad."

Though Vincent's demeanor was that of the most refined maître d' at a five-star restaurant, his face belied the illusion. A long-ago broken nose had never been fixed, a scar ran along his jaw, and one eye drooped just the slightest bit. Vincent's chestnut hair was pulled back in a ponytail, Steven Seagal fashion. All this sat atop two hundred and seventy-five pounds. If I'd first met the man in a dark alley at night, I'd have run in the opposite direction.

"I'm leaning toward having a nice Bordeaux with dinner. What would you say to a bottle of '95 Clos de Marquis?" he asked.

"Sounds like heaven to me." I considered it astounding good fortune to have wound up in his building. Apparently nobody else had wanted the place due to the preexisting tenants: an army of roaches as stubborn as ghostly "never surrender" Confederate soldiers. It wouldn't have surprised me to discover their bodies arranged to spell "Yankee, Go Home" one day. It had taken all of Terri's housekeeping skills to clear the place out, but I knew it was a temporary victory. The day Terri left, the infantry would be back in full force to reclaim their territory.

As for Vincent, he was a man of many talents—most of which lay in the adult entertainment field. He'd originally started out as a porno filmmaker, cashing in on such timeless classics as *MacBabe, King Leer, Tits 'n Ass Dronicus, Much Ado About Dick*, and *The Merchant of Booty*. Unfortunately, his odes to Shakespeare ended up spoiling him. After their success, he refused to produce or direct any other films unless he considered them of a literary or artistic nature. Needless to say, his star in the porno industry instantly plummeted.

He'd taken his profits and plowed them into his own topless bar, which he'd termed the Shakespearean pub of the eighties. However, even that undertaking eventually lost its allure—mainly due to the mob, which muscled its way into the money-making venture.

Vincent then searched for a venue where he could go it alone, yet express himself artistically. One look at his thick neck rising above beefy trapezius muscles, and the choice was a no-brainer. He successfully became a professional wrestler.

Soon he was no longer Vincent Margules, but Mad Dog Vin, AKA the Body Snatcher, wrestling for the WCW in Atlanta. His career lasted for a few years, until Vincent's body began to feel as if it had been chewed up and spit out by a meat grinder. From there it was a natural progression to founding the Mad Dog Vin School for Professional Wrestling in his hometown of Memphis.

Vincent considered the institute the capstone of his career. It was here that he took young up-and-coming wannabes and molded them into the entertainment stars of the future. The regimen included grueling hours of wrestling moves and microphone skills, along with the latest in stylish costume selection and—Vincent's own specialty—how to pick a crowd-pleasing persona. He'd tapped into a virtual gold mine. The wait list just to be evaluated for admittance already ran well over a year.

I'd once told him I didn't understand the allure of watching two sweaty guys pummel each other into the ground. Rather than being insulted, Vincent had taken the time to explain the finer points that he felt I was missing.

"This isn't just about a couple of bozos beating each other up. What you're witnessing is an entirely new American art form, known as sports entertainment. On its most basic level, you've got athletics, rock music, and soap opera plots all rolled into one neat package. But of course, what actually is taking place goes much deeper. I like to compare it to what the mythologist Joseph Campbell once wrote," Vincent said thoughtfully. "Humans inevitably re-create ancient myths with each generation. Well, that's exactly what wrestling does these days. The characters interact while working out a variety of primordial urges involving jealousy, rivalry, feuds, and rebellion.

We solve all our differences in the ring without guns or knives, or even the whisper of murder. Personally, I like to think of what we do as a therapeutic form of public service."

It was just possible that Vincent was on to something. I'd gone to visit his school once, and bumped into a student dressed as an executioner. Under his arm was a mannequin's severed leg. I'd been crazy enough to ask what he was doing. He proceeded to explain that he was modeling himself after his favorite pro wrestler—one who carried around a head.

"But don't you think that's a little gruesome?" I'd inquired.

"Not if you view it in psychoanalytic terms. Actually, my wrestling idol, Al Snow, says that what I'm expressing is healthy. I'm projecting a nonverbal cry for help. Isn't that cool?" he said, grinning from ear to ear.

I'd asked no more questions, but let the make-believe serial killer keep on walking past.

"Here are more munchies for you to nosh on. I know you're probably hungry."

Vincent added a platter of scrumptious fried calamari to the table.

Hmm. The word *nosh* hadn't been in Vincent's vocabulary before Terri's arrival.

"Which reminds me, Rachel—you're looking a little pale these days. I don't think you're getting enough vitamins, the way you eat. Here's a list of supplements I want you to take. You can look it over while Terri helps me in the kitchen," Vincent added.

Terri threw me a kiss and wriggled behind the

ponytailed behemoth. Talk about being slow on the uptake! I now realized what Terri's infatuation with Memphis was all about. Evidently he and Vincent were whipping up more than a soufflé every day while I was at work. Much as I hated to admit it, I was envious of their relationship. On the other hand, maybe Terri could teach me how to go about meeting a straight version of Vincent.

Perhaps my line of work was restricting my social life. After all, my days were spent hanging out with the likes of Hickok, along with a cast of characters who viewed the world through the scope of a rifle.

A rhythmic knock at the door broke into my thoughts, and I got up to answer it. I was presented with Miss Gena Withers's sinuous arrival. One arm casually snaked its way up the wall, further lengthening her already knockout figure. She pushed off like a luxury liner about to set sail, and slithered into the room to give me a peck on the cheek.

"Hello there, darlin'. Long time, no see," she purred in throaty greeting.

I didn't bother reminding Gena that we'd had dinner together only last night. Instead, I observed her slinky entrance in a tight lime-green dress with fingernails perfectly painted to match. A head full of long cornrows swayed with each sensuous roll of her hips. At twenty-eight years old, she was one of the most gorgeous women I'd ever met. Gena worked her way to the sofa, where she lowered herself onto the seat with the slightest hint of a provocative moan. Then she flashed me a smile as bright as a traffic light.

"So, what do you think?"

"Very Eartha Kitt." I nodded approvingly.

"Great! That's just the effect I was going for." The next moment, her eyes lit upon Vincent's tempting array of appetizers. "Wow, look at all this terrific stuff!" Gena proceeded to dig in as if she'd never heard the word *calorie*.

God, how I hate people who have a fast metabolism. I was also beginning to think twice about hanging out with women under thirty.

Gena was the tenant on the top floor, right above me. She'd been working as a bookkeeper for one of the largest junkyards in the South when I'd moved in. That changed after she accidentally opened a drawer she wasn't supposed to, and discovered that the owner kept two very different sets of books—one which recorded the junkyard's true profits, and one for the IRS. Gena quickly decided that a career change was in order if she didn't want to wake up one morning and find herself in jail. Vincent came to the rescue by pulling strings with one of his former porn stars, who'd started a small overnight shipping company called World Express after losing the battle with cellulite.

Memphis is the busiest cargo hub in the world, with fifty thousand imports and ninety thousand exports passing through its portals each day. Not only did Gena's new job with World Express give her security, but there was also never any question about having to work evenings. An important factor, since that was when she indulged in her life's greatest passion.

Gena loved to sing the blues more than anything else. God must have known it, as well. She'd been endowed with the kind of deep, throaty voice that sensuously wrapped itself around each note and didn't let go until the music was throbbing. As if that weren't enough, it also drove every man in the room crazy with lust. Anyone with her looks and talent was destined for great success. She was building a devoted following at a local club where she sang a few nights each week. The place was off the beaten tourist track and patronized by true music aficionados. Owned by her cousin Boobie, the Blue Mojo was a down-and-dirty dive. But the joint was beginning to be packed weeknights, as well as on the weekends. It wouldn't be long before she left for bigger pastures.

Terri came out of the kitchen with a Caesar salad in hand. "Now *that's* the way I want to look in my next life!" he said, gesturing toward Gena. "Like a young Vanessa Williams."

"Well then, you better be sure you get yourself a black mama," she saucily retorted. "And while you're at it, put in an order for a good dose of soul."

"That and a set of free weights would help. Gena's been sticking to the workout plan I set up for her," Vincent pointedly added as he walked into the room. "She's also taking the same supplements I recommended for you, Rachel."

"Ooh, yeah. A few bottles of vitamins, along with some liposuction and plastic surgery, and I'm sure we'll be able to pass ourselves off as twins," I retorted.

But I secretly vowed to get the supplements and start taking them right away.

Vincent announced that it was time for dinner, and we took our places at a table so beautifully decorated it would have made Martha Stewart weep. As I was feasting on homemade ravioli, I suddenly realized the wealth of information that was probably sitting right there with me.

"Vincent, how much do you know about caviar?" I inquired.

"Only that it's a gift from the gods. Each tiny gem is a perfect pearl of nature. Every bite, black velvet on the tongue. Its morsels erupt in a taste sensation incomparable to anything else in this world," he rhapsodized. "What else could you possibly need to know?"

There was no doubt about it; I'd found my caviar connoisseur connection.

"What are you, crazy or something? I'd never stick those disgusting little things in my mouth." Gena shivered.

"Maybe that's because you haven't tried the right kind of roe," Terri responded, ever the peacemaker.

"Oh, bullshit! You can call it whatever you want, and it won't make any difference," Gena insisted. "It's still nothing more than revolting, unfertilized fish eggs."

Vincent uncorked another bottle of Bordeaux and refilled everyone's glasses. "That's fine. Either you like it or you don't, and Gena has a right to her opinion. But if you're going to indulge, the important thing is to know exactly who you're buying from."

"Why is that?" I questioned, eager for a thumbnail education.

"Because otherwise you can get stuck paying big

bucks for what you think are primo eggs, such as beluga. Unless you're a connoisseur, it's all too easy for someone to pass off inferior quality caviar."

"So do you think there's a lot of consumer fraud going on?" I probed.

"Undoubtedly." Vincent swirled his wine, sniffed, and sipped. "But there are other reasons for making sure you eat only the very best roe."

Gena grabbed that and ran with it. "Probably because the stuff can make you sick as hell. Maybe even give you mad fish disease, right?"

"Not at all. This isn't bad hamburger meat we're talking about. The fact is, there are those who claim that good caviar has special powers," Vincent said tantalizingly.

Okay. Now I really *was* interested. "Such as?"

"Well, it's said to work as a laxative, as well as to prevent hangovers. But what it's most famous for is being the one food which truly is an aphrodisiac."

"I'm all for that!" Terri piped up.

I noticed Vincent's hand slide over and give Terri's leg a squeeze.

"Where do you guys get these fractured fairy tales?" Gena demanded. "That and oysters! Have you ever noticed that it's only slimy things sliding down your throat that are supposed to get you all hot and bothered? Personally, I don't need any help when it comes to turning a man on, thank you very much." She toasted us with her glass. "We had a box of those things break open at work the other day, and the room smelled like a scummy fish tank for hours. They were all over the damn floor, and believe you me, our janitor wasn't any too happy about having to clean them up. The stuff is repulsive!"

That piece of information instantly caught my attention. "How were the eggs packed?" I inquired.

"You see? Now there's an intelligent question. If more people asked the proper way to do things ahead of time, we wouldn't have to deal with these problems," she huffed. "Some idiot put them inside a foam container, which naturally broke. To make matters worse, the shipper didn't even label the damn thing properly."

A little bell rang in my head, clueing me in that I might have stumbled upon something interesting. "How was the package marked?"

"Just as seafood. There was nothing that said a bunch of squishy eggs were inside."

"The consignor must have been pretty upset when they found out that their shipment was destroyed."

"We weren't able to notify them," Gena said. "I tried to call, but it turns out their phone had been disconnected."

To my mind, that translated into one thing—the eggs were being smuggled.

"What about through their credit card? Couldn't you track down the sender that way?"

Gena arched a knowing eyebrow. "Sure, under normal circumstances. But in this case, 'Mr. Ferrante's' credit card also happened to be bogus."

This was getting better and better. "Out of curiosity, where was the package being shipped?"

"You're gonna love this: some import company in Minsk, all the way over in Belarus. You know, one of those republics that used to be part of the Soviet Union."

"Then the eggs that you saw weren't really caviar," Vincent said knowingly.

"What are you talking about? Of course they were." Gena looked puzzled.

"Not in the true sense they weren't." Vincent explained: "*Real* caviar comes only from sturgeon swimming in the Caspian Sea. The eggs you found had to have been from fish caught here in the States."

"I don't care *what* kind of fish they were from; all I know is that they stunk, I had to help clean them up, and if I ever catch the joker who packed them, I gonna give him a good ass-kicking!" Our blues mama declared.

Gena had a way with words that I totally loved. "You didn't happen to see this Mr. Ferrante, did you?" I figured he'd be easy to describe. A fat, pot-bellied, overalled skunk who walked around without any underwear.

Gena poured herself another glass of wine. "No, and I hope I never do. Otherwise, I just might have to kill him."

This was my kind of woman. She'd make a hell of an agent if she ever wanted a seven-day-a-week, twenty-four-hour job.

After dinner, Terri, Vincent, and Gena decided to continue the party at a blues club on Beale Street. I begged off for once, and went upstairs to think about the money I'd received today from Woody. Charlie had said that working undercover would play with my head. That was all right. My mind was looking to take a little vacation anyway.

The City of New Orleans pulled out of the train station, whistling that it was time to go to sleep, as the Main Street trolley clanged by. The jangle of each note carried me deeper into the Land of Nod until I drifted off, dreaming that my head was resting on a cloud of tiny fish eggs. The billowy cushion sprouted a pair of wings, transporting me across the sky. I wondered where we were headed, and my answer came as one egg metamorphosed into a tiny fish that swam up close to my ear.

We're off to the land where your grandparents came from. We're taking you back to Minsk.

Five

Terri hadn't been to bed by the time I awoke. Either that, or he'd forgotten to tell me that he'd be spending the night with a friend. I got up, showered, and scoured the kitchen for a Pop-Tart. But Terri's evil twin had apparently thrown them all away. He was clearly in cahoots with Vincent to make me start eating healthy. Boy, were they in for a surprise. I'd had the foresight to prepare for just such a possibility.

I dug through my bedroom closet and victoriously pulled out three boxes of cereal: Cap'n Crunch, Frosted Flakes, and Froot Loops. There was just enough left in each box to combine them and end up with one decent-sized bowl of cereal. I polished off my essential quota of morning sugar and headed out for the day.

I knew Hickok would expect me to show up at the office, so I chose not to go. I was afraid he'd had plenty of time to change his mind, which meant the only thing for me to do was plant myself even deeper into the case. Woody had said he'd gotten the paddlefish eggs for his brother, Virgil. That seemed as good a place as any to start. I jumped in the Excursion and hit Highway 51, heading toward an area called Chickasaw Bluffs.

I hadn't met Virgil before, and couldn't say I was looking forward to it. He'd become some what of a local legend, having been locked up in jail several years ago after a blind date turned decidedly sour. Evidently, Virgil and the girl couldn't agree on what to do for the evening. He wanted sex and she insisted on having dinner. Virgil brought the dispute to an end by raping his date and then throwing her off a bridge, after which he went and got himself some barbecued pork ribs.

Fortunately, the mud in which she'd landed was soft and the woman survived, enabling her to promptly ID her attacker. Virgil was thrown into jail, where every unsolved rape in the county automatically landed at his door, though he vigorously proclaimed himself innocent.

Deciding the odds were stacked against him, Virgil composed a note one night damning both dating and the legal system for turning him into a victim and making him an angry man. Then he bashed a guard over the head with his dinner tray, broke out of jail, and went on the lam.

When the guard awoke, he found the note. He immediately moved to Nashville, where he turned it into a successful country-western song. Soon every radio station in the South was playing "My Name Is Virgil Hardy and the World Done Me Wrong."

Meanwhile Hardy eluded local authorities with uncanny ease, having disguised himself as a woman.

Months went by and still there were no tips as to where Virgil had disappeared, even though *America's Most Wanted* aired the story. Then one day a sharp-eyed saleswoman spotted Hardy in her store, and promptly phoned the police. His downfall was that he'd attempted to shoplift a very expensive silk blouse.

Virgil served the remainder of his cell time reading up on copyright law, and he eventually sued his former jailer for unpaid royalties. Upon his release, he announced that he'd found God, deemed himself a preacher, and opened his very own church—the Dixie Rebel House of the Lord. Evidently Virgil had embraced a very tolerant form of religion; not only was his church a house of prayer, it also operated as the Sho Nuf Bar seven days a week.

I made a left onto Hobe Webb Road and headed there now. The country lane grew exceedingly narrow, and before long, the blacktop disappeared altogether and my tires crunched over gravel. Soon I was driving between two oceans of cotton fields, their rich, black soil turned over and ready for planting.

I passed a four-row cotton picker that appeared to have been abandoned. Nearby sat a dingy steel container with peeling yellow paint. Corrosive rust crawled up its walls, steadily eating away at the veneer. Clinging to the dirt below were discolored nuggets of snow that stubbornly refused to melt. I blinked my eyes and looked once more. They were renegade cotton bolls; the ground all around was littered with them.

The only relief from the endless miles of unbroken monotony were the occasional telephone poles. They brazenly ascended skyward, with arms out thrust, as if to say, *This land that you're traveling on is mine.*

A shiver ran down my spine when I saw that a sharp knife had inscribed a message on each one of the poles. Three little letters spelled out *KKK*. I pressed down on the accelerator and raced away.

Before long, the gravel vanished and I was on a dirt path that sloped downward as I descended a steep bluff. Trees clustered together and closed in around me, making the day seem dark. Even more unnerving, each limb, each branch, each trunk was smothered in an impenetrable maze of vines. Though only sixty miles north of Memphis, I had entered a no-man's land.

The ground suddenly vanished off to my right in a precipitously treacherous drop. The only thing that would have softened my fall was the rampant kudzu blanketed about. One moment it resembled a witch's tattered cloak, the next, the long, unkempt hair of a crone. It clung to everything it touched, creating an eerie twilight zone.

Originally imported from Japan, the vine has quickly taken over the South. It spreads as much as a foot a day, covering everything in its path. I'd even heard tales that the vine will suffocate a man if given the chance. Superstitious folks close their windows at night, lest the kudzu sneak into their house.

The path leveled off and I knew I was getting closer. There was no need for a sign to guide the way; empty beer bottles littered the ground. Virgil's clientele clearly didn't believe in the slogan "Help Keep America Beautiful."

The track branched off and I veered to the right, following the Hansel-and-Gretel trail of bottles. Finally a

white clapboard structure appeared up ahead. The
only indication that I'd arrived at the Dixie Rebel
House of the Lord was the large wooden cross haphazardly nailed on the front door. The notice posted
beneath read, "The Sho Nuf Bar—No Niggers or
Game Wardens Allowed."

Talk about your warm, friendly greeting. There was
only one way to deal with Virgil's crude warning: I
grabbed my gun, got out of the Ford, and ignored it.

I walked up to the front door, and pulled on the handle. Damn! Hardy's church was closed up tight—lock,
stock, and barrel.

Psst! Over here!

I could have sworn I'd heard a whisper coming
from the window. Imagination is a wonderful thing—
especially when it works in your favor.

I sidled over to a pane of glass smeared with
enough dirt to have passed as "stained." There are few
things in this world that can't use a little improvement.
I kept that thought in mind as I spat into my hand and
cleared away a circle. Then I peeked in to view a
"church" with scuffed floors, a bar, and a couple of
ramshackle tables. There wasn't a single statue of Jesus or the Virgin Mary in sight, but a large fish with a
bottle of Bud stuck in its mouth was mounted on the
wall. I decided to mosey around to the back of the
building, and see what other kinds of spiritual relics
Virgil kept about.

The odor of dead, rotting fish was the first thing to
hit me, its aroma growing stronger with each passing
step. That made sense; the Sho Nuf Bar is situated

along a tributary of the Mississippi. But there was a more acrid odor. I peered inside two trash cans and found the remains of rubber tires slowly smoldering. On the riverbank, stacks of inner tubes lay in the red Tennessee mud like a pile of putrefying corpses. But the highlight of the Sho Nuf's backyard was a broken-down Chevy Impala, whose battered, rusted carcass looked like a victim waiting to be carted off. Empty bottles of beer were placed at the vehicle's base like reverential offerings, and long straight lines were slashed into the Chevy's hood. It looked as if stiletto-sharp fingernails had drag-raced across the surface, turning the drab green paint into abstract art. Rumor had it, this was where the local boys came to cut their lines of cocaine. I wondered if they said "Amen" as they snorted up.

Having finished paying my respects, I returned to my vehicle to go in search of Virgil's house. While the mini-tour had been interesting, it was the man himself I wanted to find. I headed back to where the trail forked and followed it in the opposite direction; it didn't take long before an Air Stream trailer came into view.

The mobile home was a two-tone extravaganza, painted yellow on top and purple on the bottom. I parked near the makeshift porch, and saw that its interior was paneled in fake knotty pine. Decoratively tacked onto the walls were the skins of beaver, red fox, and mink. A single bulb dangled forlornly from the ceiling as if it had been lynched. On a nearby pole hung a Confederate flag. Adjacent to that was a paint-

by-number portrait of Jesus. Casually slung over a peg
was a pair of cammo pants.

Virgil's heap of a car sat defiantly in the front yard.
The Oldsmobile Delta 88 observed Hardy's two-tone
philosophy, touting those ever-popular shades of red
rust and brown paint. Virgil must have experienced
some trouble from folks who were envious; he'd
slapped a sticker on the rear bumper that declared,
"Keep Your Damn Hands Off! 'Cause This Car Ain't
Abandoned!"

I looked around for further evidence that Virgil was
home, but the only sign of life was a pen filled with
hogs. They paid no more mind to my presence than to
emit a couple of loud grunts. Other than that, nothing
appeared to be out of the ordinary—not until I got out
of my Ford Excursion, at least. That's when a whirl of
brown fur came racing across the ground toward me.

The small dog ran as fast as her four little legs could
scurry, as if Death were nipping at her heels.

I didn't have time to close the Ford's door before
the dog anxiously leaped up and jumped into the driver's seat. Though I tried to scoot her back out, the
pooch obstinately remained. She stopped any further
action on my part by standing on her hind legs, placing a paw on each of my shoulders, and staring into
my eyes as if desperately trying to communicate.

One pat on the head was all it took to launch the
mutt into a frenzy of licking. Having finished covering
every square inch of my face, the pooch attempted to
clamber onto my chest, as if begging to be cradled.
The next moment, I realized what she was trying to
escape from. The bloodcurdling squeal of a hog shat-

tered the air around us in a skin-prickling drizzle of terror and pain. I held my breath, awaiting the next harrowing sound, but what followed was even worse—the deafening shriek of silence. The stillness was soon replaced by a dull, steady, rhythm. *WHOMP! WHOMP!* It was the heavy, metallic thud of a cleaver systematically chopping through meat and bone.

The dog crawled into my arms, where she rolled herself into a tight little ball and shivered. All the panic and horror that had permeated the air settled into my veins with cold-blooded perseverance. It was as if I could feel the blade's deadly bite ripping through my own muscle, and sinew, and flesh.

I held the dog until the wave of terror subsided within us, then gently placed her back down on the ground. Even the hogs had stopped eating long enough to tilt their heads and listen. I walked over to them with the pooch following close on my heels.

Hogs are highly intelligent creatures who happen to enjoy rolling around in the mud. They were busy rooting through the slop now in search of slivers of food, even though their trough still held remnants of barley, oats, and corn. Their bulky bodies bumped up against one another, each easily weighing well over three hundred pounds. I thought of all the barbecue places I'd eaten at since landing in Memphis, and wondered which little piggy was destined for someone's plate next. They might have been pondering the same exact thing in their chorus of grunts, snorts, and groans.

I was so immersed in watching the hogs that I was startled by the sound of someone approaching from behind. I turned to see a giant hulk of a man slowly walking toward me, having emerged from around the back of the trailer. Half the carcass of a freshly slaughtered hog was tossed over one shoulder, and he bore the load as easily as if it weighed no more than a sack of feathers.

The man carried his large frame with the awkwardness of an overgrown boy. The rhythm of his movements was off-kilter, as though he hadn't yet mastered how to handle his massive form and unwieldy limbs. He was attired in denim bib overalls and a fiery red flannel shirt, both of which must have been at least a size triple X. The clothes accentuated the choppy movement of his legs and arms, making him appear all the more robotic. What he reminded me of was a cross between Lenny from *Of Mice and Men*, and the trademark logo for Bob's Big Boy Burgers.

Even his hair seemed surprised at finding itself on top of such a humongous body. The short, stubby bristles stood straight up in the air like an army of exclamation points. His eyes were unusually small and set far apart, topped off by wild, bushy eyebrows, while his nose was broad and its end pushed up, providing me with a lovely view into his nostrils. And that's when it hit me: his nose was formed in the shape of a snout. Meanwhile, his skin was as pink as a newborn baby's. I looked once again at the hogs, and then back at the man who continued to approach me. There was no doubt about it. Amazing as it seemed, Virgil Hardy closely resembled a walking, talking, king-sized porker.

As he got closer, I saw that his milky-blue eyes were watery and unfocused. I also noticed the wooden cross that hung around his neck. The religious symbol had been crudely made by hand and was stained black. At first glance, it appeared to be branded into the pink skin on his chest.

"Something I can help you with, ma'am?"

His voice was as cold as a block of dry ice, and had a quality that pierced through my flesh. Each word felt as if it were rimmed with sharp little hooks.

"I'm Rachel Porter with the U.S. Fish and Wildlife Service."

His eyes instantly clicked into focus and his demeanor changed, as if a storm had kicked up from out of nowhere. Thunderclouds gathered and flashed across his face. His pink skin intensified to a deep red, and an angry scowl rolled over his features.

It didn't make me feel much better that the hogs had once again stopped eating and were now staring.

Virgil glared, seeming determined to conjure up the mother of all lightning bolts. The last thing he resembled was any type of preacher who exuded the milk of human kindness. He appeared to have more in common with a holy roller exhorting hellfire, damnation, and brimstone.

"I'm looking for Virgil Hardy," I said, sure I'd found him.

"That's me. Is there some kinda problem you got?"

Yeah—being forced to deal with a guy with an out-of-control pituitary gland, rather than being home with a piña colada in my hand.

He continued to scrutinize me as if I were some piss-poor excuse for a game warden. I guessed Woody hadn't yet bothered to fill Virgil in that he'd gone and bought himself a real, live U.S. Fish and Wildlife agent. If Woody didn't feel it was important enough to alert his brother, I certainly wasn't going to be the one to break the good news. As far as Virgil knew, I was still the enemy. I decided to use it to my advantage.

"Listen, Virgil. I could stand here and play games with you, but I can tell you're not the kind of man to be taken in by that sort of thing. I'd just be wasting both of our time and not giving you the proper respect you deserve."

The storm clouds began to soften. Whoever said women are the only ones taken in by flattery? Men's egos are the size of overblown basketballs.

"So, I'm just going to lay it on the line and be honest with you. After all, from what I hear, you're the main man around these parts."

I was almost certain that I saw Virgil's lip begin to quiver. Yep. The bigger they are, the harder they fall.

"I've been told that Woody is supplying your bar with paddlefish roe. You must be aware that he doesn't have a license, which makes that illegal. And since your business is profiting from the sale of illicit property, I'm afraid you're an accessory to the fact. That means, besides paying a large fine, you'll have to show me a complete accounting of the Sho Nuf's records."

It was a good thing I'd tried to soften Virgil up before hitting him with my verbal bat. Otherwise, I'd hate to think of how he would have reacted. The clouds quickly regrouped, bigger and badder than ever. He squinted, causing his peepers to disappear under two folds of fat.

"Who in the hell would tell you a bald-faced lie like that?" Virgil thundered. He began to rock back and forth on feet the size of small boulders.

I wasn't sure if he was about to explode, or getting ready to lunge for my throat. I was just glad my gun was within easy reach.

"Your brother passed on that little tidbit," I informed him.

Virgil lifted the butchered hog off his shoulders and raised it high above his head, then threw the bloody carcass at my feet.

"That no good, lying, useless sack of shit!" he erupted. "And you fell for that crap? You can't actually believe my customers would eat lousy fish eggs, when my place is world-famous for good barbecue!"

If this was the way Virgil treated the food he cooked, I could only imagine the sanitation level in his kitchen.

"In that case, I'll be sure and call ahead for reservations the next time I'm in the area," I quipped.

Bad move—Big Boy's nostrils actually started to flare.

"Goddammit to hell!" Virgil furiously bellowed.

He took out his anger by kicking at the dog, who'd made the mistake of standing between us. Virgil missed by a sliver of an inch, and the pooch let out a terrified yelp as she scampered behind me. She remained there, quaking against my legs, pathetically whimpering. Raping women and abusing little dogs. Ooh, yeah. Virgil was quite the guy.

"All I know is what your brother told me," I responded, determined to stand my ground. "Unless you can prove otherwise, I don't see any reason not to believe him."

"And just how do you expect me to do that?" Virgil sullenly demanded.

Glory hallelujah! I love it when gathering information is this easy. But then, I'd laid a fairly decent trap. I pretended to ponder his question.

"Well, there is *one* way. If he's not selling the eggs to you, then maybe you can tell me who he *is* selling them to. That would help get you off the hook."

Virgil hesitated, his eyes slowly moving from left to right as he thought it over. He'd almost become a little too quiet for my liking, when he voiced his opinion with a loud, obnoxious snort.

"That is, unless you prefer I go through all your records with a fine-toothed comb," I added, providing a helpful nudge.

Virgil's stare moved along my figure, steady as an elevator working its way up from the ground floor. I got the distinct impression that it was quite a while since he'd been with a woman. Call it a wild hunch, but I'd bet that his source for blind dates had pretty well dried up.

When Virgil finished his visual tour, his little piggy eyes locked onto mine. A crude snigger that could have passed as the punctuation mark at the end of a dirty joke followed.

"Okay. Why not? Like you say, it'll get me off the hook. Besides, I don't see nobody else watching out for my rear. Woody's selling paddlefish roe to a woman by the name of Mavis Newcomb."

Mavis Newcomb. The name had a familiar ring. It took a mere second before I realized why. Not only did she own one of the largest junkyards in the South, but it was the place where Gena had worked. Regardless of that, it was impossible not to know her name if you lived anywhere around the Memphis area: cheaply made commercials advertising her junkyard flooded the local airways day and night. The Memphis paper had gone so far as to publish an editorial denouncing what it called Newcomb's "barrage of visual pollution."

Every spot featured a middle-aged woman buried beneath a beehive of heavily lacquered blond hair. The joke was that she always sat on top of a new pile of junk. It appeared as if the "inventory" couldn't fly out of her place fast enough.

"If you want junk, we got it," she gushed in an accent straight out of *Petticoat Junction.* "And if you got junk to sell, why then, y'all come down and see me about that, too," Mavis added with a coy wink.

But, paddlefish roe?

"Are you talking about Mavis Newcomb, the junk queen?" I asked in astonishment.

"Sho 'nuf," Virgil sneered. "Rumor has it, she had her last husband knocked off in some sort of hunting 'accident.' She'd taken one hell of a life insurance policy out on him, from what I hear. Something like two hundred grand. I guess that's how she set herself up in the caviar business. People say she's even buying those really illegal eggs these days."

The information dangled like a Hostess Twinkie in front of my nose.

"*Really* illegal eggs? As opposed to what? The ones that *aren't* so illegal?" I countered.

Virgil must have been feeling mighty good about handing over Mavis; he actually seemed to be enjoying the repartee.

"*You* know what I'm talking about, Porter. Eggs from paddlefish that have been caught in Alabama, Mississippi, and Louisiana. Not that Woody's doing any of his fishing there."

Of course not.

The problem was, the demand for caviar continued to escalate along with the New York Stock Exchange, while the supply of sturgeon and paddlefish proceeded to steadily go down. Paddlefish were just about gone from Tennessee waters, causing poachers to venture further south. Alabama, Mississippi, and Louisiana had had the foresight to prohibit the taking of all paddlefish in their waters, determining it was the best way to save the species. Naturally, that also made those states the best places to poach.

"Why *wouldn't* Woody be involved in something like that?" I asked.

"Hell, you've seen how he lives! That brother of mine is so damn useless, he can barely catch enough *legal* fish to feed his family. There's no way he makes decent money from poaching. All he's doing is picking up small change here and there," Big Boy shot back.

I gazed across Virgil's own palatial estate and found it interesting that he could so easily pass judgment on his brother. His hogs seemed to grunt in agreement. But then, Virgil didn't realize that ten grand of Woody's illicit money was already in my hot little hands. It made me wonder how much loot Big Boy might possibly have stashed away.

"Thanks for the tip about Mavis. But, out of curiosity, why did you decide to pass on so much information about her? Giving me her name would have been enough."

Virgil spat on the ground, and the repugnant splatter landed on the butchered hog. Mmm. Someone was going to be getting extra special sauce on their ribs tonight.

"Because that bitch is my ex-wife. She deserves whatever she gets."

Now *there* was a religious, forgiving man for you.

I headed toward my Ford, casting an occasional glimpse back to make sure Big Boy wasn't sneaking up on me. It was only as I started down the road that I let out a sigh of relief—until I glanced in the rearview mirror. Virgil's little dog was running after the Excursion with all the determination of a born-again greyhound. My breath caught in my throat and my eyes began to burn. I knew it wouldn't be wise to further alienate Virgil by stopping and taking the dog with me. Not yet, at least. She slowly gave up, until she stood defeated in the middle of the path.

Damn Virgil! Damn Woody! And damn all the others who would abuse and misuse any living creature.

I continued on until the dog finally disappeared from sight.

Six

Mavis Newcomb had just been catapulted to the top of my To-Do list, but first I needed a little pick-me-up. It was midmorning and my Froot Loops and Cap'n Crunch combo had already worn off. Fortunately, I'd replenished my glove box stash. I pulled out a Nestlé Crunch bar and proceeded to down it. My energy quotient immediately shot through the roof, so I didn't have to break Terri's newly imposed health regimen by drinking a fourth cup of coffee.

I flew past the kudzu and turned south on Highway 51 without having the slightest idea where I was going. Though I'd seen Mavis Newcomb's commercials hundreds of times, I'd never paid the least bit of attention to where her place was located. The other nugget of information I needed was whether Miss Mavis might actually be a registered caviar dealer. If so, she'd be on record with the Tennessee Wildlife Resource Agency as having purchased the required license for two hundred and fifty dollars. Not that it would make any difference, should she be buying illegal eggs, but it would give her a better cover.

The problem was that calling state agents would raise a red flag of suspicion. There'd be all those annoying questions: *Why did I want to know? Was there a problem?* The fewer people who knew what I was up to, the better. Besides, it wasn't only Fish and Wildlife that considered me a loose cannon; for the first time in recorded history, the feds and the local authorities had actually begun to agree on something. Who would have figured I'd be the one to bring them together? That left me with no other choice than to call the Boss Man. A list of registered caviar dealers might possibly be buried beneath all that crap on his desk.

"Well, well. It's nice of you to call and pay your respects," Hickok growled into the receiver. "I was beginning to wonder if you'd taken the day off and gone to get yourself a pedicure."

Hickok had seen my feet once, and never let me forget it. I had an impressive collection of bunions and corns from my days of wearing high heels as an actress. He'd made a comment; I'd snapped back that at least I wasn't a human homing device for chiggers. Then we'd buried the hatchet over a couple of candy bars and beer.

"Listen, Bronx. You ain't got a snowball's chance in hell of pulling this thing off unless we work together as a team. Going undercover isn't a one-man operation—it calls for logistics and strategy. And as far as I know, you ain't got no training in either. Two brains have to be working together on this thing. Otherwise, you're gonna find something coming back to bite you in the ass just when you least expect it. Which means, I want to know where *your* rear end is at all times!"

"Gee, Charlie. Does this mean you really, really like me?" I teased.

"What it means is that I don't intend to have my retirement plans flushed down the toilet. Now, where in the hell have you been this morning?"

I figured he was bound to find out sooner or later. Besides, he'd want to know why I'd decided to focus on Mavis Newcomb as a suspect.

"I paid a visit to Virgil Hardy."

"That el cuco cuco? And you walked out alive?"

Hickok actually sounded impressed. I smiled and gave myself a mental pat on the back.

"Congratulations, Bronx. You're both lucky and stupid," he jabbed, promptly deflating my ego.

"I called for something other than your undivided moral support, Charlie."

"Oh, yeah? And what might that be?" he inquired.

It didn't require mental telepathy to click in to the fact that he reveled in holding all the cards.

"I need a list of licensed dealers for paddlefish eggs." I paused, before nonchalantly delivering the second part of my request. "And by the way, I could also use the name and address of Mavis Newcomb's junkyard if you happen to have it handy."

My inquiry was met by a moment of silence. Well, not really. I was sure I could hear Charlie quietly chuckling to himself.

"Now, ain't that interesting. What are you planning to do? Redecorate that warehouse you live in? Or could this somehow be connected to that list of caviar dealers you want?"

Maybe my problem was that I'd been working alone for too long. Obviously, I was going to have to learn how to play well with others, whether I liked it or not.

"Virgil claims his brother Woody has been catching and selling paddlefish eggs to Mavis for extra bucks on the side. Evidently she's grown tired of being queen of the junk trade and has decided to branch out."

"You got that tidbit from Virgil?"

"I swear on the Dixie Rebel House of the Lord."

Hickok clicked his tongue, and I knew he was shaking his head.

"Just goes to show that even a blind hog can find an acorn every now and then."

"How about just giving me the information I want?" I asked testily.

Charlie must have felt a flicker of remorse; he came up with both her home and her work addresses. Then he told me to hold on and laid the phone down. I could hear him rooting through papers as he cursed under his breath. I passed the time by scrutinizing my collection of candy bars and deciding which one to eat next.

Hickok finally picked the phone back up. "Okay. I found it."

A moment later he exploded into a second round of colorful expletives.

"Goddammit to hell," he grumbled. "They print the type on these damn things so small you need a damn magnifying glass to read 'em."

In other words, Charlie was now going to have to embark on a hunting expedition for his glasses. The ones that no one was supposed to know he wore. I heard a drawer open and then slam shut.

"Let's see here. Huh! This is interesting. Seems there are only six licensed dealers for paddlefish eggs in the entire state. And guess what? Mavis Newcomb ain't one of 'em."

He cleared his throat and began to rattle something against his teeth. Probably the dreaded glasses.

"You know what Bronx? This dog just may run."

That was Charlie's way of telling me that we might have one hell of a good case.

"I think you oughta get the lead out and pay Our Lady of the Junkyard a visit."

I gritted my teeth to stop myself from saying, *No kidding!*

Hickok began to munch on something that sounded distinctly like peanut brittle.

"And what are *you* doing to keep yourself busy this morning?" I needled.

"The usual. Just fighting crime and stamping out lawlessness. By the way, I want your rear end in the office after you've finished your chat with the junk queen. I'll even sweeten the prospect by buying you lunch."

That would be a first. Maybe Charlie really was beginning to appreciate me. I hung up my cell phone, polished off a Mars bar, and took off.

Seven

Mavis Newcomb's home address was in the upscale Central Gardens District, but her shop was an entirely different matter. If you take Highway 51 far enough south, it turns into Elvis Presley Boulevard. I followed that now, as the charm of downtown Memphis disintegrated into a ticky-tacky strip of run-down storefronts. Elvis would have been appalled to see what had become of the boulevard anointed in his memory.

It wasn't until I approached Graceland that the boulevard resumed its former glory, fueled by the moneymaking power of its namesake. I flew past Graceland Plaza with its souvenir shops selling Elvis tee-shirts, coffee mugs, and key chains. Nearby sat the Heartbreak Hotel, along with his two private jets, the *Hound Dog II* and the *Lisa Marie*. If that wasn't enough, one could always pop into the Elvis Presley Automobile Museum. Finally, there was Graceland, itself. Should you choose to visit his home, an eighteen-dollar ticket provides a recorded tour narrated by ex-wife Priscilla, who lovingly relates Elvis's fondness for guns, karate, and gospel music.

I continued until I caught sight of the red light in the Krispy Kreme Doughnuts window. It signaled that a batch of one of the world's most perfectly realized creations was fresh and piping hot. I'd already passed up numerous convenience stores tempting me with their array of Little Debbie Snack Cakes and Moon Pies, but this was asking way too much. I slammed on my brakes, ran in, grabbed a sack full of the glazed wonders along with two cups of coffee, and continued on.

Soon after, I turned onto the side street where the Best Little Junk Shop in Memphis was located. There was no need for the sign out front; all it took was one look to know I'd arrived at the desired location. An explosion of garbage littered four of God's little Tennessee acres.

Old refrigerators, screen doors, and window frames stood next to battered bicycles and ancient pick-up trucks. Cable jumpers, boxes of screws, hammers, and pliers declared that it was possible to fix up anything. Lava lamps, empty cigar boxes, and crutches "found at Lourdes" defied gravity by tottering dangerously on top of a you-can't-buy-this-for-less Scandinavian coffee table. Luck was certainly on your side if you happened to want a broken-down freezer. Handy at fixing washing machines? Then this was your spot.

I spied a sofa that looked suspiciously like the one in my own living room. Both were upholstered in a dark burgundy fabric splattered with little white flowers. As for the odd pieces that made up my eclectic set of dinnerware, I think I had just found the rest of their matching ends. There were mirrors, cookie jars, and ceramic figurines. I'd landed in tchotchke heaven. A junk archeologist could have written a thesis on this place.

Grabbing the donuts and coffee, I ambled past a sporty little red Mercedes convertible. It was the kind I'd dreamed of owning as a kid. Of course, I'd also planned on being rich and famous, happily married, and living in a New York City penthouse. Who knew I'd be hanging out with an overweight dirt magnet who didn't believe in putting on underwear, and his brother, the cross-dressing rapist?

I wandered up a pathway adorned with plastic pots, broken rakes, and a swing missing its seat, to step inside a shop whose every square inch was crammed full of bric-a-brac. But the sensory experience didn't end there. Dust balls covered the floor like a ghostly clan of down-and-out Okies, and eau de mildew filled the air. I kicked my way through the aisles until I spotted the queen of junk herself.

Mavis Newcomb appeared just as she did in her commercials, with a helmet of blond hair piled high. Not only was she probably destroying the ozone layer with a full can of spray-on lacquer each morning, but by the looks of it, her hair would be the one thing left standing after a nuclear attack. Bent over a hefty stack of paperwork, she was adorned to the hilt in an eye-catching array of baubles, bangles, and beads.

A stunning pair of diamond earrings sparkled on Mavis's lobes, clearly meant to complement the five-karat ring that lodged like a lethal weapon on her finger. A thick gold necklace hung down over her breasts, where it brushed against the solid gold Rolex strapped to her wrist. This was obviously a gal who believed in wearing her weights, rather than lifting them.

She was dressed in a lemon-yellow pantsuit, and sported high heels that were as bright as the sun. To say the effect was overwhelming would have been selling her short; especially since Mavis was as wide as she was tall. What she most resembled was an overgrown marshmallow chick that had successfully escaped from its Easter basket.

Mavis glanced up, examined me through her rhinestone glasses, and then focused back down on her work.

"Sorry, sugar, but I ain't buyin' any junk today. One more item and this place of mine is gonna explode."

"What I've got in mind won't take up much room. I was wondering if you might be in the market for some roe?"

I placed the Krispy Kreme bag in front of her, along with a cup of black coffee. Popping the lid on my own container, I took a sip, then opened the sack of goodies. Mmm. The glazed donuts were still hot and gooey, their aroma almost sweet enough to overpower the scent of mildew. I pulled one out and took a bite.

"So, what do you say? Are you interested?"

Mavis slowly put down her pen and looked back up. "In case you haven't noticed, what I've got here is a junkyard."

I pushed the bag closer toward her. Mavis daintily reached in and extracted a donut. She held it between her thumb and index finger, keeping her pinkie curved ever so properly in the air. The sugary glaze spread smooth as Chapstick over her lips as she began to nibble on it.

"What makes you think I'd be interested in something like that?" she asked, polishing off the donut.

"Because your ex, Virgil Hardy, told me so."

Mavis popped one finger after the other into her mouth, and scrupulously sucked off all remnants of icing. Then she peered back inside the bag and eyed another couple hundred calories.

"Well, you don't look like any kind of fisherman to me. So, what's in it for you, even if I *did* happen to be interested?"

She'd just begun to reach for another tasty morsel when I broke the good news. "Plenty. You see, I'm your friendly U.S. Fish and Wildlife agent."

Mavis's fingers flew out of the bag as if they'd just touched a burning ember.

"Goddammit to hell!" she exploded. "That lowlife, scum-sucking piece of turd! Did he send you out here to harass me?"

Hmm. Those were familiar fighting words. I wondered what else Mavis and Virgil shared, besides a fondness for colorful adjectives. A dress or two, perhaps?

"I understand that you and Virgil's brother Woody are in the caviar business together—which presents a problem, since neither of you has a license. Come to think of it, that gives me enough probable cause to get a search warrant executed on this place, and have all your records removed."

Mavis pinched her mouth tightly closed and glared at me.

"Virgil also informed me that you're buying roe

from fishermen who are poaching paddlefish in closed states. I'm sure you're aware that's a big no-no." That ought to help loosen her up a bit.

"Oh, he did, did he? Well, that sonofabitch ought to know what he's talking about. Except *I'm* not the person who's doing it!" she barked.

"Then maybe you'd like to tell me who is?" I cordially offered.

Mavis's scowl relaxed into a Cheshire cat grin as she reached into her desk drawer and pulled out three packets of Nutrasweet. She gave the bags a precise tap before meticulously ripping each one open and carefully pouring its contents into her coffee. Then she took her time scrutinizing the remaining donuts before choosing one to her liking.

"First of all, you do know Virgil is crazy, don't you?" The tip of her tongue licked the glaze off her lips as her eyes studied me with almost as much interest as they did her donut. "Besides, if you really had something on me, you wouldn't be standing here talking. You'd already have a subpoena in your hot little hands and be tearing through the place."

I wondered how Virgil had ever managed to hook up with her. Newcomb was one smart cookie.

"You're thinking about this the wrong way, Mavis. I can make your life a living hell, or decide to give you a break," I conned.

Mavis wet a finger and picked up the crumbs scattered on the table. "And why would you want to do that?" she asked with feigned indifference.

"One simple reason: information."

"Oh, yeah! That would be a real smart move on my part," she scoffed. "Like I told you, I've got nothing to say."

"Maybe I didn't make myself clear. Either we come to an understanding, or you'll have a lot more than just me to worry about."

Mavis continued to smile, but a look of worry had begun to take root behind her rhinestone glasses. "What are you going to do? Have me picked up on littering charges?" she mocked with forced laughter.

"No, I'm thinking more along the lines of murder. I understand that you had quite the hefty life insurance policy taken out on your husband."

"What smart woman doesn't?"

"Yeah, but it's not every wife who's suspected of murder," I countered. "I just might have to get permission to exhume his body."

"If every wife were investigated because her husband accidentally died, the police wouldn't have time for anything else. But if you still insist on taking a look at George, be my guest. His ashes are right over there."

She pointed with her thumb to a cloisonné urn that sat on the shelf behind her.

"Excuse me. But is that a price tag I see on it?" I asked in disbelief.

"Hey, if someone wants to buy the jar, I'll take him out and stick him in another container."

"In that case, maybe I'll pay a visit to the hunter who *mistakenly* shot him," I warned.

Mavis removed her glasses and methodically began

to polish the lenses, as if she were practicing a form of meditation. "Sure. You can find Frank Hayes sitting in the next aisle. Talk about your bad breaks—seems he was so distraught over hitting poor George that he offed himself the very next day."

"You didn't also happen to have a life insurance policy out on him, did you?" I inquired dryly.

Mavis didn't bother to answer. But then, she didn't have to. She so clearly resembled the cat who ate the canary that I was tempted to reach over and pluck the feathers out of her mouth. It was time to skip straight to hardball.

"All right. Let's cut the crap and get down to business, Mavis. I happen to be privy to a little-known fact that would have the IRS attached to your ass faster than your husband hit the ground."

Bingo! I knew I'd hit my mark as her eyes flew up and met mine.

"Oh yeah? Anything you care to share?" she non-chalantly asked.

Her fingertips were the giveaway; all ten nails dug into the desk like miniature jackhammers.

"Just that the profits you report don't come anywhere near your actual take."

"People love to spread rumors like that about those of us who run our own business. Especially when the owner is female. You should know that," she chided. "By the way, what did you say your name was, hon?"

It was a blatant attempt to corral me into a guilt trip of "We women have to stick together." I had to hand it to her; Mavis knew how to play every chord.

"Rachel Porter."

"Well, Rachel. I'm sure you face the same sort of thing in your own line of work. It was probably a man who passed on that nasty piece of tittle-tattle. Am I right?" Mavis purred with a knowing glance.

"Actually, it was a woman," I replied.

She instantly turned tail. "They're even worse! They can't stand to see one of their own kind make it!"

"Time's up, Mavis. I know you've got two different sets of books for this shop. Either you decide to work with me and start supplying information, or I place a call that will end up costing you a lot more than your life insurance stash," I warned her.

"It's your word against mine," Mavis countered. "I'd like to see anyone try and find two sets of books."

"Why, did you cremate them? Or is that in your plans for the near future?"

She nonchalantly shrugged and reached for another donut. I abruptly jerked the bag away.

"Perhaps you don't realize it, but you've made more than your fair share of enemies in this world, Mavis. One of them managed to 'borrow' the evidence and had it photocopied. And guess what? They were nice enough to give me a duplicate," I bluffed.

Mavis caved. "Was it that bitch niece of mine?" she asked angrily.

Wynona was turning out to be quite the popular family member.

"You know, I can't seem to remember *who* it was. There are just too many people out there who don't like you. So, do we have a deal?" I pressed.

Mavis's fingers began to play a drumroll on the table. "What do I get in return?"

"What! You mean besides the fact that I won't investigate your husband's questionable death any further, or sic the IRS on you?" I asked in mock amazement.

"Junk's not the only thing I sell, sugar. If you want information, we gotta bargain for it." She punctuated her point with a wise-ass smile, producing two dimples that burrowed themselves deeply into her rotund cheeks.

"I guess that all depends on what you have to offer."

Mavis leaned back and kicked off her shoes. Even her toenails were painted yellow. "Okay, here's a tidbit for you. Both Virgil *and* Woody used to work for me. That is, for the little bit of paddlefish roe I ever bought," she cautiously added. "But all that ended the day another dealer moved into the area and stole them away."

"How did that happen?" I asked.

Virgil was even dumber than I'd imagined, sending me here. Either that or he never dreamed Mavis would actually spill the beans.

"Easy: he's paying them more than the going rate. Every caviar dealer in the area is up in arms about this guy. He's swiping fishing crews right out from under local dealers' noses. All a fisherman has to do is agree to work only for him, and he's automatically put on the payroll," Mavis revealed.

The idea seemed both brilliant and unbelievable.

"You mean fishermen won't sell paddlefish roe to any other dealer but him?"

"You got it! The bastard's screwing us all. Meanwhile, he's on his way to cornering the entire Southern caviar market—and I'm talking both the legal *and* illegal trade! Thanks to him, I can barely manage to make ends meet. That's the only reason why I'm still sitting in this hellhole! You wanna know what happened to the American dream?"

I nodded my head, not wanting to interrupt her verbal vendetta.

"I'll tell you what happened! I used up all my husband's life insurance money trying to break into the caviar trade, hoping to mingle with a better class of people. Instead, I got wiped out by some goddamn foreigner!"

She had just fully lassoed my attention.

"Who is this guy?" I questioned.

"Uh-uh! First we gotta come to an agreement."

"I've already made a more than generous offer," I reminded her. "What else could you possibly want?"

"Full immunity and protection."

Now I *knew* I was on to something good.

I slowly shook my head and sighed deeply. "I don't know, Mavis. That's an awful lot to ask for. What you've told me so far is interesting, but it's not enough to cut that kind of a deal."

Mavis smirked. "Okay, Porter, I'll give you a bit more. After all, I'm nothing but a small fish. There's a much bigger barracuda out there for you to hook onto your line—namely, that sonofabitch dealer I just told you about. He's now got an entire network of good ol' boys going out each night, poaching paddlefish. And I'm not just talking about here in Tennessee; I mean where the waters are closed in Mississippi, Louisiana, and Alabama. Then he's tinning the paddlefish roe right here in Memphis and passing it off as genuine Russian caviar."

Mavis had dropped her bomb with the precision and timing of an expert. I only hoped that she couldn't see my pulse pounding straight through my skin; my body felt like it had turned into a giant tom-tom.

"I think I can pretty well guarantee that we have a deal in that case. I'll just have to get my boss to sign off on it," I said casually. The trick would be getting him to agree. My mind was working on the best way to approach Hickok. "*Now* will you tell me who the guy is?" I prompted.

Mavis eyed the sack of donuts, and I placed it back on the table. Reaching in, she pulled out another glazed wonder and began to munch on it.

"The new guy in town is a Russki by the name of Sergei Galinov. The bastard is strong-arming most of us local dealers right out of business."

Talk about your intrigue! Ninety percent of the world's finest caviar has always been produced in the Caspian Sea—at least when strict fishing quotas were rigorously enforced by the Kremlin. But all that changed when the Iron Curtain fell and the communist government came tumbling down.

Poachers have taken control of the billion-dollar trade, maintaining their hold through the use of guns and missiles, helicopters and speedboats. Bandits have turned the Caspian Sea into the wild, wild West, and shoot-outs are common occurrences as they plunder the area. As a result, the species has nosedived as prices skyrocket, causing the rape and pillage to become more rapacious than ever. Consequently, the sturgeon and its highly prized roe are expected to vanish within the next two years.

Having depleted their own stock, these black marketeers were now looking for the next stop on their gravy train. Paddlefish eggs were a dandy substitute, making it easy for a smart dealer to pass them off as the pricier Russian caviar.

"If this Galinov is playing dirty, why haven't all the local dealers banded together and figured out a way to fight back? You know, strength in numbers?" I asked.

"We already thought about that, but it ain't gonna work in this case," Mavis replied sullenly.

"Why not?" Southern dealers were generally a scrappy bunch.

"Because the guy's got too much firepower on his side. He's backed by the Russian Mafia."

The words turned my blood icy cold. The Russian Mafia is considered not only the cruelest of all crime organizations, but also the smartest. They'd already been linked to an international money-laundering scheme involving a major bank here in the U.S. In addition, they traffic in weapons, refugees, nuclear materials, and drugs. The mob's reach is now global, running from Moscow and Budapest, across the ocean to Miami, Brighton Beach, and Los Angeles, in a multibillion-dollar enterprise. Still, who would have guessed they'd set up a base in Memphis?

"Are you certain that he's part of the Mafia?" I questioned.

I suddenly found myself short of breath due to pure, unadulterated exhilaration. Though part of me prayed that Mavis was wrong, the other part wanted total mob participation. This case could be the one that bumped me up to an entirely different level! Maybe even onto a playing field where I'd be able to hobnob with the big boys.

"Oh, yeah, I'm sure. He's already sent the message by knocking off a few of our illegal dealers who made the mistake of crossing him," Mavis said. "You remember that drive-by shooting a few weeks back? When Jimmy Bob Tucker got whacked in his driveway? Everyone thought it was gang-related, but it wasn't our own boys—it was the work of that damn commie pinko!"

I'd suspected Jimmy Bob of being involved in the illegal trade. It appeared I'd been right.

"What makes you so certain it was the work of Galinov?"

Mavis shot me a look that suggested I'd been born yesterday. "Because he gave the rest of us a broad hint that the same thing would happen again if we pissed him off. I heard that Galinov also wiped out two dealers down in New Orleans. Check it out, if you don't believe me."

She'd made her point.

"But you know what really burns my panties?" she asked.

I looked at the woman sitting across from me, and wasn't sure I really needed that kind of information.

"It's that some lousy foreigner is getting away with

all this. If there's a fortune to be made off paddlefish roe, it damn well should be an American who reaps the rewards!"

No one could say Mavis wasn't a patriotic kind of gal.

"And I'll tell you something else: there used to be plenty of paddlefish around these parts before the Russkies knocked off their own supply. Now they're sashaying over here, taking whatever they want. There aren't gonna be *any* fish left soon unless you get off your fanny and do something about it!" Mavis exclaimed indignantly.

Unbelievable! Now this was all *my* fault?

"If you feel so strongly about the situation, why didn't you report it to me before now?" I retorted.

Mavis opened her mouth to speak, and immediately closed it. Then she thrust back her shoulders and placed an authoritative finger on the bridge of her glasses.

"I'm telling you now because it's gotten out of hand, and I don't think it's right. There are a lot of hardworking Americans who are losing their jobs!"

Uh-huh. Why did I get the feeling I was suddenly being looked upon as her personal cleanup patrol?

Mavis got up and curled a finger at me to follow. "Come on. I want to show you something that I think you'll find interesting."

Those were the magic words that always got me in trouble. I trailed her down a set of stairs and into a basement, which was even darker and danker than the room above.

"You see that over there?"

I followed the direction of her finger toward two vertical filing cabinets.

"All the stuff I just told you about? Well, you get me that deal, and every bit of documentation in there is yours. I'll give you till noon tomorrow. If I don't hear from you by then, our agreement is off. The files will also have disappeared. And trust me—you won't be able to find them."

My eyes had sufficiently adjusted by now to see that a large refrigerator stood in the far corner.

"Is that where you keep your paddlefish roe?" I inquired.

"*Kept*, you mean," Mavis retorted caustically.

I accompanied her across the room and watched as she opened the tomb. The fridge was empty but for a small, one-ounce tin that sat alone on a shelf. Centered on its sea-blue cover was the painting of a sturgeon resting on a bed of pearly eggs. The logo, Czar's Choice, floated in yellow letters above it. Below were inscribed the words, *Prime Caspian Beluga Caviar.*

Mavis reached in and removed the tin. "This is Galinov's work. There's about as much Russian caviar in here as I've got priceless antiques in this place."

Galinov's work was impeccable, down to the Cyrillic lettering on the label.

"He's getting eighty-five bucks a pop for this crap," she said in disgust.

Were I to buy it as a consumer, I'd never have known the difference. I reached to take the tin from her hand, but she swiftly pulled it away.

"Uh-uh-uh!"

"What do you mean? I can't even examine it?"

"You've seen all you need to for now. Come back with a deal and I'll give it to you as a gift," Mavis said. "What I *will* tell you is that there's a hell of a lot more going on than you have any idea of."

Mavis placed the tin back in the fridge and closed the door, signaling our meeting was over.

"I still can't believe that miserable piece of slime gave you my name!" she fumed, cursing Virgil as she walked up the stairs.

Only after I'd left, and replayed our conversation in my mind, did I realize that Mavis had been desperate to make a deal. Given Galinov's tactics, the woman must have been scared for her life.

Eight

It was time to head into work for another round of *Let's Make a Deal*, and see how far Charlie would let me go before bringing out the hook.

This time around, Fish and Wildlife's office was situated in a prestigious area—on the southern campus of the University of Memphis. However, it was in one of the school's less desirable locations, a ramshackle former military hospital. The building was all but deserted; even the rats had jumped ship for more pleasant surroundings.

I parked in the lot and walked up to the second floor, entering a hallway that had become a graveyard for old windows that had been replaced years ago. They leaned against the walls like a bunch of sodden drunks.

Also piled in the corridor were ancient, mustard-yellow chairs and wooden desks—the kind under which schoolkids hid during atom bomb drills in the fifties. Ah! The good old days, when Americans still believed that kneeling beneath a piece of plywood could protect you during a nuclear attack.

I walked past a graveyard of filing cabinets so corroded that their handles were falling off. The paneled ceiling above was pockmarked with bullet holes, and drooped from excessive water damage. It reminded me of my old office back in Las Vegas—after it had been bombed.

I made my way toward my new office, a cheerless space that had previously been used as a patient's room. The interior was decorated with secondhand furniture that even Mavis would have turned down. The stuff went well with the gray industrial rug on the floor, its nap stained with enough greasy skidmarks to have passed as a landing strip. Peeling paint provided the final touch—along with a cartoon of Barney Fife cradling a gun. Beneath it was the quote, "Make My Day." The picture was slapped on the front of Hickok's desk; I couldn't imagine a more fitting place.

Hickok looked up as I entered, and grinned. "Glad to see you made it. You're just in time for lunch."

It was a good thing I hadn't counted on a sit-down at the Rendezvous for ribs; I'd have been in for a big disappointment. Laid out on the poor excuse for a table that was my desk were two pop-top cans of Van Camp's Beanee Weenees, and a tin of Vienna sausages. No napkins or paper plates were in sight. But at least he didn't expect me to eat with my hands—Charlie tossed me the plastic spoon from his coffee cup.

"Help yourself."

"Wow, I see you went all out."

"Hey. You wanna be a real agent, ya gotta learn to eat like one," Hickok grunted.

He pulled out his pocket knife and speared a Vienna sausage with the zeal of a big-game hunter. Good thing for him I was hoping to score some brownie points, otherwise, I'd have been tempted to tell him exactly what the item he was shoving into his mouth looked like.

"So, what did you learn from Our Lady of the Junkyard?" he asked between chomps.

"It seems the local roe dealers have some competition these days. Mavis informs me the Russian Mafia is not only horning in on the trade, but that one of their representatives has set down roots in the area. And if that's not enough, he's tinning paddlefish roe right here and shipping it out as beluga." Maybe now Charlie would buy me some lunch.

Hickok stared while balancing a Vienna sausage in mid-air. "Shit! That's absolutely, goddamned brilliant!"

At least we agreed on something.

"I'd heard rumors of paddlefish roe being sent over to Russia. Seems they're adding in a few dabs of the Caspian shit there, re-tinning it, then sending it back to the U.S. to be sold for big bucks. It don't take much to fake some Russian labels, alter export documents, and pay the right people off. They've been catching some shipments coming in through New York. Of course, they've got all that manpower up there. They'd never think of little ol' me pulling off anything really big down here."

Hickok looked happier than a pig in shit as he stuffed some Beanee Weenees into his mouth.

"Don't you mean *us*?" I corrected him.

"Yeah, yeah. You know what I'm talking about," he groused. Sho 'nuf.

Hickok reached back into the can of Beanee Weenees and extracted a couple of cold chunks of mystery
meat. They quickly disappeared down his gullet. Then
he tossed back his coffee, gave his stomach a few pats,
and followed that up with a burp. The scent of cheap
bourbon filled the air. No wonder he could eat this
stuff.

"I'll be damned! So the Russian mob is coming to
the South to play hardball, huh? Well, I'll just have to
show those Russkies a thing or two—teach 'em what a
real Southern rebel can do. They'll learn soon enough
how the cow ate the cabbage!"

There it was again, Hickok's three favorite words.
Me, myself and *I.*

"Great. Then I take it *you'll* also be the one going
undercover and putting your life on the line?" I caustically inquired.

"Hell, no. Don't worry; that's still you. After all,
someone's gotta remain in one piece and be the brains
behind this project." He guffawed.

I decided that now was as good a time as any to hit
him up with Mavis's request.

"Mavis Newcomb apparently has documentation
on a number of the deals that have been going down."

"How did she get it?"

"I don't know."

"Good one, Bronx." Hickok snorted. "No wonder
the big boys sent you back to work with me again.
Must be that damn Yankee streak that makes you such
a *slooowww* learner."

I let the remark slide; sometimes the smartest thing

one can do is simply to let men cling to their mis-
guided fantasies.

"What she *did* say is that she'll give us access to all
of her records. It seems the Russians are not only mo-
nopolizing the trade but have also started moving further south into closed waters."

"And what does the junk queen want in return for
this information?" Hickok shrewdly inquired.

"Total immunity, with a guarantee of protection."

"What!" Hickok exploded. "Who the hell does she
think she is? Sammy 'The Bull' Gravano? She'll get a
deal like that when John Gotti gets involved in the
trade!"

"It would be easier if it *were* our own Mafia dipping
their toes into the local water. I'd prefer that to taking
on the Russian mob any day. Besides, Mavis implied
this is only the tip of the iceberg. She said there's
more going on than we have any idea of." I paused,
trying to read his reaction. "I'm not sure what that
means, but the woman is really afraid."

"Yeah. She's afraid someone else is gonna hog all
the roe and leave her fat ass sitting on top of that heap
of junk," Hickok retorted.

I looked at Charlie without saying a word. How did
he happen to know Mavis was trying to get out of the
junk trade?

Hickok edgily stood up and walked over to get
himself more coffee. Once there, he slipped a flask
from his pocket. Part of its contents were poured into
his cup. Charlie turned around in time to catch me
watching.

"It's some damn medicine I have to take. Doctor's orders." He lumbered back to his chair and eased himself down in the seat. "Shit! I'm getting older than dirt," he grumbled.

I knew that Charlie was also afraid—and exactly what terrified him. He feared time was running out before he'd be able to make his own indelible mark. I knew that for one very good reason: I felt exactly the same way.

"Are you worried you don't have the leverage to get this deal on Mavis approved?" I asked, fully aware the question might spark a firestorm.

Hickok surprised me by continuing to silently drink his coffee.

"Listen here, Bronx," he finally responded. "I pick and choose my battles carefully. That's the secret to surviving in this outfit. I'm just trying to make up my mind whether this is worth blowing the rest of my marbles on. What you don't seem to realize is that victories aren't overwhelming in this business. They come in itty-bitty pieces."

"True, but you've also told me something else. That you have to choose whether to go along, get your little promotions, and stay out of trouble. Or decide that you have the drive to make a difference in this world. This is the big one, Charlie—I can feel it! This is the case you'll always be remembered for. You've only got eighteen months left. Why not go out with a bang?" Appealing to his ego was the best shot I had.

Charlie studied me closely before allowing a conspiratorial grin to escape. "Damn, Bronx. Maybe you really *do* have some South in you, after all. What the hell—Mavis Newcomb's only a little fish. Let's turn up the heat and see if we can snag Moby Dick on our line."

I smiled—until I popped open my Beanee Weenees and saw the cold beans and hot dog meat suspended in thickly congealed brown syrup. This seemed a good time to actually stay on my diet.

"Now, here's what we're gonna do. You head back up to Woody's and tell him you've decided that you want a cut of everything he and Virgil are making."

Oookay. No wonder Hickok was in a better mood. He'd cleverly hit upon a plan to have me eliminated as soon as possible. That way he'd be back in New Orleans by Mardi Gras time.

"And what makes you think they'd agree to something like that?"

Charlie grinned while pulling two packets of Cheddar cheese crackers out of his drawer. " 'Cause you're gonna offer 'em a deal they can't refuse. You're gonna be the Cheez Whiz on top of their hound dog burgers. What you've got is access to important information that they don't have."

Hickok lobbed a cracker into his mouth and my stomach started to rumble.

"You'll know exactly where state wildlife agents will be trawling their boats every night. You're gonna offer them Hardys the inside scoop in exchange for a piece of the action. Tell those two morons that way they won't have to worry about getting caught. The upshot is you'll gain their confidence."

Charlie bit into another cracker, spraying crumbs in my direction. He finally noticed that I was hungrily eyeing his cheese snack.

"Anyone ever tell you, you look pitiful when you beg?" he grumbled.

"Yeah, but it works every time," I retorted, grabbing the packet of crackers as it came flying my way. Mmm, this was more like it.

"*Now* can we get back to business?"

"Absolutely!" I happily agreed, polishing off a cracker in one large bite.

"Give it that extra little push by explaining it all boils down to good business sense. Woody and Virgil will be able to fish all night long without any headaches, and make more money. Of course, Beavis and Butthead aren't ever gonna take it out of their own pay, which means it'll have to come out of the Russki's pocket. And he's gonna want to have a sit-down with you before he does anything like that. So, a meeting will have to be set up. My suggestion is that you use those womanly charms that I suppose you got hidden somewhere."

"And what might those be?" I asked, knowing it would make him squirm.

Hickok immediately began to fidget in his seat. "For chrissakes, Bronx. *You* know that you're a damn fine-looking woman. You might as well use it for something, instead of letting it all go to waste."

Boy, was I glad I'd asked.

"Get to know who this head guy is and work your way into the action. Pretend you're Mata Hari—you were the big New York actress," Charlie snorted. "Just take the initiative and use the gifts God gave you. That's how we'll find out what's going on, and be able to lay our trap!"

The reality of what I was about to do finally hit home. Up until now, I had thought of it as nothing more than just talk.

"This *is* the Russian Mafia that we're dealing with," I reminded him. "I understand they're not the most trusting people around."

Hickok picked up on my misgivings. "What's the matter, Bronx? Suddenly getting cold feet? I thought you were gung-ho to get out there and lock up all the bad guys. You still sure you got what it takes?"

I could feel my face turn red. "Just tell me where the state agents will be making their run tonight," was my cold response.

I pulled the can of Beanee Weenees toward me. Picking up the spoon, I ate every single last bite as I listened, and then walked out.

Nine

A chorus of mournful howls was my welcoming committee as I parked next to the Coon Dog Express. But the fun didn't stop there. No sooner had I exited my Ford than Woody's two towheaded boys appeared.

"You got any more candy?" asked Spunky, by way of greeting. He used his fingers as a tissue for his runny nose, then wiped them on his pants.

I flashed the kid a dirty look that left no doubt he wasn't getting so much as a single Raisinet.

It took Little Prince Charming to rise to the occasion.

"My pa says you're just like one of his coon dogs now. He's got you trained to do whatever he says," he sniggered.

Ah, kids! You've got to love them; they *do* say the darnedest things.

"Is your father at home?" I asked the two budding hoodlums.

"Pawpaw ain't here and we ain't gonna tell you where he is!" Woody's younger son brayed.

"No candy, no information," Prince Charming seconded.

Then they ran off to play with their new toys—a steel trap and a dismembered broomstick.

I went to the house, hoping to have more luck with Tammy. Once there, I pounded on the door to be heard above the screams of her infant. Tammy finally answered, looking even more harried and bedraggled than she had yesterday.

"Is Woody here?" I asked, wondering if she ever managed to snatch a few needed Z's.

Tammy V listlessly shook her head.

"If you could tell me where he is, I'd appreciate it."

Tammy wearily nodded. "You can find him around Black Bayou, along Reelfoot Lake. He's out there setting traps." She hesitated for a moment, as if weighing the consequences of what she was about to say next. "You wanna come in for a cup of tea?" she finally asked.

For the first time, I heard the note of melancholy in Tammy's voice that clung to her words like a country-western singer's teardrop. I had the feeling she wondered what life might have held had she followed a different path. Her eyes caught mine in a silent plea, clearly hoping that I'd stay for a while and chat. It had to be lonely out here for someone her age—especially with only Woody and her kids for company. A shriek from outside and the loud snap of the trap made me jump, abruptly ending my speculation.

"Thanks, but I really need to get going. Maybe another time," I declined, and almost instantly regretted my decision.

Tammy V mutely nodded and looked away, as if she'd just been condemned to remain forever inside her solitary prison. I was tempted to tell her to pack her bags and get out while she could, but I already knew what her response would be. It was one for which I had no answer.

Where will I go? What will I do?

I walked away as she closed the door, each of us retreating into our own separate cocoons.

I drove past the tourist area of Reelfoot Lake, with its fishing camps and RV hookups. A cluster of bait-and-tackle shops dotted the shoreline, as deserted as out-of-season beach houses.

Nearby stood a small wooden building, home to city hall and the police department. No cars were parked out front, and the shades were down. Either the town officials had called it an early day, or the local good ol' boys no longer deemed any kind of authority necessary. I'd heard enough stories to know that even state wildlife agents refused to work this area alone, but my approach is somewhat different. I believe in going where I want, and never letting anyone know I'm afraid.

I turned toward Black Bayou and drove until I spotted Woody's truck. A beige Dodge Ram, it sat parked at the edge of the woods. I pulled up next to it and got out. Walking over, I peeked inside and spied a box of Little Debbie Snack Cakes. I reached in and took one out, then broke the cake into pieces to mark my path along the way.

I headed deep into the woods, following the bare bones of a trail while searching for any sign of Woody. Not a bird was to be heard, or even the rustle of a snake. I had nearly decided to turn back when I caught sight of an old fishing cabin. Nearby stood a gnarled tree that eerily resembled an evil crone. Its withered trunk was bent, and crooked limbs beckoned to me like long, arthritic fingers.

Come here, little girl. Don't worry. I won't hurt you. Oh, that's right. You're the one who's not afraid.

I hurried past, knowing it was nothing more than my active imagination—but not wanting to take any chances, either.

I continued along what I hoped was the path. The track had steadily narrowed, then finally disappeared, making it impossible to distinguish the trail from the rest of the wooded grounds. To make matters worse, my Little Debbie Snack Cake had run out when I heard the snapping of twigs. I stopped and nervously glanced about, checking for ghosts. Nothing was there. I breathed a sigh of relief. I took another step, only to hear the noise start up again in the distance. I knew it had to be Woody.

I followed the sound until I came upon his bib-overalled form bent over a snap-spring trap, a Krispy Kreme donut in hand. He looked like a big old bear waking up from his winter hibernation, rummaging around in search of a midday goody. I watched as he ever so carefully reached inside the trap, where he placed the tempting morsel as bait. A coon also watched from afar, sitting up on its haunches.

The critter remained perfectly still, except for compulsively rubbing its paws one over the other, as if trying to figure out Hardy's ploy. I silently snuck up behind Woody's rotund butt and stole a glazed goody from his sack. I waited until Hardy's hand was free and clear of the trap's vicious bite, then threw the treat toward the coon. An explosion of leaves erupted as the critter grabbed the donut, stuffed it into its mouth, and took off.

Hardy jumped back in surprise, letting loose a loud yelp. That immediately set off a chain reaction, spurring the trap into lethal motion. The spring promptly snapped closed with a deadly WHAP! For a moment I thought Hardy was going to keel over in shock, and I began to worry I'd gone too far this time. I was trying to figure out how I'd ever haul Woody's hefty carcass back to his pick-up, when he turned and faced me with an infuriated glower.

"Goddammit, Porter! What the hell'd you go and do that for? Not only did I lose that damn four-legged pelt, but you nearly scared the living daylights outta me!"

"Sorry about that." But I hoped it had taught him a lesson. Perhaps the next time Woody baited a trap, he'd stop and think about how an animal felt right before its windpipe was crushed.

Woody consoled himself by reaching into the donut sack and munching on some of his bait.

"I thought you'd stopped trapping. You told me the fur trade was dead these days," I reminded him.

"It is, dammit," he groused. "But what the hell else am I supposed to do with myself?" Then he narrowed his eyes and looked at me. "Whatchoo doin' out here, anyway?"

He finished the donut and started another.

"Maybe you should slow down on those things," I suggested. "Otherwise, people are going to think it's you, instead of Tammy, that's carrying the baby."

"That's real funny, Porter," Woody said, still

munching away. "But you know what they say: When you got a big tool, you need a big shed. Or maybe you don't know about those things, seeing as how you can't seem to get yourself a man these days. So, did you buy something good with all that money yet?" Hardy asked, with the hint of a sneer.

"Funny you should bring it up. That's exactly why I'm here."

"Whatsa matter, Porter? Have trouble sleeping last night? Don't worry, you'll get over it," Woody advised. "Besides, it's kinda late to try and return the money now. You've already shown your true colors."

"You've got it all wrong, Woody," I promptly replied. "I came for exactly the opposite reason. I've decided I want more money."

"What the . . . Goddammit to hell!" Woody roared. "I shoulda known better than to have been so generous. You know damn well that wasn't our agreement!"

"And exactly what agreement was that?"

"It was a onetime deal! Ten grand for you to keep off my ass. For chrissakes, what the hell do I look like? Some big ol' sugar daddy?" Hardy sputtered.

I bit the inside of my cheek to keep from laughing. What he looked like to me was a flailing, angry walrus.

"Take it easy, Woody. It's not as if I don't have something to offer in return," I quickly placated. "Besides, that ten grand was just a down payment for my silence. What I'm presenting you with now is a way to make a whole lot more money. More than you've ever dreamed of. Unless you're already happy with the way things are, that is."

Woody bent down and pulled the mutilated remains

of his bait from the trap. Brushing off some loose fur, he ate it. I took that to mean he was willing to listen further.

"The information I've got will allow you to catch all the paddlefish you want. Think about it, Woody: I'm offering you the best of both worlds. Not only will I never rat you out, but I can give you a rock-solid guarantee that you'll never get caught."

Hardy wiped his hands across his overalled belly, leaving behind a sticky residue. "Oh yeah? And how you gonna do that?"

"I can tell you where state wildlife agents will be making their runs on the river each night. That way, you'll know in advance exactly where to set your nets without any worry. What I want in exchange is a cut of the action."

"Whadda ya, crazy? You should be doing it for free as part of the ten grand!"

"I guess you should have thought about that earlier. Don't be so cheap, Woody!" I threw up my hands in disgust. "You know what? Maybe we should just forget I ever mentioned it. I'll offer this to someone else who'll better appreciate what I can do for them."

I turned to head back to my vehicle.

"Hold on there a second, Porter! I didn't say I wasn't gonna do it," Woody whined.

"Do we have a deal, then?" I pressed.

"I don't know yet," Woody said, stalling for time.

I took a lesson from Mavis's book. "Fine. I'll give you twenty-four hours, then I offer it to somebody else." I flashed Hardy the sweetest of smiles. "But I really wouldn't wait all that long, if I were you. There are plenty of other people who'd be only too happy to jump at this deal."

Hardy actually started to look worried. "Listen, Porter, I'd do it right now if I could. It's just that I gotta pass it by Virgil first. Why doncha come to the Sho Nuf Bar tomorrow around noon, and we'll finalize it then."

I lowered my head, as if thinking it over.

"Come on, Porter! I'll even buy you lunch," Woody said jovially.

Uh-huh. Where had I heard *that* offer before?

"So you and Virgil are both working this thing together? Why didn't you tell me that from the start?" I demanded.

Woody reached into his shed and adjusted his tool. "Because I didn't think you needed to know. I don't have to tell you everything that's going on."

Boy, did Hardy have a surprise waiting for him at the other end of the rainbow.

"Okay, Woody. I'm going to give you a freebie in the spirit of goodwill," I offered. "Throw your nets off the waters of Mud Island tonight—there won't be any state agents trawling their boats there. That should give you a taste of what you can get for your money. But I expect your answer by noon tomorrow," I warned. "Any later than that and the deal is off."

I headed back the way I'd come, trying not to look as lost as I felt. I searched the ground for any sign of my Little Debbie Snack Cake crumbs, knowing they were the only proof that I was on the right path. I just hoped some critter hadn't gotten to them first.

I passed by the fishing cabin once more, where the

old crone of a tree stood in wait. But this time, I distinctly felt another set of eyes bearing down upon me. I hurried to my Ford as fast as I could and left.

I was all the more anxious to get back to Memphis as it started to turn prematurely dark. The sky grew black and I inexplicably found myself in a melancholy mood. At times like this, there's only one thing to do. I pointed my vehicle straight for Beale Street, and the heart of the blues.

I parked in a lot and ambled down Beale's three revamped blocks, where each blues and jazz club beckoned for me to enter. Though it was still winter, there were already far too many tourists cruising the strip for my liking. I basked in the glow of neon signs as I passed shop after shop hawking souvenirs, tee-shirts and fortune-telling items.

I stopped and inspected the window of A. Schwab Dry Goods, the oldest authentic store on the beat. What I liked best was that it carried everything anyone could possibly ever want, from ladies' dresses in size sixty to straight razors and suspenders. Next door was Tater Red's with its array of voodoo products, including my personal favorites: Other Lawyer Be Stupid candles and Bitch Be Gone incense. I continued on until I hit my usual dive on Beale—the ever-funky Blues City Café.

Slipping into one of the lumpy, ripped vinyl booths, I placed my elbows on the sticky white Formica table. The place had just the right amount of shabbiness to make me feel completely at home. A group of overhead fans creaked out their own rickety rhythm as I took comfort in the sight of the kitchen's laden metal counter. "Put some South in your mouth," commanded the menu. I did just that, ordering the fried catfish with a side of red beans and rice. The first beer went down easy. By the second, I was feeling even mellower. But there was still someplace else that I needed to go tonight.

I ditched my Ford at home and began to walk. Though Beale Street is fun, it's mainly a beacon for tourists. For real blues and juke joints, you have to venture off the beaten path. I needed to feel the sting of a hot blues guitar, and the cry of a wailing voice flying smooth as lava up my spine. The best place for that was near the crossroads of Calhoun and South Main, at the Blue Mojo.

A former whorehouse, it had evolved into a late-hours nightclub specializing in blues the way they were meant to be heard. In the past, such tunes had been considered nothing more than "chittlin' music for poor people." But it's the only music I know that can so fully express every human emotion. It speaks of loves that are lost, jagged holes in the heart, and other dark and gnawing feelings. Tonight I wanted to be wrapped tight in the warmth of its cloak. I entered the Blue Mojo's shabby storefront, bellied up to the bar, and took my place on one of the stools.

The owner wasn't around tonight. No matter; Boobie wasn't the person I'd come to see. I ordered a longneck and waited until Gena took the stage. When she stepped forward, it was into a shower of pale red light, causing a ripple of excitement to shimmer through the audience. She had poured herself into a dress that most women would have killed to look half as good in—and every man in the room would have died to get her out of.

Gena had been trained by the best, singing spirituals in Reverend Al Green's Full Gospel Tabernacle choir. Her voice knew just where my heart needed to go. She belted out a tune overflowing with love and hate, passion, yearning, and desire. When God handed out gifts, Gena had been twice blessed. Besides being beautiful, she could interpret a song like no other vocalist. She shut her eyes and slid into a low, guttural groan, and the sound conjured up a deep, primal underworld of haunting delta ghosts.

I'd once looked up the phrase "having the blues" and found its derivation went all the way back to eighteenth-century England. Then, those painwracking emotions that burrow deep down into your soul had been called "blue devils," a slang term for melancholia. A bunch of those little suckers were having one hell of a party dancing around me tonight.

I let the music bury itself inside me, with its whisper of what I was missing. Then I polished off my beer and headed out the door. I walked home alone, where I lay down, concealed in semidarkness. But nothing could take away the feeling of loneliness that wrapped around me like a shroud. Or the feeling that I was still being watched.

Ten

The next morning, I picked up the phone and gave Mavis a ring as I downed my newly purchased forbidden Froot Loops. I wanted to let her know that our deal was on. Okay, what I really wanted was to get my hands on her mystery files as quickly as possible.

Receiving no answer at her home, I tried reaching her at the Best Little Junk Shop in Memphis. Wouldn't you know? Busy. She was yapping up a storm, probably planning when to shoot her next TV commercial. After a while I got tired of redialing, and decided to head on out. I took a look at my chipped cereal bowl as I placed it in the sink. Hmm. Maybe it was time to break down and buy more dishware.

I sped along Elvis Presley Boulevard, where I mentally saluted *Hound Dog II* and the *Lisa Marie*, only to be cut off by a Graceland shuttle bus. I slammed my hand on the horn and passed it, catching sight of the angry tourists inside. Some shook their fists, while others wagged their heads in disapproval. The rest voiced their opinion of my behavior by way of digital salute.

I was in such a rush to get hold of Mavis's files that I didn't even bother to stop at Krispy Kreme. I flew past and didn't ease up on the gas until I swerved into the junkyard.

Once there I hurried inside, but the junk queen was nowhere in sight.

"Mavis! It's Rachel Porter. Are you here?"

Either she was playing coy or, for some reason, she couldn't hear me. Then I realized that her Mercedes convertible hadn't been parked out front. I made my way over to her desk and discovered her phone was off the hook. My pulse instantly quickened.

Okay, slow down. Don't jump to any conclusions.

Perhaps she'd simply walked away and left an annoying customer hanging. God knows, I'd been tempted to do it to Charlie many times. I lifted the receiver and listened to the recorded message that continuously requested that I please hang up. I was happy to oblige, and then began to poke around the table.

Mavis's paperwork still sat in the same hefty stack, giving the impression she'd made little headway on it since my visit yesterday. I called out once more and then made a beeline for her basement. As far as I was concerned, our deal was in place, and I was determined not to leave without her records.

The cellar door stood wide open, and a glimmer of light bled steadily up the stairs. Bingo! It looked like I'd just discovered the whereabouts of Miss Mavis. The next second, my euphoria crumbled into panic. I didn't put it past Newcomb to "edit" a few incriminating items from her files at the very last minute.

I flew down the steps, determined to wrestle her to

the ground, if necessary. But Mavis wasn't there. To top it off, her filing cabinets stood open, completely empty.

I didn't know whether to feel stupid or angry at having been played for a fool. Mavis had clearly pulled a fast one. One possibility was that she'd lied from the beginning about having any documentation. That would have bought her some time to get me temporarily off her tail. The other scenario was that she had sold every scrap of evidence to the highest bidder. Either way, I wasn't a happy camper. On top of which, I now had to deal with Hickok.

"I'll be back!" I called out, à la the Terminator, still certain she must be around. I slowly walked out, listening for the slightest sound that would betray her. But the shop remained oddly silent.

Now I had plenty of time to kill before meeting Woody at the Sho Nuf Bar, but that wouldn't be hard to do. Hickok had demanded that I first come by and show my face at work. I decided to sweeten the visit by stopping off at Krispy Kreme, where I purchased a mixed dozen of glazed, powdered, and jelly donuts. Maybe I could keep Charlie so busy eating, he'd forget to ask any pertinent questions.

Barney Fife was the first thing to greet me as I walked in the door. Hickok's smug face was the second.

"Unless you've got those files disguised as a bunch of donuts, I'd say something's *reeeaaally* screwed up."

Oy vey. I placed the bag of Krispy Kremes in front of him.

"Mavis doesn't seem to be around this morning. She's probably just running some errands," I offered.

"Yeah. Like changing her mind and selling her information to that damn Russki," Charlie replied in a pissed-off growl.

It wasn't all that comforting to know that our minds worked in exactly the same manner.

"She'll turn up," I declared. *Even if I have to tear through every cotton field in order to find her.*

I was about to help myself to a donut when my telephone rang. I lunged, praying the caller was Mavis.

"Hey, Porter! It's me. You've had plenty of time to check out that information I gave you. So, when am I getting my money?"

I was almost able to catch a whiff of fried bologna through the phone line. It was none other than Woody's daughter.

"Like I told you before, Wynona, I need more than just a snapshot of raccoon's eyes. I talked to your father, but there was no proof of anything around. I even looked inside his Coon Dog Express trailer."

Hickok began to laugh so hard, he nearly choked on his powdered donut. I flashed him a vexed don't-screw-me-up expression.

"The best thing you can do is to let me know when he plans to make another run. That way I can catch him in the act of transporting rabid coons, and then we'll talk money."

"Oh, yeah. I'll be real sure to do that," Wynona barked. "Whadda ya think? I'm some kind of hillbilly dummy? Why should I trust you now that you've been paid off?"

"What?" I asked in amazement.

Hickok had turned out to be right once again. Hardy was flapping his gums, bragging to the world about how he'd gone and bought himself a genuine federal agent. It wouldn't take long for poachers to decide the coast was totally clear, and start having themselves a field day. The only consolation was knowing that the fear of God would be rammed into them once they learned what I'd really been up to.

"Don't play dumb with me, Porter. Daddy told me all about the deal he made to shut you up. What *I* think, is you owe me at least half of that money."

Wynona was wasting her talent on this penny-ante stuff; she could have gone into the legal profession and made herself a killing.

"That money is tied up. But believe me, I still plan to help you. However, the first thing you've got to do is to get me proof to go on."

"Yeah, right! I'd have a better chance of getting the money if I'd stuck with my original blackmail plan," Wynona grumbled. "Or maybe my boyfriend and I'll just come after *you*," she added ominously.

"Are you threatening me?" I asked, squaring off. "Because if so, I'm warning you right now: Don't even think of trying anything."

"All I'm saying is you'll be getting yours soon enough." She slammed down the receiver.

"That sounded like it went real well," Hickok affably observed. "Rabid coons, huh? That don't surprise me none. Woody and his clan are the horses' asses of all horses' asses. Here, have one of these. It'll make you feel better."

I caught the donut in mid-air, but the tension in my grip made me squeeze it too hard, causing raspberry filling to seep through my fingers like cold, coagulated blood. The effect was more than enough to turn my stomach. I actually threw a donut in the garbage for the first time that I could ever remember. However, the Krispy Kremes seemed to have worked their magic on Hickok. His mood had definitely improved from when I'd walked in.

I glanced at my watch. There was enough time to make one quick call, and then I was out of here.

"Mad Dog Vin's School for Professional Wrestling. Others bark, I bite," rang out Vincent's baritone.

"Hi, Vincent. It's Rachel. Listen, I have a favor to ask."

"What? Some guy bothering you? Just say the word and I'll be glad to make his acquaintance with a monkey flip, before getting to know him better by way of a pile driver. After which I'll cement our friendship by holding him in a full nelson, while you open a can of whup ass on him," he graciously offered.

"Thanks, that's nice of you. But I was thinking more along the lines of a caviar lesson," I responded. "Would it be possible for you to give me a crash course this evening? I'll gladly foot the bill."

"Splendid!" Vincent replied. "I'd be delighted to do so."

I glanced over at Hickok for his approval, and Charlie sourly nodded his head as he bit into a glazed beauty.

"I'm always looking for a good excuse to treat myself. In fact, let's do it up right. The champagne is on me," Vincent proposed. "After all, you can't have one without the other. Then we'll follow it up with a light dinner. See you later, and stay out of trouble." The warning had become part of his normal farewell.

I hung up to find Charlie darkly glowering at me.

"Anything else we here at the U.S. Fish and Wildlife Service can do to help you along with the case? Maybe get you some paté and truffles to go with your fish eggs? Or how about a nice bottle of champagne?" he sarcastically inquired.

"No, thanks. That's already been taken care of," I said cockily.

Oops. Maybe that hadn't been the right approach to take. Hickok's eyes locked onto mine like two torpedoes in search of something to nuke.

"I got news for you, Porter: you better pull this one off. 'Cause I'm making sure it's your neck and not mine that winds up on the chopping block," Charlie warned, beginning to slide into one of his black moods.

He was obviously disgruntled that I hadn't come through with Mavis Newcomb's files. I wasn't too thrilled about it, either.

"So if I were you, I wouldn't take too much advantage of the situation," Hickok warned.

"Don't worry. I'm not about to screw up," I said, hoping I sounded a lot more confident than I felt. I was damned if I'd give him the satisfaction of failing. I did my best to pull off the charade by reaching into one of the Krispy Kreme bags and grabbing a donut I didn't want, then I left.

Eleven

I drove back along the road I had traveled yesterday, passing the corroded steel container pockmarked with sullied cotton bolls. A chill wind whipped across the barren fields, and the long, low sky was identical to the day before. So were the telephone poles, with their nasty carved *KKK*.

Nothing had changed—other than myself, that is. Lurking inside was the feeling you get when fingernails screech with abandon down a chalkboard: your nerves are set on edge, and your skin begins to crawl, making the very teeth in your mouth ache. It was a sure sign that I was heading for trouble. I shoved the premonition aside, and did my best to ignore it. Give in to fear once, and you'll question yourself every time. I already had enough demons to contend with.

I drove down the bluff and into the maze of kudzu, which swiftly closed around me with grim determination. It didn't require much imagination to feel it reach in through the window, to clutch at my arms, my legs, and my hair. I held my breath, not daring to exhale until I was safely out of its grip.

This time I arrived at the Sho Nuf Bar to find that I wasn't alone. Ten other cars were haphazardly parked in the lot, each faced in a slightly different direction as in a game of bumper cars. It almost looked as if the drivers had jumped out of their vehicles before bringing them to a complete stop.

I parked next to Woody's pick-up and walked past the forbidding sign: "No Niggers or Game Wardens Allowed." Its angry tidings echoed in my brain, and a voice within me whispered a cautious warning.

Sure enough, there was a bunch of good ol' boys sitting at a dozen rickety tables, chugging beers and drinking what looked to be moonshine. Homemade liquor was big in these parts, since this was a dry county. Several men had their faces buried in plates of ribs, and everyone was talking loudly. Until I entered the room, that is. Then all activity promptly came to a halt. Either their investment adviser from Paine-Webber was about to speak, or *I* was the lucky gal who had become the focus of so much male attention. I looked out over the sea of forbidding expressions and unkempt bodies. It was enough to make any sane woman glad to have remained blissfully single.

I tried my best to appear unruffled as I glanced around the room, where my eyes lit upon two signs— one proclaimed, "David Duke for President," while the other advised, "We Don't Bother Calling 911." Wasn't *that* reassuring.

I casually wandered over to the bar and stood beneath the mounted fish with a bottle of Bud in its mouth. The next moment, I looked up and very nearly plotzed. I could have sworn the damn thing winked at me. Either that, or it was the nervous fluttering of my eyelids as the silence continued to mount. It couldn't have been more apparent that an unwanted visitor was in the room. The whoosh of an angry cleaver was the only sound to sever the malevolent stillness, further emphasizing the point.

I was tempted to break the ice by asking how many game wardens it takes to screw in a lightbulb. Fortunately, I was saved by Woody, who popped his head out of the kitchen.

"Hey, Porter! Set yourself down at one of the tables and I'll round us up some lunch."

That seemed to do the trick. The crowd proceeded to ignore my presence and focus back on their chow.

I headed for an empty table in the corner of the room and took a seat. But, wouldn't ya know? My rear end landed in a chair that rocked back and forth like a boat tossing about in a storm. One huge, whiskered customer nailed me with a look, as if to say, *How uncouth!* Then he got up and began to walk toward me.

This is it! I thought. Woody and Virgil had put out the word. I'm a woman, a wildlife agent, and, even worse, a New Yorker to boot! Their plan had been to lure me to the Sho Nuf Bar, have me knocked off, and then throw my body into the murky waters of the Mississippi.

Mr. Z Z Top seemed to be contemplating just that as he loomed like a sinister giant above me. I was prepared to give him a quick kick in the shins, when he saved me the trouble by falling down hard onto a bended knee. Oh no! It was even worse than I'd thought: This was a church, and I was about to be mar-

ried in a bizarre delta ritual to prove I could be trusted!
I got ready to jump up and run as Mr. Z wiped the barbecue sauce from his face. The next thing I knew, he'd
lifted one side of my chair off the ground, with me in
it. Then he placed a matchbook just so beneath the
wobbly leg.

"There, that ought to do it," he said, and gently set
me back down.

Ohmigod! A real live gentleman!

"Thank you," I croaked.

It had been a long time since I'd had an actual date.
That's the only excuse I could come up with as to why
I found myself imagining what Mr. Z would look like
with a decent shave and a haircut.

Woody broke the spell by approaching with a couple of brown paper bags. He set them on the table and
headed over to the bar, returning with two plastic cups
half filled with RC cola. When he sat in his chair, it
rock-and-rolled worse than my own had. Reaching
down, he retrieved a pint of Early Times bourbon from
its hiding place inside his stretched-out sock.

"This stuff is cheap but it does the trick," he said
with a wink, and spiked both our cups.

I grabbed one of the paper bags and began to un-
wrap my lunch, only to have Hardy stop me.

"Hold on there a second. I can already tell you
don't have the damnedest clue what to do when it
comes to barbecue. There's a right way and a wrong
way to eat a rib sandwich. Watch and learn, girl.
Maybe some day you'll even be able to pass yourself
off as a Southerner."

I was all for that.

"First, you take it outta the bag and stuff the brown paper in your pocket, 'cause you're gonna need it later on. Now you cup the top slice of bread in your hand, scoop up the slaw, and eat it real quick, being that's your vegetable. Then grab those four slabs of meat inside, and gnaw to your heart's content on the bones. That leaves you with one last piece of bread. Whatcha gonna do is use it to wipe all the sauce off your face, and then eat it. Finally, throw the leftover bones in the bag and take 'em home for your dog. And that's how we eat barbecue here in Tennessee," Woody lectured.

"For chrissakes!" Virgil spat.

He hauled a chair behind him like a caveman dragging his woman around, and slammed it into place between us. No wonder all the seats in this place sounded as grouchy as a bunch of arthritic old men. Virgil straddled the chair and scowled, causing goosebumps to rise on my neck as he caught my eye. His lips curled into a snarl, and I felt the screech of nails racing down a chalkboard once again.

"Enough fun and games. Let's cut the crap and get down to business," he growled.

I decided to get the ball rolling in the right manner. "So, how did your fishing go last night? I take it you went to the area I told you to hit."

"It was good, but not good enough," Woody diffidently responded, ever the game player.

"Whadda ya talking about? It sucked!" Virgil heatedly announced. "The paddlefish are running low and the ones we're catching are too young, without any

eggs in 'em. Hell, all we're doing is slitting 'em open
and throwing 'em back in the water. You want a share
of the money, Porter, then you gotta do better than
that. I don't need to go out on the river and waste my
time." His nostrils flared, much like a large, angry
hog's.

"Look, I told you what I could do," I retorted. "If
you want to find protected areas where the fish haven't
been hit yet, you're going to have to head further
south."

"No shit, Porter. Whadda ya *think* we've been doing?" Virgil bitched.

"That's right, Virgil. We have been doing that,"
Woody soothingly agreed. "But we still need Rachel
here to point us in the right direction and supply us
with protection. She's our guarantee that we won't be
caught."

"I can do both those things for you," I confirmed.
"But, of course, it'll cost you more money."

Virgil leaned in close. "Listen here, bitch. First you
gotta meet the man we work for. He has final say. He's
also the one who controls the purse strings. So save all
that smart talk of yours, and use it to sell *him* the idea.
And after that, you goddamn better make sure that you
do come through. Or you'll be the next thing that finds
itself swimming with the fishies." He drew a jagged
fingernail across his fleshy throat.

I leaned in an inch closer and stared straight into his
milky-blue eyes. "You're right, Virgil, intimidation
does brings out the bitch in me. So let me warn you
now: I'm not like those other women you pushed

around in the past. Not only do I push back, but I make sure not to take any prisoners." I held his gaze, unwilling to let him know how much he was getting to me.

"All right. That's enough from both of you," Woody jumped in. "You've each marked your territory. Now let's try and work together on this thing. You okay with that, Virgil?" he asked diplomatically.

Virgil sat back. "Sure. I got no beef with her yet." Then he smiled at me. "In fact, I kinda like you."

Knowing his past history, that wasn't very comforting.

"Okay. Now, we got a meeting set for ten o'clock tonight. Make sure to be there on time, 'cause this guy doesn't like to be kept waiting. Here's the address."

Woody slipped a piece of paper into my hand. The location was south of Memphis, not far from Graceland.

"Do I get to know the man's name?" I asked, wanting to make certain this was the Russian Mavis had told me about.

"You'll hear it when you get there. Not before," Virgil gruffly replied. Then he licked his bottom lip, in what I imagined was his idea of foreplay.

I was tempted to ask if he'd heard from Mavis since yesterday, but decided to hold off. It was possible she didn't want him to know that we'd been in touch. Besides, I was still hoping that our deal was in place.

"Fine. I'll see you there tonight." I left the rib bones lying on the table and quickly walked out.

Once inside the Ford, I took a deep breath. The exhalation turned shuddery as I suddenly realized one other possibility: perhaps Mavis *hadn't* gone to the

Russian at all, but had run straight to Virgil with her files. Maybe she still felt a twinge of loyalty to her ex. If so, *he* was the one now in control. For all I knew, Virgil already suspected I wasn't really crooked but was only pretending. Acting on the hunch, I headed for his trailer now to see if Mavis was hiding out, there.

I arrived to find Virgil's little dog chained to a metal pole in front of the trailer, looking as forlorn as a mutt counting down the days it has left in a pound. The pooch couldn't have appeared any more pitiful as she visibly shivered—though I wasn't certain whether it was due to the cold, or from a residual sense of fear. I walked over and gave her a few reassuring pats, and she gratefully reciprocated with a rush of licks. Then I straightened up and gazed around.

There was no sign of a little red Mercedes, which came as a relief. It looked like Hickok once again had proved to be correct: undercover work was already playing with my head and making me paranoid.

Then again, maybe not. There was still the yard behind the trailer to check. The dog followed as far as she could before the chain ended and yanked her back. She lay down to await my return, as I approached the rear of Virgil's home.

Nope. Mavis's car wasn't there, either. But I *did* stumble on equipment for making moonshine. Sitting on the ground was a fermenting tank, along with a large black pot and a coil of three-inch copper tubing. I had no doubt that if I took the time, I'd also uncover bags of cornmeal, sugar, yeast, and malt. The ingredients for making the "mash" were probably stored in the same shed from which Virgil had emerged carrying half a hog. I decided to skip that part of the search; I wasn't in the mood to poke around in a slaughterhouse today. Besides, I didn't really care that Hardy sold illegal alcohol. I only wished he made enough money from it to leave the paddlefish alone.

Turning around, I returned to the dog, knelt down, and began to pet her. When she wriggled in gratitude, I sat on the ground and the pooch curled up in my lap. The scene was so peaceful—even the hogs were quiet and content. As I watched them lolling lazily in the mud, my eye caught sight of something peculiar. Though just a tiny speck, its color was unusually bright. Peeking out from the pool of brown mud was an object the color of a runny egg yolk.

I gently pushed the dog off my lap, only to have her scramble back on. We played the game a few more times until I finally won, then I headed over to the pen to investigate further. Though the hogs glanced up and grunted, they didn't bother to move. Leaning over the rail, I tried to get a closer gander at the mystery object, but whatever I'd seen had just as quickly disappeared—until I started to turn away. Then the lemon-meringue item playfully popped back into view again.

I returned to my Ford, where I pulled out a pair of latex gloves and two heavy-duty garbage bags. Hey, what can I say? I follow that old Boy Scout motto to always be prepared. I put a foot inside each Hefty sack, wrapped the plastic tightly around my legs, and held the bags in place with two large rubber bands that I'd scrounged from inside the black hole of my glove box. Having suited up, I returned to the pen feeling like a fifth-rate astronaut out of an old black-and-white Japanese movie. A broken broomstick lay nearby on the ground, and I picked it up and hoisted myself inside the pen.

The hogs protested with angry grunts and snorts, eyeing me in much the same way as Virgil. I ignored their complaints and headed straight for the spot of yellow. Once there, I lowered the broomstick and began my fishing expedition.

Voilà! I hooked my prey on the pole and, ever so carefully, lifted the sodden treasure out of the muck and waste. My breath caught in my throat as I stared at what I'd exhumed, not quite knowing what to make of it. Dangling from the end of the pole was what appeared to be one of Mavis Newcomb's muddied yellow high heels, which I'd seen her wearing only yesterday.

My stomach constricted until it was taut as a vise. Lowering the stick once more, I began to methodically probe the mud, not wanting to admit what I was after. By the time I was through, pinpricks of sweat dappled my skin like morning dew, turning my clothes cold and clammy so that they stuck to my flesh. I was no longer an astronaut heading up into the sky, but a diver delving under a sea of putrefying slime in search of what I hoped not to find—namely, a cadaver. The sensation of suffocation didn't end until my task was through. Only then did I finally breathe a deep sigh of relief.

Maybe I really was crazy. Still, Mavis had definitely been pissed at Virgil for ratting her out to a Fish and Wildlife agent. All I could figure was that she'd shown up here yesterday, gotten into a fight, and whacked Virgil with her shoe during the ensuing battle. Most likely, he'd retaliated by throwing her high heel into the pigpen. I was beginning to think the two truly were soul mates. God knew, they were greedy enough to deserve each other.

I slogged past the hogs with my trophy and hauled myself out of their sty. I couldn't help but get the giggles as I thought about how much I'd scared myself—not to mention how I must look in my stunning new outfit. Removing the plastic bags from my legs, I wrapped Mavis's shoe inside one, then headed for the Ford. Virgil's dog begged me to stop by breaking into a chorus of pitiful whimpers. I did everything in my power not to listen, but the pooch's cries grew increasingly louder and more pathetic by the minute.

I climbed inside my vehicle and started the engine, provoking the mutt to let loose with a heart-wrenching wail. It was as if I were consigning the critter to eternal damnation. I'd sworn on my life never to let myself get attached to anything ever again. Not after my dog Pilot, in Nevada. Still, I couldn't help but sneak a peek. The canine played me masterfully, breaking into an eerie howl as if on the verge of dying.

There are some things over which we have little control in life. Though my head told me to drive away, my heart kept my foot on the brake, refusing to let me leave. I finally gave in, knowing there was no other way I'd ever be able to live with myself.

I trudged back across the yard with metal snips in hand and gave Virgil's dog her freedom, knowing all too well what would happen next. The pooch made a mad dash for my vehicle and jumped inside the cab with a flying leap. Then she happily sat in the passenger seat, wagging her tail while waiting for me to join her.

I pulled myself up behind the wheel and sternly stared at my new companion. "Okay, let's get something straight right away. I'm the boss. That means I'm the one in control here."

She played me for the patsy I was by cheerfully licking my face.

"All right! Enough already," I gruffly replied, blinking the tears from my eyes as I once again turned on the engine and left.

I now had a lot more baggage than when I'd first started out this morning. Namely, Virgil's mutt, Mavis's muddied yellow shoe, and a barbecue rib sandwich that lay like a log in my stomach.

Twelve

"**Y**ou realize you're crazy, don't you?" Terri asked, after I'd bathed the dog and taken a shower.

"Is that a question or a statement?" I inquired.

"In your case, it's both. What are you going to do with a dog? You couldn't even take care of a cockatoo."

I didn't bother to respond, but simply watched as Terri proceeded to feed our new boarder some leftover chicken. Then I went into the bedroom and finished getting dressed, in preparation for my caviar lesson.

"So, what are you going to call her, anyway?" Terri questioned.

I walked into the living room where the two of them were sitting on the couch together. I shrugged, not yet willing to name the pooch for fear of becoming too attached.

"I haven't really thought about it. How about just Dog?" I suggested.

"Oh, right. I get it. You're Holly Golightly and we're about to have breakfast at Tiffany's," Terri retorted. "Absolutely not. The dog deserves better than that."

"Then why don't *you* name her?" I proposed, as if

that would release me from any emotional bond, and place the weight of commitment on Terri.

But Terri shook his head. "Oh no, you don't. On second thought, Dog will do just fine for now. You'll name her when you're ready."

Terri and I headed for Vincent's, only to be stopped at the door by a heartfelt moan. Dog sat with her head cocked to one side and gazed at us with mournful eyes. Then she started to wobble as if she just might topple over, unable to bear the thought of being left alone.

Terri and I looked at each other in a moment of silent communion before blurting out in unison, "Oh, all right. Come on!"

Dog jauntily followed us out the door. We rang the bell and Vincent waved us into his abode, until he spotted what was tagging along at our feet.

"Oh dear God. You've finally done it, Terri. You went and got a dog. Does this mean we're now one of those New Age nuclear families?" he asked apprehensively.

"No, it means Rach has picked up another stray which I temporarily get to take care of." Terri sent a knowing look my way.

"Just tell me the creature's housebroken. That's all I ask." Vincent dramatically pointed toward his beautiful antique Persian rug.

"Don't worry, she's perfectly well-behaved," I assured him, hoping the pooch wouldn't prove me a liar.

"In that case, let's start our lesson, shall we?" Vincent led the way into the dining room.

Before us was a table laden with enough silver and crystal to make me believe I actually *had* landed at Tiffany's.

"This is absolutely amazing!" I exclaimed in delight.

Four separate mounds of caviar, nestled in faceted cut-glass bowls, sat in sterling silver servers that acted as ice chambers. Vincent pulled out a chair and held it as I took my seat. Then he did the same for Terri. Dog seemed to sense this was an important test; she lay down and placed her chin on my feet.

"Now, as I said the other night, one of the most crucial things is to know who you're buying from. Your caviar connection should care about you as much as your plastic surgeon."

"I'm all for that," Terri agreed, and gently patted the skin around his eyes.

"The other thing to remember is never let caviar come into contact with metal," Vincent instructed.

"Why is that?" I asked, wondering how else you were supposed to spoon out the stuff.

"Because a chemical reaction ensues when the two elements meet. That's why the insides of their tins are always coated with epoxy glaze. Just look at those tiny, fragile globes. Good caviar should make your taste buds burst into the strains of a Chopin waltz. It should fill your veins with romance. That's not about to happen if the roe has a metallic taste."

I could see his point.

"That's why all the spoons tonight are mother-of-pearl, and the caviar is served in crystal. Now, let's move on to how the eggs should look," Vincent suggested.

I glanced at Terri, who sat with his chin in his hands, gazing at the wrestler with unadulterated rapture. It was the first time I'd ever seen him like this. For a moment, I felt the slightest twinge of envy. Even Dog had begun to snore in contentment at my feet. Boy, was I feeling sorry for my lonely, unattached self.

Drop the self-pity, and get your mind back on the lesson!

Vincent gently lifted a diminutive egg between two sausage-sized fingers. "You see how the roe is firm? That's exactly the way you want it to be." He slipped the sample into my hand. "The eggs should never be broken or mushy. Now go ahead and take a whiff."

I lifted the eggs and carefully inhaled, afraid if I sniffed too hard it might fly up my nose.

"How does that smell?" he questioned.

"Just like the sea."

"That's exactly right. And the scent should have a fresh and clean aroma."

Vincent picked up a mother-of-pearl spoon and dipped it into the closest mound of roe.

"Each of these four bowls contains a different type of caviar. It takes a certain amount of skill to differentiate between them, so I'm going to try and make this as simple as possible."

He extracted the spoon from bowl number one and offered me a taste. I placed a few of the eggs in my mouth. But try as hard as I might, I didn't hear any strains of Chopin, nor did I feel a throbbing rush of romance course through my veins. Instead, it tasted akin to belly lox—except this stuff was probably a whole lot more expensive.

Vincent opened a bottle of Veuve Clicquot, easing out the cork with a gentle sigh. Then he poured its contents into three crystal flutes. The bubbles raced to the surface of each glass like frantic survivors desperate for air.

"Cleanse your palate with a sip of this," he instructed.

I reached for the flute.

"Always hold your glass by the stem, Rachel. That way the warmth of your fingertips won't flatten the bubbles, and you'll impress the hell out of a true gourmand."

He handed a glass of champagne to Terri with an affectionate wink. No wonder Terri was falling for this guy. Not only could he kick ass, but his taste was impeccable.

"Okay. Sample number two." He slid a different spoon in my mouth. "How would you describe this one?"

These eggs were more yellowish-golden in color than the first sample I'd tried.

"It has a kind of nutty, earthy taste to it," I offered. Ooh, yeah. I could see *that* review being printed in the *New York Times*. It sounded like I was critiquing a kid's cereal.

"Very good!" Vincent praised. "Your description is perfect. That was osetra. It's one of the three types of Russian sturgeon from the Caspian Sea. Take a sip of champagne and we'll move on to the next."

Mmm, I was really beginning to enjoy this lesson. I slipped the third spoonful of roe into my mouth. The eggs were smaller than the last batch, and lighter gray in color.

"These seem to have rather a briny taste," I tentatively offered.

"Right again!" Vincent beamed. "Those are sevruga. You're a natural at this. Now here's the last sample."

However, rather than handing me the spoon, Vincent deposited a few of the eggs along the base of his thumb, as if they were snuff, and tested the roe with a small lick before eating them.

I had no idea what the hell he was doing, but it certainly looked impressive. I naturally followed suit. These eggs were steel-gray and the largest of the four samples, with a taste like that of wonderfully creamy butter.

"Those are my favorite," I said boldly.

Vincent nodded approvingly. "They're the rarest and most expensive eggs of all. What you just tasted is beluga."

So *these* were the eggs that Mafia gangs were battling Russian marine guards over. The flavor instantly lost its appeal. The beluga sturgeon had little time left before it would officially be declared extinct.

"I can't stand it any longer! Enough with the lesson! Can I join in and eat some of this now?" Terri held a hand to his forehead, pretending to feel faint.

"Absolutely." Vincent laughed. "Why don't you bring the toast points and crème fraîche out from the kitchen?"

"You never told me what the first batch of eggs were," I realized.

Vincent smiled knowingly and had me sample them once again. "This is what we call our local caviar. It's paddlefish roe. Can you tell the difference between it and the others?"

The taste wasn't all that different from the sevruga. "Yes," I hesitantly responded. "But only the slightest bit."

"Don't feel bad; it has nothing to do with your taste buds," he said. "It takes a connoisseur to immediately make the distinction. Especially when black market dealers mix it with one of the more expensive varieties."

Terri placed a spoonful of roe on his sliver of toast, topped with a few drops of lemon juice. "That's why I only eat beluga. At least that way I know what I'm getting," he proclaimed and happily licked his fingers.

Even Terri didn't stop to think about where the eggs on his toast came from—or of the sturgeon's inevitable march toward extermination.

"The problem is, you can't always be certain that what you're buying is pure beluga these days—even at its rarefied price." Vincent sighed. "That's why it's so important to deal with someone you trust."

"But how do they know what *they're* being sold?" I asked.

"Smart girl," Vincent observed with a nod. "Sometimes they don't. Which reminds me of one last trick I want to show you."

He pulled two of the bowls toward us—the ones holding osetra and beluga.

"My caviar connection tells me that osetra is regularly being pawned off as beluga these days, since their population is in far better shape. However, there *is* a way to tell the difference. You just have to know the secret."

Vincent placed one of each egg on the white surface of his plate and then lightly pressed down on them. The beluga exuded a gray oil, while the liquid secreted from the osetra was tinged with yellow.

"There! That's the best two-second test you can possibly perform to detect fraud. Now, do you think you can remember everything you've just learned?"

I put the champagne flute down. My head was beginning to spin from trying to retain too many facts.

Vincent gave my hand a reassuring pat, and began walking toward the kitchen. "Don't worry, I plan to feed you dinner now. That will make you feel better. Then we'll go back over everything once more after we eat."

Thirteen

By nine-thirty that night, I was in my Ford chugging south along the Blues Highway, the flat road humming beneath my wheels. Visions of paddlefish, osetra, beluga, and sevruga sturgeon danced inside my head. The living fossils performed a prehistoric ballet, slapping the water with their tails, as thousands of eggs spurted out of their bodies. I pushed the bizarre image from my mind, wondering if I was beginning to identify just a little too much with the archaic species. I tried focusing instead on the abandoned stores and clapboard houses with fallen-down porches which flew past, but even that couldn't distract the horde of little blue devils who continued to dance around me.

I'd heard the delta was a place of missing things. The image came to life tonight as I drove by the South's very own version of the Great Wall—the levee holding back the Mighty Mississippi. A ghostly swirl of blues chants rose off the water, as if springing from the restless souls of those long-dead men who had given their lives to build it. Their spirits filled the air as the Ford began to shake, whipped by a blast of wind that mournfully howled across the broad delta floodplain. The cry became that of a woman betrayed, and I shivered as it crept inside my body.

I turned off the main road and followed a serpentine street, finally arriving at my destination. A wrought-iron gate barred the way up to the house, requiring that I press a buzzer for entry. I waited to hear a dis-embodied voice request my name, rank, and serial number, but my presence was obviously expected tonight. The gate automatically swung open.

Towering live oaks lined both sides of the long drive-way, creating the perfect setting for a horse and carriage transporting Scarlett O'Hara. I was in for a greater surprise when I arrived at the house, for this was no Tara: it was a cloned Graceland. I spotted Virgil's broken-down Olds 88 sitting alongside Woody's dented pick-up; the clunkers were parked next to a dark Lincoln Town Car and a hot-pink 1955 Caddy. Either Mary Kay was permanently interred here, or its resident had a serious Elvis fetish.

I walked up the steps, past four grandiose white columns. When I rang the bell, its chimes jived to the strains of "Jailhouse Rock." If an Elvis impersonator opened the door, I was definitely out of here. The last time I'd bumped into the King's likeness was when I'd nearly gotten hitched at the Graceland Wedding Chapel in Vegas.

The man who answered the door did look like he was straight out of Central Casting, but he'd apparently stumbled off the set of *The Beverly Hillbillies*. A pair of beat-up jeans hung off his hips as though they were intent on hitting the ground running. The man's eyes looked as red and sunken as those of a basset hound that had been sniffing glue. A matted lock of hair fell over his brow, while two cowlicks stuck straight out on either side of his head. On his feet were worn-out boots with dented metal tips.

He stared at me for a long moment as if trying to figure out not only *who* I was, but *what* I was, before wiping his hand against his nose and slowly asking, "Kin I help youuuuuu?"

"My name is Rachel Porter," I replied, enunciating each word carefully, though I wasn't sure why. "I'm supposed to meet the Hardy boys here tonight."

The realization of what I'd said hit me, and I started to giggle. Maybe I should have introduced myself as Nancy Drew.

The man blinked, as if trying to decipher both the information and my reaction, before finally nodding his head.

"Ooookay. Now I know whooo youuu are."

He rubbed his hand on his pants and extended it toward me—the same one with which he'd cleaned his nose. I reluctantly gripped his palm. Not only was it damp, but a thick strip of dirt was buried beneath each of his nails.

"I'm Billy Paw."

Then I remembered that Woody and Virgil had never said the man they worked for was Russian; I'd simply taken it for granted. I was beginning to wonder if Mavis had made up the whole Mafia story. Could *this* be the mastermind behind the devastation of the paddlefish? No way! Something was definitely wrong with this picture.

"Why doncha come inside?"

I walked into a hallway lined with ornate smoked mirrors that reflected the light from a gaudy chandelier.

"Your friends are in here."

Billy Paw walked before me with such a loose gait that it appeared his bones were about to collapse beneath his flesh. He led the way into a living room that featured a white sofa as long as a train caboose, along with two white chairs and white wall-to-wall carpeting. Royal-blue drapes fringed with gold tassels gave the decor a retro seventies feel. But best of all was the sight of Woody and Virgil, looking like two peas in a pod that belonged in a very different sort of vegetable patch.

"You kin wait in this room with your friends while Mr. Sergei finishes his other business. I'm sure he'll be with ya'll in just a minute," Billy Paw informed us, and then bobbed back down the hall out of sight.

I breathed a quiet sigh of relief, happy to know that Billy Paw wasn't the person I'd traveled to meet. Sergei Galinov was the name Mavis had mentioned; this had to be the same man. Well, if I was going to wait, I might as well be comfortable. I planted my rear end on one of the lily-white seats.

Neither Virgil nor Woody uttered a word; their body language said it all for them. Both men self-consciously shifted their feet, as if afraid they might leave a permanent stain on the carpet.

It wasn't long before Galinov sauntered into view. Surprise, surprise. He turned out to be an overweight Russian version of Elvis. A pile of jet-black hair, slicked into a greasy pompadour, was accompanied by fuzzy sideburns. A short-sleeved sequined jumpsuit showcased his hefty, jiggling paunch, and the outfit was offset by gold chains that hung heavy as shackles around his neck. The man's eyes were hidden behind a pair of you-can't-see-me-but-I-can-see-you dark glasses. Galinov didn't belong in Memphis, but in a Vegas nightclub act.

As he approached, I noticed his arms were extensively tattooed with designs as elaborate as Russian icons. One illustrated the Virgin Mary holding baby Jesus, while another portrayed Christ with a halo encircling his head. Incorporated among these images was a crown of thorns dripping blood, and a scorpion bearing an enormous stinger. A pair of manacles were tattooed around his wrists.

Galinov's other arm was thrown across the shoulder of the man walking beside him. I tried to catch a glimpse of the man's face, but Galinov's heft blocked my view. However, I had no trouble seeing the woman who followed behind them. A tall, stunning blond, her cheekbones were so sharp they could have been used for slicing meat.

"Go to the Velvet Kitty and whatever you want is on the house tonight. Okay?" Sergei buoyantly offered in a thick Russian accent. "Have fun with one, two, even three girls if you like. Tatyana, you make sure my friend here enjoys himself."

Galinov didn't bother to look at the statuesque woman who nodded, as if it were simply understood.

"In other words, ya'll want time to check out my credentials."

The words barely made a dent. It was the voice that imploded inside me, bringing my heart to a painful halt.

"Sniff around all you want, Sergei. You'll find that my money's good. Hell, come down to my club in N'Awlins and partake in the same hospitality."

My brain shouted for me to breathe before I passed out, and I took a few shallow gulps. The stranger must have sensed he was being watched. Tilting his head, he casually looked back over his shoulder. That was all it took to jumpstart my heart. The thick tangle of curly black hair, the nose as sharp as a hawk's—the man's hooded eyes met mine and, for a brief second, their brooding darkness flashed with fireworks. The next moment, the mask fell back into place. Only a telltale twitch revealed he'd been caught as much by surprise as I was.

I was glad to be sitting down; otherwise, my legs might have given out. My fingers dug into the chair so hard I was surprised that it wasn't crying. The love of my life didn't miss a beat as he focused his attention back on Galinov.

I'd last seen Jake Santou in Miami the evening we broke up. But he'd continued to haunt my thoughts each day since—and every single night. I sat spellbound now as he once again walked out the door, this time with a long-legged blond on his arm. What was he doing in Memphis? How did he know Sergei? Had he become corrupt? And, lastly, who was the babe? I was forced to quickly gather my wits as Sergei approached with a disarming smile.

"So! You are my first federal agent who wants to be bought off. That is good. Please don't take offense, but first I must check you out."

What does this guy want, to see my driver's license?

Galinov pulled me to my feet, and his pudgy hands methodically began to frisk me.

"What the—" I angrily sputtered, and jerked away.

Sergei instantly stopped. "So sorry. But this is the only way to make sure you are not wearing a wire. I understand if you don't want me to do this. But then any deal is off, and you walk out of here right now."

Damn! I reluctantly resumed my place and let his fingers continue their journey. The sound of heavy breathing took me by surprise. I looked over and saw that Virgil was watching intently. Terrific. Galinov then removed the .38 from the back of my pants and handed it to Billy Paw.

"No guns are allowed inside. You can retrieve it when you leave." Having finished, he took hold of my hand and kissed it. "It is wonderful to meet you, Rachel. I may call you that, no? And you must call me Sergei. Now, let's go talk where it's more comfortable. Except for you, Billy Paw," he pointedly added. "You wait in the kitchen."

Billy Paw shuffled off with what appeared to be a slightly resentful gait. Then Galinov led the way, keeping me by his side as Virgil and Woody followed behind. We ended up in a duplicate of Elvis's Jungle Room, complete with the custom stone waterfall and green shag-carpeted floor and ceiling.

"Here. Come sit by me." Galinov patted a space on the sofa beside him. "I see you've noticed that my house is an exact replica of Graceland. It is because Elvis is my idol."

I sat down and felt the seat jiggle beneath me. Galinov's knee was bouncing away a mile a minute.

"My friends here tell me that you think you can be of help," Sergei began.

"I believe I already proved that last night," I asserted. "Not only do I know when and where state agents will be making their runs along the river, but I can also provide information on protected areas for finding paddlefish in closed states. In addition, you won't have to worry about me being on your tail."

"But I might like that," Sergei blatantly flirted. "Of course, I'd be willing to pay extra for that service."

Wouldn't you know I'd wind up with a lecherous version of Elvis in his later years?

"Well, we'll just have to see about that," I parried, flashing my best Mata Hari smile.

"Then it's settled! Welcome to my family."

Virgil leaned forward and finally spoke. "Yeah, but her cut ain't coming outta our pocket, is it?"

Sergei's smile twisted into a blood-chilling sneer. "Listen, my friend. Be glad that you have a pocket at all. You know the rules. Make the wrong move, and I cut *you* open in search of caviar."

Though the words had been softly spoken, they hung heavy in the air.

"Now, let's celebrate, shall we?"

Sergei shepherded us into a kitchen that was part Graceland, part Brady Bunch, and pure 1970s Americana, where we sat at a counter.

"Billy Paw! Bring out the vodka and caviar!"

A bottle of chilled Stoli was placed in front of us, along with a bowl of caviar nestled on ice.

"Let me do the honors." Sergei poured the vodka and then spooned some roe onto a toast point for me. "*Tchornaya ikra*. These are black pearls from the Caspian Sea, the best beluga in the world. Enjoy."

I took a bite, expecting to relish the same exquisite buttery flavor I'd tasted at Vincent's. Instead, my palate was hit with an earthy tang. Sitting nearby on the counter was the tin they'd been taken from. The sea-blue lid featured a sleepy sturgeon on a blanket of roe. Czar's Choice. Removing a few of the eggs, I placed them at the base of my thumb and took a lick. There was no doubt about it; Sergei was attempting to take my measure.

One good turn deserved another. Placing a few of the eggs on my napkin, I gently pressed down. Yellowish oil oozed onto the fabric in a small, greasy pool.

"Somebody must have sold you a mislabeled tin. What you've got here isn't beluga but osetra caviar."

Sergei's mouth dropped open in surprise. Woody and Virgil inched away, their glance silently wishing me good-bye. I was beginning to wonder if I'd made a fatal mistake when Galinov exploded in a belly laugh and lifted his glass in salute.

"You've got what you Americans call 'balls,' Rachel Porter. I like that! We will work well together. Now drink up!"

Woody and Virgil simultaneously lunged for their glasses.

"Billy Paw, bring out the real beluga now!" Sergei's

eyes twinkled at me in amusement. "I believe you've earned it."

After the bowl had been set down, I reached to take the proffered sample from his hand. But this time Galinov brought the caviar-covered toast point to my lips.

"Open," he softly commanded.

I did so, and he slipped it into my mouth. The buttery eggs were even better than those I'd tasted earlier this evening. I followed that up with a sip of the ice-cold vodka, which easily slid down my throat.

Neither Virgil nor Woody had touched the eggs, but focused on their Stoli. I silently raised a questioning eyebrow. Galinov noticed and laughed, covering my hand with his own.

"What can you expect? They are barbarians."

I glanced over at the Hardy brothers as Virgil's eyes burned angrily through me. After a few minutes, I stood up to take my leave. I knew it was time to go home.

"We will do this again soon, Rachel," Galinov promised, as Billy Paw returned my gun.

Virgil and Woody followed me out the door. I walked quickly to my vehicle but a fist dug hard into the small of my back, pressing me up against the Ford. A hot breath tinged with vodka slithered as venomously as a rattler along my ear.

"Just remember that snitches get stitches," Virgil angrily whispered. "Don't try pulling anything funny, Porter."

Fear nipped at my flesh as I knocked the hand off my back and spun around. Virgil's piggy eyes were ablaze, accentuated by his unruly eyebrows.

"The next time you sneak up with a threat, you'll live to regret it," I warned heatedly.

But Virgil didn't budge.

"Woody, call off your attack dog!" I warned.

"What are you trying to do? Get us killed? Just leave her the hell alone," Woody nervously muttered and pulled Virgil aside.

I got in my Ford and headed straight to the Blue Mojo.

The owner, Malcolm "Boobie" Baylford, was there when I arrived. Boobie was decked out in a red suit, with his hair pomaded against his dark skin. I slapped his upraised palm in greeting and then headed directly for the bar.

"Hey there, darlin'. What's up this evening? You look like you've seen a ghost," he observed, slipping onto the next stool.

Santou's face danced before me in the room's dim light—perhaps a little more creased for wear, but with the same smoldering intensity.

"I believe I have, Boobie," I admitted, unable to brush the vision away. "Someone from my past."

Boobie took a drag on his cigarette, and the smoke sensuously transformed into Santou's lopsided smile. "Did this apparition happen to speak to you?"

"No, he just floated by. Though we did exchange a glance."

"A man you used to be with, huh?" Boobie surmised. "Damn if that ain't the worst kind of apparition. What you need is a special concoction in order to get your mojo working." Boobie hopped off the stool and walked behind the bar.

I drank what he made without any question, then another as the yowl of a blues guitar sliced through the air. A male voice wailed of betrayal and insecurity as I nursed my drink like a long-lost lover. All the emotions I'd kept pent up for so long now rose to the surface. Like a genie, they pushed their way out of the bottle, unleashing all my hurt, vulnerability, and sorrow.

When I went home that night I tossed and turned, my dreams tormented by visions of Santou making love to a beautiful blond.

Fourteen

I woke to a throbbing headache and the sensation of a warm body lying beside me. Had Santou snuck into my bed, like a thief in the night? Rolling over, I came nose to nose with something that was wet and had bad breath—Dog was soundly snoring with her head on my pillow.

Dragging out of bed, I showered and dressed before having my morning fix of sugar cereal. Dog joined me in the kitchen with a yawn and a long, lazy stretch. Oh, what the hell. At least *she* deserved a decent breakfast. I scrambled a couple of eggs for the pooch.

Terri's room was empty. No problem; I knew where to find him. Dog and I traipsed down to Vincent's. The two men were draped in original Sophie kimonos, dining on eggs Benedict. Terri gave me half of his fancy Egg McMuffin, which I gratefully accepted.

"So, how'd your caviar lesson work out last night?" Vincent inquired.

"Perfectly," I replied.

"Then why do you look like hell? Something's wrong, and I don't want you to lie about it." Terri softened his words with a hug, and I instantly melted.

I knew the professional thing was to not say a word,

but I'd burst if I didn't tell someone. "I saw Santou."

Terri nearly jumped out of his kimono. "You did? Why didn't you tell me? He tracked you down and wants you back! I just knew it!"

I held up a hand to evade further questions. "It was while I was working undercover."

Terri's bubble instantly burst. "Oh dear. That must mean he was somewhere he shouldn't have been," he correctly surmised.

"You got it. Do you know if he's still working homicide these days?" I prayed that the answer would be yes.

But Terri shook his head. "I heard that he'd left the police force."

It was just possible Santou had gone back to his former life of drugs and booze, having found a more lucrative way to pay for his bad habits.

"I've got another favor to ask you, Vincent."

"You want me to beat the crap out of this Santou guy?" he volunteered.

"No, but do you know anything about a place called the Velvet Kitty?"

Vincent picked up his glass of freshly squeezed orange juice. "It's a nudie lap dancing bar featuring Ukrainian and Russian women. Any further contact a customer wants happens in the back room. The club's open twenty-four/seven and rakes in big bucks."

My stomach churned, and I pushed my plate away. "Where can I find the place?"

Vincent supplied directions to the Mount Moriah area, east of Memphis, off Elvis Presley Boulevard.

"You know, you really should drop by the school

and brush up on your wrestling moves," Vincent advised.

"Better yet, keep a really big gun with you at all times," Terri recommended.

I don't know what I expected to find at this time of morning. Maybe Santou. Maybe not. But I headed for the Velvet Kitty like a homing pigeon on a mission. It made sense that Galinov would be the owner; the Velvet Kitty was probably how he laundered his money.

I'm only doing this because of the case. But my heart knew better. I had to discover what Santou was involved in, no matter where it led me.

I drove through a strip of tacky stores and run-down bars before spotting the Velvet Kitty. The place would have been difficult to miss. Its neon logo featured a voluptuous cat with large, perky breasts. Beneath it was a sign that read, "Let Our Kitties Pamper You with 2-for-1 Drinks!"

I parked my Ford next to a bunch of other cars, wondering who would be here at this hour. I received my answer as I walked inside to find a group of unshaven rednecks lapping their drinks. The red walls matched their bloodshot eyes as a lanky brunette danced for their pleasures. The girl muffled a yawn while she listlessly ground her hips and lethargically whipped off her G-string.

Galinov ran quite the class act. The place reeked of stale beer and perspiration. Even the floor felt sticky beneath my feet. I chose not to imagine what that could be due to. Relieved not to find Santou facedown at the bar, I turned to skedaddle, when my eyes lit on a woman sitting in a leopard-print booth. It was the long-legged blonde from Galinov's place, still dressed in last night's outfit—skintight black leggings, a little midriff top, and high heels. She also had a jacket draped over her arm.

I had to find out what she'd been doing with Santou, though I was almost afraid to know. Taking a deep breath, I walked toward her. She carefully averted her gaze.

"Hi. My name is Rachel. I saw you at Sergei's house last night."

The woman's head never moved; only her eyes cautiously slid in my direction. "Then, you are one of his friends?" she hesitantly asked with a Russian accent.

"Let's just say we're doing business together," I replied with a smile.

A flicker of fear flashed in her eyes, which further piqued my interest.

"Are you going somewhere?" I questioned, refusing to let the conversation drop.

The woman visibly flinched.

"All I meant was that you're holding a jacket," I softly observed.

The blond shrugged in embarrassment. "My shift is over. I'm waiting for a cab to take me home."

"I'm leaving myself. Why don't I give you a lift?"

A pair of sad green eyes gazed at me in surprise. "Oh no. Please don't bother."

"Don't be silly. I insist—Sergei would want me to make sure you got home safe."

That seemed to do the trick. The woman reluctantly stood up.

I decided to press my luck. "Why don't I buy you some breakfast?"

"No, I must get home right away," the babe said adamantly.

I waited until she was buckled in her seat and I'd been given directions, before asking any more questions. "You haven't told me your name yet."

The blond hesitated. "Tatyana," she finally murmured.

"Pretty name," I commented, beginning to wonder just what the hell was up. "Have you been in America long?"

Tatyana shook her head.

Okay. Evidently, the trick was not to ask any yes or no questions. I pulled two Hershey bars from my pocket, and offered her one. She quickly stashed it in her purse.

"So, how do you know Sergei?"

"From home."

"And how did you end up in Memphis?" I continued.

Tatyana nervously looked away. "With Sergei's help," she answered evasively.

Ooh, yeah. Our tête-à-tête was going really well. I decided to skip the chat and get right down to business.

"The man that you left Sergei's with last night, is he also a friend?"

My inquiry was met by total silence. I knew that trying to push her further would do no good. Instead, I allowed the stillness to gather, until the sound of a quiet whimper caught me off-guard. Suddenly, it was no longer just Santou that I was worried about.

"Did that man do something to hurt you?" I asked anxiously, bombarded by apprehension, anger, and jealousy.

Tatyana quickly wiped away a tear. "No, no. He did nothing. He only wanted to talk. Please don't say anything about this to Sergei."

"Then tell me why you're crying," I insisted.

Tatyana turned her tearstained face defiantly toward me. "Because he asked me too many questions. Just like you."

This was the first spark of life she'd shown, but it just as quickly disappeared.

"I am very sorry, but I'm tired. My house is over here."

I pulled up in front. Tatyana's home was a ramshackle place, with black tarpaper slapped over paneless windows. Tic-tac-toe patches haphazardly dotted the screened-in porch. A little girl opened the front door and shyly peeked out. She had dark hair and big brown eyes, and I guessed her to be around eight years old.

"Is that your daughter?" I asked.

But Tatyana had already jumped out and was running toward the porch. She shooed the little girl inside and quickly closed the door behind them.

Fifteen

Mavis had yet to return my calls, and I was beginning to worry. I seriously doubted the Memphis police would put out an APB on a woman last seen wearing one yellow shoe, which meant some snooping around on my own would be necessary. I placed another call to her junk shop and hung up after the tenth ring. It was time to head to Mavis's home.

The Central Gardens District was a far different world from the one where I'd dropped Tatyana off earlier. Stately old mansions tranquilly sat on quiet, tree-lined streets, each a crown jewel. It's a neighborhood where people of good breeding reside, among them some of the oldest and most prestigious families in all of the South. So what was Mavis Newcomb doing there?

Her house was a two-story Tudor on Belvedere, the prettiest street in the District. Her red Mercedes wasn't parked in the drive. I rang the side bell anyway and, receiving no answer, decided to try the doorknob. Well, whadda ya know? It just happened to be unlocked. Mavis didn't strike me as the trusting kind, and I walked in to see what was up.

The door opened directly onto the kitchen. Either

Mavis was one hell of a lousy housekeeper, or she'd had unexpected company. The sink was piled with dishes that obviously hadn't been washed for days, their surfaces dry and crusty. A bucket of fried chicken lay uncovered on the floor, where a gang of roaches were feasting on it. My eggs Benedict began to rebel, and I quickly left.

I walked into a living room that could have been decorated by a Spanish matador. Every piece of furniture was covered with cheap velour of toreador-red. Hung on the walls were black velvet paintings depicting bullfights in all their gory splendor. By the look of things, a bull had jumped off the velvet and torn through the place. Every knickknack lay broken on the floor.

I picked up a photo and gazed through the shattered glass at a man as short and rotund as Mavis. The only visible difference between them was their hair. A few wisps had been carefully combed across the man's bald pate, and a thick stogie was jauntily stuck in his mouth. He exuded the demeanor of a good ol' country boy with a heart as big as the South. This was probably the poor sucker that Mavis had set up on a deer hunt and then knocked off.

I tiptoed through the minefield of slivered porcelain and glass to venture upstairs into Mavis's bedroom. Clothes were strewn all over the floor, but more disturbing was her doll collection. Each doll's dress was roughly pulled over its head—those that still had heads left. The place had apparently been the target of a whirlwind search-and-destroy mission.

A cushioned ledge was stretched in front of an old

bay window, and I sat down to think. The street below appeared as serene as an unruffled lake; there was scarcely a sound. It made the scene before me all the more macabre.

I leaned against the window, pulling away from the brooding sense of violence that still filled the room. The wood squeaked beneath me. I squirmed and it happened again. Either termites were eating away at the house, or I was sitting on a storage space. Standing up, I uncovered a hinged window seat. I lifted the lid and began to rummage through it.

Out came an assortment of odds and ends, including a hammer, a baseball bat, and other goodies. I kept going until I hit rock bottom, where one final item waited to be excavated—a blue cardboard box dotted with pink roses. Opening it, I discovered the box was filled with old photos.

I sifted through black-and-white snaps, finding pictures of Woody in his younger days, before he'd developed his paunch. Though he wore overalls, a shirt was neatly tucked underneath, and a lovely young woman hung on his arm. "Woody and Tammy II" was written on the back.

The next batch featured a happy and much slimmer version of Mavis, in the company of a tall man with a devilish expression. I recognized the upturned nose and the bristly hedgehog hair; it was Virgil staring back at me through space and time.

I dug some more. My reward was a number of photos in which Virgil was impeccably dressed as a woman. Others captured Virgil and Mavis with their arms flung around each other, looking like two giddy girlfriends—except that one of them was a man on the lam. I quickly moved through the rest until I came to one that appeared to have been taken at Reelfoot Lake. It featured Virgil standing next to a fishing cabin. Turning it over, I read the inscription: "Home Sweet Home on Black Bayou."

I returned the photos to their vault, and once again thought of the yellow high heel I'd uncovered at Virgil's. I felt ever more certain that Mavis's disappearance was linked to the man. Closing the lid on her coffin of mementos, I lowered it back inside its grave. An uneasy feeling stayed with me long after I made my way out of Mavis's house.

Sixteen

I was deep in thought as I drove down the road, when my cell phone rang.

"Hey, Bronx. I gotta tell you that our deal with Mavis Newcomb is off."

Damn! That could mean only one thing. The top brass in D.C. had learned what I was up to and were shutting us down.

"What happened?" I asked warily.

"Newcomb's car has been pulled out of the Mississippi. Some fisherman thought he'd hooked himself one helluva big one." Hickok snorted. "Goddamn if he didn't stick on a diving suit and go down to see what it was. Probably peed in his pants, hoping he could keep the Mercedes!"

"Was Mavis inside?" I managed to ask. The muscles in my throat had become tightly constricted.

"Nope. But she might turn up as a floater in a coupla weeks."

A giant primeval soup, the Mississippi is the stuff of legends. It's impossible to see what's lurking beneath the river's murky surface, which is why it's called the Big Muddy. The Mississippi is used as a dumping ground for everything from pesticides to PCBs to raw sewage to dead bodies.

"Where was her car found?" The lump in my stomach began to burn hot around the edges. Now I really *was* one of the guys—I'd have killed for a slug of Mylanta.

"In the water off Chickasaw Bluffs."

Not far from Virgil's place.

"Keep your nose out of this one, Bronx," Hickok instructed. "This is police business. Have I got your word on it?"

"Yeah, yeah," I muttered, keeping my toes and fingers crossed.

I pulled into the nearest Piggly Wiggly, where I bought some Mylanta and drank it straight from the bottle while standing at the register. Clearly, any possible evidence would have vanished by the time the boys in blue got around to investigating Mavis's disappearance.

Though lunchtime was nearly over I felt sure Virgil would still be busy at the bar, which meant his house would be empty. I pointed my vehicle toward Chickasaw Bluffs, knowing in my gut who Mavis Newcomb's killer was.

The hogs took an interest in my presence as I pulled up next to their pen and parked. They looked up and wagged their little corkscrew tails before sticking their snouts back in the slop. But nothing could dispel the funereal pall that hung like a black magic spell over the grounds. Virgil's car was nowhere in sight, so I got out.

I passed a deer carcass lying in the dirt near the pig-pen. It seemed a strange way to treat meat he planned to eat—not that I cared what Virgil stuck in his gullet. Apparently, neither did he.

There were any number of areas to look, so where to begin? Since the shed was where Virgil slaughtered things, that seemed a good place to start.

I approached the slaughterhouse and found a board lodged across the door. Lifting the plank from out of its holders, I laid it on the ground. Then I pulled the wooden door toward me, unleashing whatever demons lay within. It groaned forebodingly at my intrusion. I let my eyes adjust to the dark, and slowly entered the room.

A ray of sun became impatient with my lagging pace and raced ahead, reflecting off a shiny surface. A cleaver; probably the one Virgil used to slaughter his hogs. The knife lay on a primitive altar, where an ominous shadow hovered over the shrine. I looked up and my blood froze into tiny daggers of ice. An enormous black cross was nailed to the wall, awaiting a sacrifice.

A voice inside my head screamed for me to leave. *Go to the trailer, go to the Sho Nuf Bar. Just get away from the Grim Reaper, drawing steadily closer within his tattered robe*. My breath came in searing gasps as bony fingers of death tightened around my throat. It was as if an unseen force had control over my body. My limbs refused to move, and the air around me grew cold.

I turned on shaky legs to bolt, only to discover an even scarier presence blocking the doorway. It was Virgil, looking like Bob's Big Boy gone berserk. The quills of his hair stood straight up on end, as if fed by an electrical current, and his pale blue eyes unwaveringly focused on me. My Grim Reaper was no phantom in a hooded cloak, but a hormonal freak in bib overalls. As Virgil's scowl slowly transformed into a sneer, I realized the black cross hanging from his neck was a miniature of the one that loomed behind me.

"Whatcha lookin' for, Porter?" His voice slithered through the air, like the black plague.

I knew I'd be a goner the moment I showed the least bit of fear. I could tell he was sizing me up even now, figuring out what kind of fight I'd put up, calculating how long it would take to subdue me.

I stared the man down. "Hey, Virgil. I was wondering if you've seen Mavis lately. I appreciate the information you passed on, but I can't find her."

Virgil grotesquely licked his bottom lip. "You know how Mavis and me met? She came rubbin' up agin' me like a cat in heat. She was almost yowling, she wanted it so bad. So I gave it to her, Porter. Right then and there. Women, they do things like that. Mainly it's the devil gets in them, so they got no control. Once that happens, the only way to get rid of that kind of wantonness is through a cleansing."

I stared dumbstruck at the man, wondering what planet he was from.

"How 'bout you, Porter? You got some evil in you that needs to be washed out? Could be it comes from spending too much of your time with Sergei's hookers."

A surge of adrenaline kicked my warning system into an all-out alert. Was Virgil the menacing presence

I'd been feeling around me? "What kind of crap is that, Hardy? You don't have a clue what women want. And what's more, how do you know who I have and haven't been seeing?"

Virgil's answer was to shut the door behind him. A few rays of sun slipped through the wooden slats, giving the room a dreamlike quality.

"You got a tendency to go from zero to bitch in no time flat. That's something you should learn to control. I just might be able to help you with that."

"Open the door, you bastard!" I hissed, standing my ground.

Virgil's sneer turned into a leer as he drew closer. "That must be why you're standing in front of my cross. God knows you're impure, so He sent you here to me. It's also why He brought me home just now. Sometimes you first gotta have a taste of hell before He can save your soul."

Virgil's arm lashed out, revealing a cleaver in his hand. I whipped the .38 from my waistband in response and aimed it at his head.

"Come one step closer and I'll blow your brains out," I warned. "I swear to your God *and* mine on that!"

The cleaver hung suspended like a guillotine, as a jarring *brrriiing* fractured the air. I kept my gun trained on Virgil as I reached down and plucked the cell phone off my belt.

"Hello?" I tersely answered, hoping it wasn't Terri calling to ask if I'd tried the new moisturizer he'd bought.

"Rachel! Have I caught you at a bad time?"

It was Galinov. I'd never been happier to hear from anyone in my life.

"Hi, Sergei. No, your timing is fine. I'm here with Virgil in his shed," I promptly informed him.

Giving Galinov that information should make Hardy think twice. My logic proved correct. Virgil's eyes flashed a warning as he lowered the cleaver, opened the door, and slunk off in the direction of the hog pen.

"I'd like for you to come to my house for dinner tonight. We can talk business and get to know one another better."

His invitation presented the perfect way to advance myself into his inner circle.

"I'd love to."

"Shall we say around eight o'clock?"

"I'll see you then," I confirmed, my gun still aimed at the door.

After I hung up, I realized my hands were shaking. I got my nerves under control, then walked out with the .38 by my side in plain sight.

All I wanted to do was get in my Ford and leave. What stopped me cold was the gruesome sound of Virgil's cleaver hacking through bone. He methodically dismembered the deer carcass and threw it, limb by limb, in to the hogs. I stared in disbelief, never having seen swine ravenously eating flesh before.

Virgil spied the look on my face, and a bloodcurdling laugh erupted from his massive form.

"Surprised, Porter?" he asked, his blue eyes now as dark as thunderstorms. "Hell, these ol' hogs of mine'll eat anything. Bones, hair, flesh—even clothes in no time flat."

I stood in a fog, unable to pry my gaze away as they tore into the deer's corpse with terrifying squeals and grunts. Their snouts bristled in rage as they fought over every single morsel, setting the very air aquiver with the sound of their insatiable gorging. Everything around me began to spin as the frantic porkers merged into a formless sea of colliding bodies and masticating jowls, until I was afraid I would pass out.

I hurried toward my vehicle, propelled by Virgil's maniacal laughter racing behind me. The next thing I knew, I was tearing down the road. Only after Virgil and Chickasaw Bluffs were well out of sight did I slam on my brakes, open the door, and throw up.

I now had a good idea of Mavis's fate, and why only a single shoe had been found in the pile of slop. Shivers gripped me until my teeth chattered. I slammed the Ford's door and headed home, vowing to make Virgil pay for what he had done.

Seventeen

I walked into my loft, where Dog greeted me with a storm of wet kisses. Then she barked, letting me know I'd been away for too long.

"Sorry. I guess it's been a lousy day for both of us."

I picked up the pooch and gave her a hug, aware that we each could use one.

"Anybody home?" My question was greeted by silence. "Let's go see what Terri's up to, shall we?" I asked the brown ball of fur, knowing where he most likely was.

I knocked on Vincent's door.

"Entré!"

Vincent was garbed in an outfit that was part wrestler, part Bette Midler, his legs encased in black tights embellished with red flames shooting up toward his groin. The black hood over his head was adorned with the same fiery pattern, topped by a pair of horns. The studded collar epitomized his nickname, Mad Dog Vin. Terri was spraying every inch of Vincent's bare, magnificent torso with a light coating of oil, as if Julia Child had taken possession of him.

"So, what do you think? I designed it myself." Terri gave the wrestler's chest one last spritz. "I'm doing

169

costumes for his students after I finish next season's line for Yarmulke Schlemmer."

"The students are gonna eat this stuff up," Vincent said happily. "Speaking of which, I hope you're hungry. I've got an organic rib roast with mousseline potatoes cooking in the oven."

"Actually I have dinner plans."

"A date with anyone I know?" Terri asked hopefully.

"No, it's business. But I have to dress for the occasion. Any suggestions?"

"Wear your black dress," both men answered in unison.

"Are you going to someone's house, or a restaurant?" Vincent questioned, ever the cautious gentleman.

"His house," I responded, aware of what was coming next.

"And just how well do you know this guy?" Vincent grilled.

"It's the same man I met after my caviar lesson last night."

"In other words, the creep's a perp."

The next thing I knew, I was facedown on the floor, my arms and legs pinned, with Vincent on my back.

"Okay. This move is your classic full nelson. That character tries anything funny, this is what you do to him."

First I was nearly attacked by a twisted religious freak, now I had an oily, gay wrestler on top of me. So far my day had been full of surprises. I promised to be careful. After a few more pointers, I headed back upstairs to shower and change. What the hell—if I was going to play Mata Hari, I might as well go all the way.

I fixed my hair and put on some makeup, then surveyed the results. My black dress clung in all the right places more than I might have liked, but it would help get the job done. Besides, if Sergei got out of hand, I'd just brushed up on the right moves to contain him.

I pulled up to find the hot-pink Caddy was the only car parked in Sergei's driveway. This really *was* an intimate dinner. I listened to the chimes play "Don't Be Cruel," wondering just how crazy I was to have come.

Billy Paw once again opened the door, looking more like Jed Clampett than ever. "Ohhh. It's youuuu." His sunken red eyes gave me the once-over.

A look of displeasure flashed across his face as I stepped inside. He held out his hand for my gun, and placed it on a nearby table. I was about to ask what his problem was when Sergei rushed up, grabbing both my hands in his own.

"Rachel! You look absolutely delicious!"

"You look pretty spiffy yourself."

He was dressed in a short-sleeved white jumpsuit swimming with rhinestone studs. Missing were the sunglasses from the other night, and he exuded an even more powerful presence without them. Possibly it was my weakness for caffeine, but his espresso-colored peepers were truly captivating. If Sergei dropped fifty pounds, wore normal clothes, and lost the sideburns, he'd actually be quite good-looking.

"Champagne?" he asked, handing me a glass.

I properly grasped the flute by its stem.

"Billy Paw, get dinner ready," Sergei commanded.

"Sho 'nuf," Billy Paw responded and trudged off.

While his choice of words was unnerving, even more so was the fact that Billy Paw was Sergei's chef.

"He's your cook?"

"Absolutely! Billy Paw was the best thing to come with this house."

"Then you inherited him?"

"Inherit! Very good, I like that!" Sergei laughed. "Yes. He worked for the previous owner, and I saw no reason to fire him. Besides, he makes the type of food that I like. His mother used to cook for Elvis."

Whoa! Hold on there! "That's not possible. Elvis's chef was a black woman."

Sergei leaned close enough that his sideburns tickled my face. "Mixed marriage."

Billy Paw was proving to be quite the huckster: the guy was as white as a Klan sheet. I lifted my glass, only to have Sergei stop me, entwining his arm in mine.

"You must never drink without looking into the other person's eyes. It's bad luck."

Billy Paw wasn't the only hustler around.

"To our new relationship," he said.

By the sound of it, Sergei was planning to catch more than just paddlefish.

"Now let me show you the house. As I told you, it's an exact replica of Graceland."

"Perhaps the downstairs is, but nobody knows what the second level of Graceland looks like. That's off-limits to the public," I reminded him.

"That's true. But not to me," Sergei bragged.

"You're about to see what only a chosen few have ever been privy to—Elvis's most intimate quarters."

Lucky me. Being a regular peon, I guess I'd have to take his word on it. We headed upstairs. All the while, I could hear Sergei's engine running, even though he appeared to be in neutral.

"You know one of the things I like best about you?"

"What's that?" I asked, preparing to karate chop him if he made the wrong move.

"The fact that you're part Russian."

Well, catch me with a hook, line, and sinker. "How did you know?"

"I have my sources. It was easy to check."

Great. I wondered what else he knew about me.

Sergei answered my unspoken question. "You have an emotional nature, which is a Russian trait. I can already tell you're a very passionate woman."

With any luck, he might come to view me as his very own Russian Priscilla Presley.

"It is very smart of you to work for me."

"I prefer to think of it as working *with* you," I corrected.

"The future holds many possibilities. I have all sorts of business ventures."

"Such as the Velvet Kitty?"

It was Sergei's turn to be surprised. "How do you know about that?"

"I have my sources as well," I archly responded.

"It's merely a small club for entertaining business clientele," he said with a shrug.

"Like the man who was here the other night?"

"Who?" Sergei's hand smoothed his pompadour, as

if the answer lay in there. "Oh, Renny Folse. He's just someone from New Orleans who's interested in purchasing supplies."

So Santou was using an alias these days. "What kind of supplies might those be?"

My question remained unanswered as we reached Sergei's bedroom door. If I'd thought the rest of the house was over the top, this room took the proverbial cake. Decorated in gold, it boasted three built-in TVs and a four-poster bed with a chinchilla spread. But the tour wasn't over yet. Sergei led me to a bathroom whose walls were covered with photos of Elvis, and nodded toward the toilet.

"That's where the King fell off the throne in 1977."

"You're speaking metaphorically, of course."

Sergei looked at me questioningly.

"I mean, that's not the *actual* toilet."

"Yes, it is. The very one."

"*That's* the toilet from Graceland?" I asked in disbelief.

"Absolutely. And let me tell you, it cost a pretty ruble," Sergei solemnly informed me.

I was left with that thought as we headed down to the dining room, where dinner was already on the table.

"See? I eat just like Elvis." Sergei boasted. "Meat loaf, collard greens, mashed potatoes, and cornbread."

Everything was swimming in a pool of butter. Sergei served me first, then loaded his own plate with enough food to spur on a case of arteriosclerosis.

"You're a fascinating man. How is it that you decided to settle in Memphis?" I coquettishly inquired, as he shoveled some meat loaf into his mouth.

"A group of business associates wanted to set up a base in the U.S. I was chosen since I am the best and the brightest," Sergei bragged. "It was decided there are too many headaches involved with sending paddlefish roe over to Russia, just to mix in a little Caspian caviar and export it right back here. For instance, I had a problem the other day with a small overnight shipping firm. Some fool broke the package and ruined all the eggs."

So Sergei was the anonymous shipper Gena had tried to track down!

"It is much better to tin paddlefish roe right here, label it as Russian caviar, and distribute the product out of Memphis. That way there is no middleman. It means bigger profits, plus we corner the market," Sergei gloated.

"You're talking about an enormous chunk of the trade. Where can you get enough fishermen to do that?" I asked innocently.

"Easy! I steal them from the local hick caviar dealers." Sergei snorted. "I give them better prices, help them get girlfriends. Whatever they want!"

"But don't you worry that angry dealers might decide to snitch?"

Sergei burped and buttered a piece of cornbread. "The ones that are smart don't. And those that do? I take care of them." He lifted his knife and drew it across his throat as Billy Paw shuffled into the room.

"Clear the table and bring out dessert," Sergei ordered.

Billy Paw flung a few more invisible daggers of resentiment my way. Either he was overly protective of his master, or Billy Paw just plain didn't like me.

Dessert was another Elvis calorie buster—banana icebox pie.

I waited until Billy Paw left the room. Then, raising a finger, I began to trace the intricate outline of the designs burned into Sergei's skin.

"Your tattoos are fascinating. Tell me about them."

"What do you want to know?" he asked, his voice husky and low, his eyes following my finger's every move.

"For instance, the designs. How did you choose them? And why do you have iron manacles tattooed around your wrists?"

Sergei grabbed my finger and held it captive. "Each is very special. They were given to me as proof of my courage and loyalty for work well done. I will tell you more when you prove your loyalty to me. Then you will also get rewards."

Galinov put increasing pressure on my finger as he swiftly picked up a knife, pricked the flesh, and drew blood. I gasped in surprise and tried to pull away, but Sergei held on as he did the same to one of his own and then pressed our two fingers together.

"Make an oath that you'll never betray me," he demanded, his face hovering close. "Swear it on the name of all you hold holy."

My finger ached as he continued to press tighter.

"I swear," I finally repeated, knowing I'd probably go straight to hell.

"I always like to grab my friends by the balls so they can't double-cross me. Where are your balls,

Rachel Porter?" He laughed and kissed my finger before letting go. "Don't worry. I'll find them."

Galinov poured us each another glass of champagne. "Now, let's drink to working *together*, as you say. You like that. No?"

The liquid slid like poison down my throat. "I should tell you that I'm *also* known for busting balls. Now, I really must go."

"But it's still early! Don't tell me I've scared you away?" he teased. But his eye held a deadly gleam.

"I need to contact Virgil and Woody so they'll know where to set their nets tonight. After all, the more paddlefish they catch, the more money we make."

Sergei smiled and lifted his champagne glass, his teeth gleaming against the crystal. "You're both beautiful *and* smart. The best way to increase production is to start fishing in the protected waters of Mississippi and Alabama. Get information on those areas. I trust you'll keep our operation safe."

"I will," I promised.

Sergei tenderly kissed my hand. "Then until next time, Rachel Porter."

I retrieved my gun and headed home.

Eighteen

I drove back to Memphis under a sullen sky, accompanied by an angry mob of raindrops. Jagged lightning ripped through the night, punctuated by a low rumble of thunder. The sound echoed, as eerie as a disembodied moan rising from out of a graveyard.

You've gone too far. There's no turning back now.

I was afraid the admonition was correct. I'd wanted to play with the big boys; now I had no choice but to go the distance.

I parked the Ford near my loft and began to walk toward the Blue Mojo, too immersed in my thoughts to care about the rain. That is, until a wraith grabbed me from out of the dark, seemingly intent on dragging me back to hell with it. Whirling around, I was determined to fight off Satan in whatever form he was cloaked—Virgil, Sergei, or even Charlie Hickok. Instead, I froze in place when I saw it was the man who'd haunted my dreams and held my heart in shackles.

Even darkness couldn't hide the blistering intensity radiating off Santou, nor the lines in his face, which were etched deeper than ever. Life had apparently dealt him a few more blows since last we'd met. A crackle of lightning marbleized the sky as rain showered the street in a punishing outburst. I held back the tears that were welling up inside.

It was Santou who shattered the silence. "We need to talk. Is there somewhere we can go?"

I nodded and led the way. The Blue Mojo's sign cast a seductive glow, its colors staining the puddles below.

I grabbed a table in the dimmest corner of the room, hoping it would mask not only my wounded pride, but also the fact that I'd take Santou back in a New York minute. I momentarily closed my eyes and luxuriated in his scent, which wrapped itself around me, until something foreign touched my skin. Pulling back, I was startled to find Santou drying the rain off my face with a napkin.

He reacted likewise, covering his embarrassment by extracting a pack of Camels from his pocket. Removing a cigarette, he rolled it between his fingers, the action as intimate as if he were exploring the body of a long-lost lover. Then he placed the cigarette between his lips where it hung suspended, along with my soul, until he lit up.

"I see you still have one bad habit left. Any others I should know about?" I asked lightly.

Santou's eyes momentarily softened beneath their hooded lids, and he leaned in as if to share something, only to think better of it. He was once again the professional, keeping his distance.

"I'm not here to discuss my bad habits, Porter. I'm here to talk about you."

You were hoping he'd say "us," weren't you? Just

*remember, people don't change. And only rarely do
circumstances.*

I caught Boobie's eye and held up two fingers. He
nodded, automatically knowing what the occasion
called for. Then I set my emotional armor in place before turning my attention back to Santou.

"What could you possibly want to talk about that
we haven't already discussed at some point or other?"

If Santou felt the zinger, he did his best not to show
it. But his fingers danced across the table like a crab
with a case of the jitters.

"I need to ask if you're still working for Fish and
Wildlife?"

I threw the ball back at him. "Now *that's* an interesting question. Why do you want to know?"

Santou's hand crash-coursed through his hair, sending a shower of watery droplets into the air. He looked
at me and slowly shook his head, flashing that signa-
ture grin which never failed to tug at my heart. This
time he *did* lean forward.

"You're right. I *do* know you, chère. I know you all
too well. And my gut tells me that you're not corrupt—which means you must be involved in some
kind of undercover assignment."

Boobie placed down two glasses. It was the same
concoction he'd previously prepared to kick-start my
mojo. I hoped it worked as well tonight.

"How many drinks have you already had, Jake? I
think you're letting your imagination get the better of
you."

"And what *I* think is that you're working on something to do with paddlefish," Santou responded.

"What a fascinating leap. Why don't you enlighten me as to how you reached that conclusion?" I bantered, as if this were highly entertaining social conversation.

"All it took was one look at those two jokers you were with the other night. My guess is they're working as fishermen for Galinov. In fact, that's probably how you got to Sergei in the first place." Jake smugly picked up his drink and downed it.

Oh yeah? And what about the blond babe you were with? I smiled in amusement. "You should consider becoming a novelist in your spare time. Come to think of it, I have the perfect pen name for you. How about Renny Folse?"

Santou blinked, but didn't say a word.

"By the way, I heard you quit the New Orleans police force."

Jake took a hit off his cigarette, bathing his profile in a ghostly haze, his wound-up intensity tighter than ever. He signaled for another round and Boobie brought it over, raising an eyebrow in Jake's direction.

"I call this my apparition special," he announced, and sauntered away as Gena took the stage.

"What's that supposed to mean?" Santou suspiciously asked.

"It's his name for the house drink," I said airily, beginning to feel its effect.

An unruly curl fell onto Santou's temple, like a black sheep rebelliously straying from the rest of the flock. I instinctively brushed it back only to have Jake seize my hand, making it his most willing prisoner. His lips seared my palm, and every cell in my body burst into flame. Jake was here and, for now, that was all that mattered. Which is why I could have kicked myself as the words tumbled out of their own accord.

"Tell me what *you're* doing in Memphis. Are you working on assignment for another agency? And why is Sergei Galinov your target?"

All he had to do was say five little words.

I'm here because of you.

Just that.

Instead, Santou dropped my hand. "I can't tell you anything now. Maybe later."

I defined that to mean, *No deal. No way. No how.*

"Listen, chère. I showed up tonight to give you a warning. It's obvious you're working Galinov. And knowing you, it's probably without any backup or authorization. I want you off this case right now. You don't have the slightest idea who it is that you're dealing with."

I should have expected this. After all, this was the reason we'd broken up in the first place.

"Okay, Jake, now you listen to me. What I choose to do is *my* business. You're not my boss; you're no longer even my lover. I don't need advice from someone who's unwilling to tell me why he's here in Memphis."

"I don't see you entrusting *me* with any precious details," Santou said with a sharp, angry laugh.

I began to move away but Santou grabbed my arm, refusing to let me leave.

"Do you even know what Galinov's tattoos stand for?" he hissed.

"What's this? A ploy to extract information that you don't have?" I fired back.

Santou's eyes furiously locked onto mine. "Those markings mean the man's been in prison doing hard time. He's part of the Russian Mafia's ancient Thieves World. Galinov is an aristocrat of the profession and keeper of its code. Those tattoos are a sign of his membership. He is absolutely ruthless. He'd kill you just to show his cohorts that he can slaughter a federal agent and get away with it—which is why I'm telling you to stop whatever you're doing."

My heart raced, knowing that everything he'd just told me was probably true. At the same time, there had to be a reason that Santou wanted Galinov all for himself. He'd obviously shown up tonight to push me out of the way. Well, I wasn't going to roll over so that whatever agency he was working for could grab all the glory. Galinov was mine; I intended to keep it that way.

"If you're not worried about dealing with Galinov, why should I be? Because I'm a woman?"

Santou polished off his drink and looked me square in the eye. "Damn straight."

I glared at him and intuitively knew that Santou had sunk deep inside a bottle from which he was trying to escape. Rather than respond, I drifted into my own sanctuary filled with the blues as Gena began to sing like Tina Turner, "nice and rough." The song roused my spirits. Like Tina, I might be bruised, but I damn well wasn't broken. I finished my drink and stood up.

There was no need to look back; the sexual bond

between us was as highly charged as ever. I instinctively felt Santou's heat following closely behind. The pouring rain sizzled off my skin as I made my way down the street and opened the door to my loft. Santou walked in without any question, having finally arrived home. Not a word was said as I turned and Jake slowly lifted my dress above my legs, my thighs, my hips. I held up my arms and the flimsy material grew wings and flew into the sky. Two quick movements later, my bra and panties were off.

"I want to taste you, smell you," Santou roughly whispered in my ear, and proceeded to do exactly that.

A moan slipped from my lips as Santou satiated every square inch of my body. Then I made him do it all over again, just to make sure he'd permanently forget about long-legged blonds. This time I fell over the edge into uncharted territory, traveling deeper within myself than I ever had before. And there I discovered my love for Santou was never-ending. My need for the man was encoded in my DNA.

Jake's fingers traced the outline of my face before blazing over my stomach and down along my hips. I studied his features, bathed in a ray of moonlight. As much as I loved Santou, I needed at least one question answered before I could lay the matter to rest.

"Why did you leave the NOPD?" I asked, hoping it wouldn't destroy the magic bubble that encased us.

Santou let loose a sigh and reached for his pack of cigarettes on the nightstand. Removing one, he lit up. Jake didn't speak until its ember burned as red-hot as my body had only a few minutes earlier.

"Remember when Terri appeared on your doorstep

in Miami with a pair of eyes that looked like two black holes?"

"Yes. An old boyfriend, Bruno, had beaten him up." It happened not long after Santou and I had ended our own relationship.

"Well, Terri reported the incident to me first, before hightailing it out of town."

Funny that Terri had never mentioned that. I wondered what else he'd not told me about.

"Did his case have something to do with why you left the force?"

"My decision was due to a lot of things, Rachel. Terri was just the trigger."

The bed creaked its own night song as Santou turned, bringing his face close to mine, his words burrowing deep inside me.

"Our breakup was the main catalyst. The reality of it hit me worse than I could have imagined."

My heart began to pound so hard that I felt sure the room was shaking. "Tell me what happened."

"I screwed up, Rachel. Plain and simple. I let my anger get the better of me in the wrong situation." Jake emitted a mirthless laugh. "I went to the Whipping Post looking for Bruno, and collided with my past."

I held my breath, afraid I'd otherwise explode with a million questions. There was no sense bombarding him; Santou would reveal only as much as he wanted me to know.

"I had a few drinks while I waited for Bruno, figuring he'd eventually show. It wasn't until I came face to face with the guy that I remembered who he was. When I found out, I began to drink some more. The weasel used to be my drug lifeline." Jake grimaced at the words. "Bruno remembered me, too. After I dropped out of the scene, he sniffed around and soon learned I'd been working undercover for DEA. He also knew I'd been kicked out of the agency for liking my coke too much."

"You're a different person now," I quietly told Jake, hoping it was true.

A bitter smile tugged at Santou's lips. "Well, it gave Bruno a real good laugh. I kept knocking back Scotches while he was yucking it up, until I'd had enough. Then I began smashing the bastard's head into the floor. Guess who was up on charges after that?" He placed a finger to his head and pulled the trigger.

"Were you kicked out?" I asked, the words sticking in my throat.

Santou's fingers idly traced the tops of my breasts, riding the rim of the sheets, his face a wistful ache. "I received two weeks' suspension without pay. But you know what? It turned out to be the best thing that ever could have happened. It gave me the time that I needed to think. Bumping into Bruno again was like seeing a ghost of myself—one that I'd tried hard to forget. But there are some things you can never escape."

His gaze drifted out the window, his profile as still as a death mask. I was tempted to lean over and kiss all the pain away, but whatever Jake had to say needed to be done without interruption.

"What scared me was that I could feel how easy it would be to get caught up in that world again—where

nothing but nose candy matters." He turned and
looked at me fiercely. "I snorted a good chunk of my
life away, Rachel. It almost happened again when I
lost you. Instead, I quit the force, got some help, and
cleaned up my act. The upshot is that I've recently
been given a second chance."

"You've gone back to work for the NOPD?"

Santou pushed aside a strand of hair on my forehead and replaced it with a kiss. "No. I'm doing something else."

Then he finally whispered what I'd been longing to
hear him say.

"And even better, now you're back in my life. Have
I told you how much you take my breath away?"

The words softly stroked my soul, silky as the tip of
a feather.

Santou took it a step further than I had even dared
hope.

"I was wrong back in Miami, chère. We belong together. Please trust me, just this once. I promise to explain everything as soon as I can."

That was enough to put my remaining questions on
hold for now. I turned and wrapped myself around the
man who made my heart beat faster than anyone else
in this world. The blues were supplanted by gospel as
"Amazing Grace" drifted through my mind. "I once
was lost but now am found" took the place of counting
sheep as I laid my head on Santou's shoulder and fell
asleep. I was finally at peace, having been reunited
with my soul mate.

Nineteen

When I awoke, Santou was gone. I wondered if it might have all been a dream, until I nestled my head on the spare pillow and was embraced by his lingering scent. That was quickly replaced as Dog bounded onto the bed and covered my face in a shower of licks. Terri must have dropped the pooch off early this morning without making a sound. I removed the note attached to Dog's collar, and read that Terri and Vincent would be out of town for the next few days.

"Looks like you'll be hitting the road with me for a while," I informed the pup.

I bathed and dressed, my body still tingling. It was only as I got breakfast for Dog that I rocketed back down to earth. Though I loved Santou, it was essential I discover Mavis's information before he did. And there was one other place I could think of to try. Dog took a seat beside me in the Excursion, and we headed for Tatyana's house.

The sky was as gray as cold, discarded cigarette ashes, the sun sulking behind a cloud. A sprinkling of rain splattered my windshield.

Swish, swish. Swish swish.

Dog's head moved back and forth to the wipers'

beat, as if watching a tennis match. As we parked in front of the run-down house the sky rumbled a loud warning, sending Dog into the shivers. It was clear the pooch didn't want to be left alone.

"All right, come on. Just behave yourself."

We walked up to the porch, where the screen door squeaked like a frightened mouse. I knocked on the thin wooden door behind it. Tatyana cracked the entrance open only the slightest bit and cautiously peeked out. Freshly blue bruises marred her milky-white skin.

"It's Rachel Porter. We met the other day. Can I talk to you for a minute?"

Tatyana refused to look at me and vehemently shook her head. "I told you before. I have nothing to say."

"Tatyana, if someone is hurting you, I can make that stop."

She raised her eyes to meet mine. "You think so? And just who are *you?* No one! My life is what it is. Now please go away."

I was about to concede defeat when Tatyana's little girl poked her head out and spotted Dog, her eyes widening in delight.

"Oh Mama! A puppy! Please let it in!" She clapped her hands and looked beseechingly at her mother.

"The puppy would love to play with your daughter," I shamelessly added, taking full advantage of the situation.

"Please Mama! Please! I promise to be good!" the child pleaded.

"All right. All right, *moya malenkaya.* But only for a minute," Tatyana grudgingly relented.

She opened the door and the pooch ran inside. I quickly followed. Gone were the high heels, midriff top, and tights. Tatyana wore sweatpants and a baggy shirt, without a touch of makeup.

"Galya, why don't you play with the doggy in your room, while I talk with this lady in the kitchen?"

The girl giggled as Dog jumped up and licked her face. "Come puppy! This way!"

I followed Tatyana into a dingy kitchen, where she took a seat at a small wooden table. I pulled out a wobbly chair and sat across from the woman, whose sorrowful eyes accused me of having tricked her.

"Did Sergei do that to you?" I quietly asked.

Tatyana remained stubbornly silent. I had little choice but to take a gamble. We were both women living some kind of lie. I would trust her with my life; in return, I hoped she'd tell me the truth.

"I'm going to share something with you that can't leave this room. I'm not really a friend of Sergei's, but a federal agent with the U.S. government. I know Galinov's involved in many illegal activities. I need you to tell me what's going on at the Velvet Kitty."

"I'm afraid." Tatyana's voice trembled. "Too many people can get hurt."

"One woman is already dead. Galinov has to be stopped. I promise he will never learn that we've spoken," I pressed.

Galya ran into the room before her mother could respond, and timidly approached me.

"So sorry. But what's your little dog's name?" she shyly inquired.

I looked into the child's eyes and wondered how it was that so many trusting women grew up to be hurt.

"She doesn't have a name yet. Would you like to give her one?"

Galya nodded. "I'd call her Zouzou."

"Then Zouzou it is," I agreed.

"But why didn't *you* name your doggy?" Galya curiously questioned.

The pooch gleefully jumped into the little girl's arms, and Galya buried her face in its fur.

The answer became immediately apparent.

"Because Zouzou has been waiting for you. She's your dog now," I softly told the child.

Galya looked at me in wonder, not quite believing what she'd just heard. Her arms cuddled the dog, who contentedly lay as if in a cradle, and I knew I'd made the right decision.

She turned to her mother, her eyes brimming with hopeful tears. "Oh, Mama! Please, may I keep her?"

Tatyana looked at me, then at her daughter, and silently nodded. "Now go play."

We both watched as Galya and the dog ran out of the room. A quiet moment passed.

"Working at the Velvet Kitty. Is that the kind of future you want for your daughter?"

The question effectively stripped Tatyana of her last defense. She gazed at me with eyes as old as Methuselah, and I knew she'd experienced things of which I'd never dreamed.

"I was a stupid girl from a village in the Ukraine where there is no work. Just like all the others, I answered an ad for single, pretty women. It promised us jobs abroad as waitresses, hostesses, and models. Housing would be supplied and wages would be enough for me to send money back to my mother. Sergei also told me that I'd have a chance to meet foreign men. That was the one thing he didn't lie about."

"Then you already knew Sergei?" I asked in surprise.

"Yes. Back in Russia he was a *shkafy*." Tatyana searched for the words. "A big shot. He was my contact when I landed in America."

She looked down at the cracked linoleum floor and wiped away her tears.

"What happened once you arrived here?" I felt certain I knew, but I needed to hear Tatyana say the words.

"Sergei said I'd have to dance at the Velvet Kitty and work as a prostitute. Then he took my passport away. Still, I refused to do what he wanted. That's when he threatened to have all of my family killed."

"And you believed him?"

"Of course. He is part of the *organizatsiya*: the Mafia. They do what they want." She plucked a tissue from her pocket and blew her nose. "He told me, *I own you now*, and that I'd have to work until I earned my way out. Sergei said if I spoke to the police I'd be deported because I don't have papers. Then he'd find me again and bring me back."

I felt sick to my stomach. "And it's the same with all the other women at the club?"

Tatyana sadly nodded.

By now a lump the size of a golf ball had formed in my throat. "How many others are there?"

"Sergei keeps a stable of twenty girls. We work out of cubicles in the back of the club. Each of us services around fifteen men a day." Tatyana's voice broke. "How can I ever hold my head up again when I feel so dirty?"

"Have any of you tried contacting the police?" I questioned, holding back my rising anger.

"Yes. A few girls. But they wound up dead. So now we are all afraid to talk. Besides, we are easily replaced and Sergei says the local police have been paid off."

"What about the man I saw you with at Sergei's house? Renny Folse? What did he want?" My heart pounded so hard, it threatened to burst through my chest.

"He also had many questions. He asked how often Sergei brings in new girls and who else buys us."

That hit me like a bucket of ice water. "You mean Sergei sells you to other clubs?"

"Yes. That's what Renny Folse came to see Sergei about. He wants to buy women for his own club. He offered to pay five hundred dollars for each girl, but Sergei refuses to take less than two thousand."

Though I'd heard the words clearly, I still had a hard time believing them. Apparently, Tatyana felt the same way.

"Sometimes I think this is all a horrible nightmare and I must try very hard to wake myself. How is it possible that women can be bought and sold?"

I wondered the same thing.

"The girls live worse than dogs. They sleep four to a bed in the club's basement."

"Then why aren't you there with them?" I asked skeptically. "What is it that makes you so special?"

Tatyana leveled her eyes on mine and let the last bombshell drop. "Galya is Sergei's child. That is why I get special treatment."

If this was how the Russian Elvis treated his child and her mother, what would be in store for me should my charade be discovered?

"I promise that Sergei will end up in prison for this," I declared passionately.

A bittersweet smile tugged at Tatyana's lips. "Nothing will ever happen to Sergei. He has too much money, too much power. Don't make promises you can't keep."

She was right. Anything I said was worthless until I could prove it.

I said good-bye and walked outside, feeling shaken. I'd once again strayed into territory that scraped at my soul—the netherworld of disposable women. Sergei had found the perfect enterprise to run alongside his caviar trade. Each business paid no taxes and had amazingly low overhead. The major difference was that each tin of caviar can be sold only once. But women provide a constant money machine. Galinov was running a factory fueled by slave labor.

I headed toward my Excursion, pondering what to do next, when an arm appeared out of nowhere and wrapped itself around my neck. A gun bit at my flesh as its barrel was rammed into my ear, accompanied by a voice as cold as a serrated blade.

"I'm only going to say this once, so you damn well better listen. People who dig too deep in the delta tend to disappear. You're messing with our case, bitch. Now get the hell out of here!"

The ground came rushing up to meet me as I was jerked off my feet like a puppet and roughly slammed against the asphalt. I tried to regain my breath, but searing pain ricocheted throughout my body. Then a car screeched to a halt near where I lay. Shoes with metal tips jumped into the vehicle, which quickly spun out, kicking up a spray of gravel. I shielded my eyes against the tiny pebbles, uncovering them in time to see a standard-issue black sedan speeding down the street. What I'd begun to suspect had just been confirmed: another government agency wanted me out of the way. If the bastards thought I was going to crumble, they'd quickly learn I was harder to get rid of than overdue bills.

I stood up on shaky legs, energized by anger and fear, wondering if Santou knew what had just taken place. Even worse, had he been inside the car viewing the action? He'd once likened me to a wolverine who, having hold of something, refuses to let go. Well, guess what? I was more determined than ever to prove it.

I brushed myself off and climbed into my Excursion as the cell phone began to ring.

"Hey, Porter! Whatchoo doin'?"

As if today weren't already bad enough, now Woody was keeping tabs on me.

"Never mind what I'm doing. What do you want?" I snapped, still smarting from my run-in with the phantom federal agent.

"I hope you ain't got any hot plans looming on the

horizon, 'cause I need you to come fishin' with me tonight."

Woody and me alone in a boat together? There was definitely something suspicious about that.

"What do you need me for?"

"It weren't my idea; Sergei suggested it. Virgil's gonna be busy and I need help pulling in and setting the nets. Sergei thought you'd be interested since we put 'em in prohibited waters last night."

Sergei was right. They'd crossed state lines, making it essential that I go. It was the only way I could document exactly where the fish were being caught.

"All right, I'll come. Where do you want to meet?"

"There's an oxbow along the river in Tunica, Mississippi." Woody gave detailed directions. "Be there at ten o'clock tonight."

I hung up to find that my head was throbbing, while the knot in my stomach had grown to the size of a fist. No wonder Fish and Wildlife kept us so well-supplied with large bottles of generic aspirin. But as usual, I didn't have any with me. Pulling into a Quik Stop, I bought some, along with more Mylanta, a Diet Coke, and a pack of Twinkies. Then I phoned Charlie Hickok.

"Ain't you ever gonna learn to call in on a regular basis?" he demanded by way of friendly greeting.

"I've been kind of busy. Besides, I need to be careful," I said between clenched teeth.

"What the hell's with you, Bronx? If working undercover's too much, I can always stick you on duck duty. What are you, worried someone's gonna find out what you're doing?"

"That's not it," I retorted, partially lying.

"Then what is it?"

I hadn't told Charlie about my latest visit to Virgil's and my theory on how Mavis had been disposed of. Then there was Sergei's white slave trade. Should Hickok get a whiff of any of that, I'd be yanked off the case faster than a New York minute.

"My dinner with Galinov went well last night. Not only did he confirm that he's part of a Russian cartel, but he boasted about strong-arming Southern dealers and passing off paddlefish roe as Caspian caviar."

Hickok let loose a whistle. "Hell, Bronx. What'd you do? Sleep with the guy?"

"I believe it's known as 'milking' your source. Besides, you know how men like to brag," I retorted. "By the way, I'm going fishing with Woody tonight in illegal Mississippi waters."

"Now I know you've lost your marbles," Hickok barked. "You're actually gonna trust yourself alone on the water with him?"

"Sure. He can't be *that* irresistible." I chuckled. "Don't worry; I can handle Woody. We'll never have a rock-solid case unless I document what they're up to."

"Just be careful," Charlie grudgingly relented. "I don't need to break in another rookie at this late stage in my career."

"I'll do my best to save you the trouble."

I spent the rest of the day tending to my "drive-by" bruises, after which I tried to catch a few winks. But every time I closed my eyes, Santou loomed in my mind warning me off the case. I finally jumped in the

shower, determined to wash off the invisible layer of
dirt that insistently clung to my skin. But no amount
of soap could rid me of its taint. I knew it would remain until the Velvet Kitty had been closed and Sergei
Galinov was safely locked away.

With a few hours to kill, I wandered over to the
Blue Mojo to get an early meal. My timing proved to
be good, Boobie was cooking in the kitchen. He gave
me a plate of fried chicken with collard greens and
biscuits baked with lard, just like his mama used to
make. Then he joined me at the table with two slices
of sweet potato pie. There was so much pomade in his
hair that a fly landing on top couldn't stop, but slid
down its slippery slope and onto his fork. Boobie did-
n't miss a beat, but flicked the insect onto the floor and
kept right on eating. After that, he lit a cigarette and
took a drag.

"So, was that your apparition I saw you with last
night?"

I nodded and stuck a biscuit in my mouth. It melted
upon touching my tongue. My arteries weren't too
happy, but my taste buds were having the time of their
life.

"Mm, mm, mm. You're in for trouble, li'l girl. I can
tell just by the sight of him, that man is full of nothing
but heartbreak."

Like he was telling me something I didn't already
know.

"I don't suppose you can whip up some sort of
herbal remedy," I quipped, only half in jest.

"Nope. There ain't nothing will change a man like

that. All you can do is hang on tight and go for the ride."

That was a big help. I dug into my sweet potato pie.

"You're eating kinda early this evening. Meeting that apparition of yours for a late-night snack?"

My fork scraped up the last bit. "No. I've got a business meeting later that could go on for a while."

Boobie sucked on the end of his cigarette, then plucked a few shreds of tobacco off his tongue. Laying them on the table, he studied the flakes as if they were tea leaves.

"I know you may think I'm a superstitious old fool, but listen to me now. You'd best be careful tonight. The moon's red and hanging low: that ain't a good sign. The only thing worse would be if it were touching a gravestone."

His words pricked at my skin, sharp as dagger points.

"It's okay, Boobie. I know what I'm doing. Besides, I've been drinking plenty of your mojo specials. That should count for something."

Boobie gave me a pat on the cheek and then disappeared into the growing crowd. I suddenly felt terribly alone. Dog was gone. Who knew where Santou was? And Vincent and Terri had fled town. For the first time in a while, I was completely on my own.

I tried to dislodge the feeling, but it refused to go away. I finished off my coffee and walked out into the delta night.

Twenty

Boobie was right. The moon *was* hanging low tonight, its color as disquieting as a blood blister. I sped by Graceland and over the Mississippi line, where a row of casinos rose out of the cotton fields, as imposing as enormous headstones. Their pulsating colors flooded the land in a pool of pale red, reflecting the crimson moonlight. I could have sworn I heard a taunting whisper echo inside my vehicle, and nervously glanced back though no one was there.

I continued to drive as the silence grew more dense, finally spotting the landmark that Woody had told me about. A rickety shack stood next to a looming water tower. Beyond it was an unmarked dirt road.

I turned onto the rutted path and followed its trail, hoping it knew the way to the oxbow. Rolling down the window, I was reassured by two scents. The odor of fresh dust rushed into my nose, revealing somebody had traveled this same route recently. The second was the fetid smell of the Mississippi. Up ahead, moonlight gathered in a shimmering pool on the shiny roof of a vehicle. I pulled up and parked next to Woody's Dodge Ram.

I turned off my engine and sat still for a moment, having glimpsed a red glow bobbing up and down like a drunken firefly. The inebriated insect slowly transshaped into the fiery tip of a burning cigar. Woody had his fourteen-foot johnboat unhitched from the trailer and was setting it in the backwater channel. I hopped out of the Ford and walked over.

"Hell, wouldn't you know the damn river would be pissed tonight?" Woody muttered irritably.

"What do you mean?" I asked, wondering if he was as wacky as his brother.

"Look at this boat bobbing like a damn Halloween apple. If it's doing that here, it's gonna be murder out on the river."

"Do you want to call it off?" I anxiously hoped that wasn't the case.

"No way! Maybe it'll die down. This river's just like a woman—it changes its mind every other minute."

We climbed into the boat and shoved off.

Putt, putt, whispered the engine, as if aware it was best to remain quiet. Not that anything could have been heard above the churning, seething Mississippi. I was about to suggest we turn around, when the water mysteriously calmed down as if all its rage had been vented.

"See? What did I tell ya?" Woody champed on his cigar with supreme satisfaction.

We continued until we reached the area where Woody and Virgil had previously set their nets; then we began the arduous task of hauling in one hundred yards of eight-inch mesh. Woody shined a flashlight on our catch. Flopping around inside were a variety of

fish, wriggling and jerking, desperate to return to the
water before they died. I swiftly complied, throwing
back those that Hardy didn't want. He poked among
the bodies to find six young paddlefish.

"Welcome to Dixie, girl. We got us some Delta
Gold." Woody grinned.

I'd never seen a live paddlefish before. It would
have put Cyrano de Bergerac to shame. The paddle-
shaped snout was nearly half its body length, while a
toothless mouth made it look like an old man who'd
forgotten to put in his dentures. Woody snapped the
linoleum knife open with a flick of his wrist, and
placed the tip against one creature's stomach.

"Okay. Whadda ya say? Is it a boy or a girl?"

He jabbed the point in and sliced the fish open. A
trickle of black eggs oozed from its belly.

"Hot diggity! We got us a female!"

Woody anxiously spread the flesh apart. Removing
the glistening black mass, he placed the precious
cargo into a plastic bucket.

"One down, five to go!" He laughed and picked up
the next squirming victim.

But this fish had no roe. Whether it was too young
or of the wrong gender made little difference; its fate
remained the same. The eviscerated body was tossed
overboard.

Hardy followed the same procedure with each.
Only three fish contained Delta Gold. The others were
destroyed before ever having had the chance to reach
maturity. I stared at the bucket, now filled with unfertilized eggs. Each one represented a creature forever
lost, its fate to wind up in the mouths of the wealthy.

It's been said that we're once more at the start of a new Dark Age. Only this time, it isn't books that are being destroyed, but the irreplaceable DNA of countless plants and species. The business of extinction is alive and well and incredibly profitable. I knew I'd never be able to enjoy caviar again.

"Goddammit! We'd be able to make a lot more money if there were some big fish around here," Woody grumbled.

No shit, Sherlock. The problem was there were few elders left: they'd all been knocked off by bozos like him.

"What does Sergei pay you for this?" I asked, curious as to the going rate.

"I get a flat fee to work just for him, plus forty bucks a pound. We got about eight pounds here already, but this is chump change. I should be makin' a thousand a night easy." Hardy slapped a lid on the bucket.

"You're kidding!" I exclaimed, unable to stop myself.

"Hell, Porter, don't you know nothing? Whadda ya think Sergei's pulling in with his network of fishermen?"

"I don't know," I replied, feeling foolish.

"I'll tell you: around forty thousand bucks a day," Woody snorted.

The markup was dazzling, considering all he needed was a bunch of bubbas in boats.

We made our way further south, where Hardy spotted a marker holding someone else's gill net. He veered the johnboat over and cut it loose.

"That's known as getting rid of the competition."

He winked. "God almighty, but I love being on the water. It's like letting your mind take a shit when you're out here. Doncha think?"

"Is this how you charmed all your wives?" I cracked. "Or how you lost them?"

Woody guffawed. "Hell, I got a better way than that. One night I told Tammy IV, 'Honey, you've gained a few pounds.' The little woman answered, 'I'm retaining water.' 'That's a pile of bull,' I said. 'What you're retaining is Twinkies and Budweiser.' Right after that, she packed her bags and left."

Hardy stopped the boat. "This spot looks good. Give me a hand."

We threw the gill net overboard, and the current pulled it under. Then we headed back for shore.

"Speaking of ex-wives, Mavis's car was recently pulled out of the river."

"You don't say," Woody replied.

"I'm beginning to suspect she was the victim of foul play. What do you think, Woody?"

Hardy continued to steer the boat. "What I think is Mavis dumped that Mercedes in the river herself, in order to claim the insurance money."

"I don't believe that. Tell me, was Virgil upset when they got divorced?"

The riverbank was just ahead when Woody turned to face me with a funny look.

"That's exactly the kind of question that's gotten you into trouble, Porter. Fact is, Virgil ain't too happy with this partnership."

I saw Woody reach for something and realized it was a gun. My hand quickly slid toward my own .38.

At the same time, a swift moving current rammed the boat and I was thrown forward. Woody's gun was knocked out of his hand and into the water as the craft slammed into the bank, its nose rearing up like a flimsy toy. Startled by the turn of events, we both grabbed onto the boat's aluminum sides as the current roughly dragged us away from land. Something wet sloshed against my back, and I twisted around to find water pouring inside. A second current broadsided us with the smack of a giant hand, and the hull was sent spinning into a three-hundred-and-sixty-degree turn.

"Christ almighty! We're gonna drown!" Woody exclaimed, suddenly finding religion.

He grabbed the bucket of roe and threw me a rope attached to the boat's nose. "You gotta jump out and pull us into land!"

"What are you, crazy? Why don't you do it?"

"Don't be a wuss! The bank's just over there! Besides, I can't swim and this sucker's going down!"

He was right about that; I was already sitting in a large pool of water.

"What the hell do you mean, you can't swim? You're a fisherman, aren't you?" I yelled.

"Yeah, but I fish with my butt in the boat! Now do something before we're pulled out any further!"

Damn! I just wished Hardy's craft had a life preserver. I was tempted to swim back and leave him on his own, except that I needed the rope to hang on to.

I prayed my mojo was working and jumped into the water, which felt like liquid ice. The freezing cold stole my breath away, and my muscles angrily protested, warning they'd soon begin to cramp.

Though I swam as fast as I could, the bank seemed a hundred miles away.

Adrenaline's a wonderful thing when death is at your heels. I tapped into a source of strength I never knew I had, and kicked the current into submission. I hit the bank and pulled Woody to shore, all the while violently shivering.

"I'll get you something warm," Woody offered, jumping out of the boat.

"Take off or pull another gun, and I swear to God you're a dead man," I warned between chatters.

But Woody had a smattering of decency left; he threw a wool blanket around my shoulders.

I waited until my shaking was under control, and then confronted him. "What the hell was that about back there?"

"I told you the water was unpredictable," Woody sheepishly responded.

"You know damn well what I'm talking about. You were going to try to kill me! Was that on Sergei's orders?"

Woody hung his head like a coon dog who'd just received a scolding. "Aw, shit! No, it weren't Sergei. He don't even know you're out here tonight," he admitted. "It's Virgil. He thinks you're horning in on too much of the money. Personally, I believe there's something he just don't like about you."

Perhaps the fact that I knew he was totally crazy. "*Now* what am I supposed to do? Hell, you saved my life. It's not like I can still kill ya," Hardy dejectedly moaned.

"I take it that's your way of saying thank you," I snapped.

"Hey, don't get pissy with *me,* Porter!" Woody huffed. "I can't help it if I'm a lover and ain't a murderer. Damn! I'll take care of this mess somehow. You just better stay out of sight until Virgil cools down."

That wasn't very likely; I had no intention of letting Virgil think I was afraid of him.

"Right now, I gotta process this roe before it starts going bad."

I followed Woody to the back of his pickup, where he pulled out a bucket of water and a screen for grading eggs. He carefully washed the roe, and then added half an ounce of flour salt to each pound.

"What happens now?" I asked, wrapping the blanket tighter around me.

Woody slapped the lid back in place. "I deliver the eggs to Sergei."

"In that case, I'll take it from here," I said, and grabbed the bucket from Hardy's hands.

"Hey! That's my job!" he protested.

"Not tonight. You straighten Virgil out. I'll handle this end. Where do you make the delivery?"

"I drop 'em at Galinov's house if it's before midnight. After that, I meet him at the Velvet Kitty." Woody sulked. "You're not gonna rat me out to Sergei, are you?"

Tammy V's face floated into my mind, along with her two brats, the baby, and the bun in the oven. Underneath all the wheeling and dealing, the dirt and the stench, Woody wasn't a totally bad guy. Besides, he was more valuable to me alive and kicking. "No. Just remember, you owe me big-time."

I left Hardy behind with an empty plastic bucket for bailing out his boat.

Twenty-one

It was nearly midnight—too late to catch Sergei at his Russian Graceland. No matter; I wanted to go home first, anyway.

I locked the roe in my Ford and headed upstairs, where I showered off the rank odor of the Mississippi. Then I dried my hair into its usual jungle of curls and slipped into a form-fitting dress. The garment displayed just enough cleavage to be provocative. Heading back out, I pointed my vehicle toward Mount Moriah.

It had become essential that I act quickly to cement Sergei's trust. Clearly, another agency had become interested in him. I suspected it wouldn't be long before they'd once again try to kick me off the case—perhaps permanently, next time.

The Velvet Kitty's lot was jammed. Little wonder; the club's logo had an added attraction in the dark: the cat's nipples flashed in an ever-changing array of colors. I knew there was a good chance Tatyana would be at the club tonight. I'd learn soon enough if she'd kept my secret safe.

I parked near Sergei's pink Cadillac and approached the club's front door, only to be accosted by

one of the exiting patrons. The guy tottered as he
walked and his shirt was two sizes too small, revealing
way more fat than muscle.

"Hey there, cutie! You're lookin' luscious tonight!
How 'bout giving me a Velvet Kitty rub in my car before you start your shift?" he drunkenly inquired. "I'm
talking full contact, for which you get twenty-five
smackeroos that you don't have to split with the boss."

I began to walk past, when his hand landed someplace it shouldn't have.

"Come on sugar tits; don't be like that. I'm talking
a quickie!"

In two seconds, Mr. Wonderful was thrown flat on
his back. Perhaps our chance encounter would teach
him it's not nice to touch without an invitation.

"I hope that was full contact enough for you," I
said, and stepped over his body. "That's *my* version
of a quickie." God, Vincent would have been proud
of me!

I walked inside, feeling ready to deal with any situation, only to stop dead in my tracks. The one thing I
hadn't counted on was staring right at me. Santou sat
in a booth next to Galinov. Jake blanched and slowly
shook his head. I took that to mean I was to vamoose,
go play somewhere else. Santou smoothly focused his
attention back on Sergei.

I'd pretty much had it with people trying to push me
around, from my attacker this morning to the joker in
the parking lot. I didn't care who Santou was working
for; I had no intention of scooting away with my tail
between my legs. Galinov was square in my sights

and I refused to give up my prey. If Santou wanted Sergei, he'd have to fight me for him.

I impudently sashayed over, giving a little extra sexy sway to my hips. Sergei's face lit up as he caught sight of my approach.

Top that one, Santou! I silently gloated. I knew I'd hit my mark as Jake's complexion turned a shade paler. At the same time his eyes revealed that he'd never expected anything less.

Sergei jumped to his feet and wrapped me in a bear hug, as if I were a long-lost relative. "*Moy dorogoy!* My dear, what are you doing here?"

"I hope I'm not disturbing anything, but Woody was unavoidably detained, so I'm taking his place tonight."

Santou's eyes worked like magnets, drawing my own from over Sergei's shoulder. He'd once told me that his grandmama had practiced voodoo when he was a young boy. If so, she must have passed the art on to her grandson. Santou now held me in thrall with the ease of a snake hypnotizing its victim. I felt myself tumble down a rabbit hole, uncontrollably falling into a featherbed of sinfully sensuous thoughts and emotions.

I couldn't help but remember how Santou's fingers had expertly hit every pulse point in my body. Jake seemed to know it, as well. His hint of a smile sent a shiver of electricity rippling through me.

"Rachel, you're shivering! Are you telling me that you were alone on the water with Woody tonight?" Sergei questioned, rubbing my arms with his hands.

"Virgil wasn't available and I thought he might need some help."

Galinov's eyes narrowed as he processed this information. "And everything went all right?"

"Absolutely fine," I assured him.

"Here. Let me pour you some vodka. It will warm you up. That and sitting close to me. I have enough body heat for the both of us."

I scooted onto the bench, aware of the wound-up intensity vibrating off Santou. If he was nervous, it didn't show. He casually draped his arms over the top of the cushioned booth and leaned back, his eyes boldly traveling up and down my form as if examining a piece of merchandise. Santou was not only calling my bluff, but playing his own game of chicken.

"So, Sergei. What have we here? She's quite a looker. You going to introduce me to the lady?"

Galinov caught Santou's drift and swiftly brought it to a halt. "No, no, my friend. This one, she is not for you." He handed me a glass of vodka and raised his own in salute. "Priscilla is an associate of mine who likes to take risks almost as much as I do. In fact, she is proving to be an invaluable asset."

Priscilla? I glanced at my Elvis clone and took it as a definite sign of progress.

Galinov clinked his glass against mine. "*Na zdorovye,*" he toasted. "Drink up!"

"In other words, you want to keep her all for yourself. Not that I blame you." Santou pointedly stared at my cleavage before looking back up. He couldn't have made his disapproval of my attire any more clear, while managing to hide the fact from Sergei. "She really *must* be something special."

I glared at Santou. "I'd appreciate not being referred to as some sort of commodity. And if you have something to say, you can speak directly to me. I don't know who the hell you are, but for your information, I belong to no man." I spiked the blow with a lethal smile. Raising my glass, I downed the remaining vodka.

Sergei chuckled and refilled both our glasses. "I don't think my friend likes you, Mr. Folse. Our business is over for tonight, anyway. You push too hard and I haven't yet made a decision. Now, if you'll excuse us," he said by way of dismissal.

Jake slid out of the booth, and then picked up my hand and kissed it. "Please accept my apology, miss. I meant no harm. It's just that you're very beautiful."

My anger promptly dissipated into a clump of sawdust in my throat. For that one moment, I no longer cared who won the game. All I knew was that I didn't want to lose Santou ever again.

"How about I call you in a couple days, Sergei, and we'll see if we can't work something out?"

Santou didn't wait for a response, but turned and walked away. My eyes remained glued to his form until the very last whisper of his presence slipped out the door.

"So, Agent Porter. Now that you're here at my club, what do you think?" Galinov asked.

But I knew his inquiry was much more than a question. It was a test.

I glanced at the lap dance going on at the next table. "I'd say you've got yourself quite a gold mine."

Galinov nodded heartily in agreement. "That it is. It's good you approve."

If I'd thought the place was sleazy before, now that I knew what was really going on, it seemed downright sinister.

"You brought the eggs with you?" Sergei questioned.

"Yes. They're in my vehicle."

"Good. Let's go get them."

I followed Galinov past the painted faces of girls staring blankly into space as their bodies performed like machines. I only hoped their souls had learned to grow wings, on which they could mentally fly thousands of miles away.

I unlocked the Excursion and delivered the container of roe to Sergei.

"Huh," he grunted, calculating its weight in his hands. "About eight pounds. Not bad. Still, I think we'd better move even further south if we plan to catch the bigger fish."

That's when I knew what I had to do next. "So, tell me. How do you store the eggs? Are they kept in a portable ice chest in your house?"

Sergei looked momentarily perplexed, then his face began to darken. "Why do you ask this? What are you talking about?"

"I've had the opportunity to check out some amazing storage spaces at other dealers' facilities. But those were legitimate caviar places, of course." I directed my arrow at Sergei's pride, laying my trap.

"They're big-time players and have very elaborate set-ups. You probably don't have anything like that."

Zap! My arrow hit its bull's-eye.

"And what the hell do you think *I* am? Some fish-monger standing on a street corner in Moscow?" Galinov erupted. "You're impressed because you believe somebody has a fancier place? I tell you, there is nobody with a bigger or better business! I have a fortune stockpiled in caviar and paddlefish roe!"

"I don't mean to offend you, Sergei. But there's only so much roe a dealer can keep on hand; it has to be moved fast. After all, it's a perishable product."

It was now Galinov's turn to gloat. "That's where *you're* wrong! For most dealers, yes. But not for me." Sergei's finger tapped against his temple. "You are dealing with one very smart cookie. I have developed a method for freezing eggs which others don't know. You will come with me to the house, and I will show you something you've never seen before!"

"Tonight?" I demurely questioned.

"Tonight!" Sergei roared, reestablishing his un-questionable masculinity.

A minute later I was in my Ford, following Sergei back to his Moscow on the Mississippi. Billy Paw opened the front door before we even reached the top step. Talk about your loyal manservant! He wore a loud flannel shirt stained with what smelled like chewing tobacco, yet I could have sworn he glanced at my dress with disdain. Who'd put *him* on the Best-Dressed list?

"Can I get youuu something, boss?" Billy Paw

drawled, catching Galinov's sequined cape with one hand while holding out the other for my gun.

"No. Nothing right now. Go away. Make yourself scarce."

A beam of resentment emanated from Billy Paw that was nearly as strong as a nuclear flash. This was the first I'd seen it directed at Galinov. If Sergei wasn't careful, he might find himself with a revolution on his hands.

Sergei led me through the kitchen to a door I hadn't noticed before, where he fished a set of keys from his pocket and chose one with a large, square head. Unlocking the door, he then switched on a light and we proceeded downstairs to an enormous room filled with a stereo system, an assortment of radio equipment, and lots of knickknacky Elvis memorabilia. It could have passed as any other suburban basement except for the steady hum that issued from six commercial-sized freezers. The metal coffins lined two of the walls.

Galinov walked over to the steel lockers and flung open each of their doors. Inside were buckets filled to the brim with little black beauties, also known as Delta Gold, Chattanooga beluga, and Aphrodite's eggs. In addition, there were bucketfuls of Caspian beluga, osetra, and sevruga roe. He added tonight's catch to the millions of embryos that lay perfectly preserved in a suspended state of animation.

"Okay! Now tell me where you've ever seen anything else like this before!"

I had to admit he had me on that one.

"I have ten thousand pounds of frozen caviar. Mix

in a little beluga or osetra, slap on a Russian label, and I can pass it off as the genuine article. Do you know how much money all this is worth?"

My mind did a quick tally. Beluga was retailing for ninety-five dollars an ounce these days, and fancy Manhattan restaurants easily sold a thousand pounds of the stuff. I came up with somewhere around 1.2 million dollars. Then I multiplied it by ten. My brain began to short-circuit, just trying to add up the numbers. Wow! Sergei had as much caviar on hand as Harrison Ford got paid per picture! That really *was* impressive!

Galinov drew close, his breath hot and heavy on my neck. "Last year alone, New York consumed eighty-one tons! Just think of it!"

My mind performed another speedy calculation. That amount of caviar equaled the size of forty elephants!

"You Americans are insatiable—it is what I love best about you!"

Sergei turned me toward him, and presented me with his best Elvis sneer. "Why did you really go out on the water tonight? What were you trying to prove?"

Think *Body Heat!* I instructed my inner actress, going for a young, slim version of Kathleen Turner.

"I wanted to keep an eye on what Woody and Virgil were up to. Somebody might try to take more than their fair share when this much money is at stake. Besides, we're in business together now," I added in a low, sultry tone. "I believe in safeguarding my investment."

Sergei drew me close, until all that separated us were his protruding rhinestones. "Could it be? Maybe you really are my Priscilla. If so, you are one lucky female. Why is that, you ask? It is because just like Elvis, I know how to satisfy my women. I believe it is time we became more intimate."

Sergei's arms wrapped around me like tentacles. Maybe showing so much cleavage *hadn't* been such a good idea. Now what the hell was I supposed to do? Kick him in the groin and make a run for it?

Galinov's vodka-laced breath nearly knocked me out as his lips pressed hard against mine. The next moment, a deafening crash resounded from the floor above, and Billy Paw began to curse loudly.

"Goll darn it to hell and holy tarnation! Dear Lord and Elvis, help me now!"

That did it. Sergei flew upstairs as though having heard that Elvis had just arrived in the building. I followed, pausing as my foot hit the first step. Hidden beneath the stairwell were two metal cabinets. I mentally filed the discovery away, then hightailed it up to the kitchen, where a large teapot lay smashed on the floor.

"You idiot! That belonged to Elvis's mother!" Galinov roared. "Vern gave that to Gladys after Elvis appeared on *The Milton Berle Show!* How could you be so stupid?"

I slipped past Sergei, who dropped to his knees, bringing Billy Paw down with him.

"We're going to gather every single piece up and then glue it back together!" Galinov raged, close to tears.

I retrieved my gun and walked out the door amid the confusion.

Sleep came easier than I'd expected, enveloping me in its black velvet grip. I floated on a cloud of moonlight, while a spider wove lunar cobwebs. Each was a strand of gold and contained a translucent gray pearl in its middle. But the surprise lay in what was swimming inside—a perfectly formed paddlefish.

I plucked an egg, which broke in my hand. An iridescent stream gushed out, and the puddle rose as the water exploded. Then a whirlpool pulled me down.

The darkness was as dense as undeveloped film, until I finally hit bottom. Once there, I discovered I wasn't alone. An arm brushed against mine and I turned to find Valerie Vaughn, a former stripper from New Orleans. I'd worked on her case after she'd been murdered, her body slashed to resemble an intricate puzzle. A stream of white froth tumbled out of her mouth in a trail of glistening champagne bubbles.

I quickly became part of a circle of girls dressed in their best "fuck me" shoes and G-strings. We were attached by umbilical cords permanently forged from iron chains. They'd clearly been sold into sexual bondage, each a prisoner in a hidden trade, lost in a labyrinth with no end.

Their desperate fingers began to claw at my hair, some wanting to be saved, others intent on having me join them. Then I saw a metal freezer on the river floor, patiently waiting with its door open. I fought but couldn't stop the women from placing me inside the steel coffin, after which it was closed and locked.

I woke up in bed, screaming and covered in sweat. The lamp was off, its bulb burned out. My demons had cleverly snuck in under the cover of night, knowing I didn't expect them. I grabbed the remote and, with shaky fingers, quickly turned on the TV. But even the noise couldn't fully bring me back from my dream's watery depths. I lay under the circling blades of the overhead fan and imagined them to be a protective wheel of sabers. Just like the Mississippi, my own lair was filled with dark, mysterious secrets.

Twenty-two

I fell back into a restless sleep, only to be dragged awake by the nerve-jangling ring of the phone. I glanced at my clock. Six A.M. Who the hell would be calling at this hour? I picked up the receiver and mumbled hello.

"Bronx! Haul your sorry ass out of bed, throw on some clothes, and get over to the office right now!"

The voice shot through me with the crackling sting of a whip. I hadn't heard Charlie Hickok sound this frazzled since our days back in New Orleans.

"What's up?" I asked, my adrenaline set on high-octane and already pumping.

"Something's happened. We need to talk."

Before I could ask for more particulars, Charlie hung up. My stomach churned with the low grind of a failing car battery. I felt sure the call meant only one thing: whatever was going on, I was in some serious deep shit.

I pulled myself out of bed, and prepared for the day with an extra large slug of Mylanta. Then I showered, dressed, and made a beeline for work.

What have I done? What have I done?

"Your job! Now stop being such a wuss!" my inner voice tartly commanded.

I walked down the deserted hall and through the office door, where Barney Fife pointed his gun at me. But that was nothing compared to the rest of the firing squad that awaited my arrival.

Holy moly! I found myself confronted by what had to be Billy Paw's twin brother—only this guy had his act together. His hair was neatly combed back and he wore a suit. Even stranger was that Santou stood beside him. Meanwhile, Hickok sat slumped in his chair wearing a dire expression that clearly read, *You're about to get your ass whupped.* Talk about your Unholy Trinity.

I took another look at Mr. Clean, who exuded a lethal mix of machismo and arrogance. The morning sun streamed through the window, creating a metallic glare on the floor that captured my attention. Glancing down, I spied a pair of worn-out boots capped with shiny metal tips. My eyes instantly shot back up. This was the bastard who'd jammed a gun in my ear and exfoliated my face with a spray of gravel!

A repugnant smirk was plastered across the man's face. "How youuuuu doing, Porter?" he drawled in amusement.

I stared in disbelief, refusing to acknowledge Santou, who'd begun to fidget.

"This here is Special Agent Ed Tolliver." Hickok's voice crackled in the tension-filled air. "And I believe you already know the other sonofabitch next to me."

Only then did I shoot Santou a look of withering scorn. His eyes briefly held mine before I angrily pulled away. I could already tell what was going on. I should have realized the moment I caught sight of Billy Paw dressed in a plain gray suit: it was standard-issue FBI garb. I was clearly facing a lynch mob who were about to pull the plug on my case. That would happen over my dead body.

"I take it you recognize me?" Tolliver patronizingly flashed his badge in front of my face.

"Yeah. I'm sorry to say, you look better as Billy Paw."

Tolliver clucked his tongue and slid his ID back in his jacket pocket. "Now, now. Don't be a sore loser, Porter."

I wanted to punch the guy smack in his arrogant kisser. "Maybe I'm missing something, but when did this become a game that you've won? And by the way, do you have one of those G-men badges, too?" I fired at Santou.

Jake pulled out his ID and threw it to me. Only a twitch near his mouth betrayed that he genuinely felt sorry about what was taking place.

Santou's ID burned fiercely hot in my hands. His likeness stared at me with his predatory gaze, battle scars, and steamy sexuality.

"You take a lousy picture," I remarked, and tossed the badge back. Damn, I was mad!

"Face it: you fucked up, Porter. You should have listened to Santou when he warned you to stay away. Or at least to Billy Paw, Jr." Tolliver patted the .45 that sat holstered beneath his armpit. "As it is, we've had to waste precious time checking to make sure you weren't really crooked. We're talking a big boo-boo on your part. It's one that you're now going to have to pay for."

"Why is that?" Where did this guy get off making threats? And why wasn't Charlie sticking up for me?

"Because you're screwing with our investigation," Tolliver coolly responded.

"I have every right to investigate a case dealing with the illegal trade in paddlefish," I replied, choosing to play dumb.

Tolliver shot straight to the heart of the matter. "Not without the proper authorization, you don't. You never got clearance to work undercover. Plus, you've situated yourself in the middle of *our* investigation on the white slave trade!"

"Goddammit to hell, Bronx! Why didn't you tell me what you'd plopped those dogs of yours into?" Hickok barked. "Haven't I always said not to put your foot down before checking exactly where it is that you're stepping?"

"Agent Porter deserves more credit than that. Don't think for one second she didn't know what she was doing," Tolliver retorted. "That's why we're dealing with this mess. We were making good headway until Porter stuck her nose in where it didn't belong."

"Please, let's give credit where credit is due," I returned the compliment. "The only headway *you've* been making is perfecting your meat loaf recipe and learning to grill peanut butter and banana sandwiches."

Hickok's lips quivered and a snort escaped.

"I'm glad you're whooping it up, Grandpa," Tolliver snapped. "Especially knowing what this little prank is probably going to do to your retirement."

That shut Charlie up.

Tolliver turned his animosity back to me. "The problem is, you're trying to pretend to be something you're not."

"And what would that be?" I retorted, knowing full well where this was headed.

"You're living out some fantasy that you're a female James Bond. Well, here's a wake-up call. You're nothing more than a glorified game warden who should be answering phones and fielding investigations to qualified agents."

"Gee, I bet you wouldn't be half so mad were it anyone other than a female U.S. Fish and Wildlife agent who not only stumbled upon this case, but also managed to gain Galinov's confidence. Apparently that's something the FBI hasn't been able to do," I responded with a wicked smile. "From what I can tell, Billy Paw is dismissed from the room every time the subject of business comes up!"

"All right, you hotheads! That's enough!" Hickok broke in, knowing it was Tolliver who needed protection.

"No way! She's on a roll," Santou declared, ending his silence. "Say whatever's on your mind, Porter. I'm sure you think Galinov's got a problem with me, too, so go ahead. Give it your best shot."

I was taken aback until I realized Santou probably knew I needed to vent my rage.

"Must be the Russki just don't like coonass Cajuns," Charlie smartly cut me off. "All right, enough of this crap. Let's get down to business. What you don't know, Bronx, is that there's been another murder."

A sickening feeling rolled over me. *Please don't let it be Tatyana,* I prayed, worried Galinov had somehow discovered that I'd talked to her. "Who was it?"

"A fisherman snagged Woody Hardy's body near Chickasaw Bluffs early this morning," Hickok said with a near imperceptible shake of his head.

It suddenly felt as if all the air had been sucked out of the room, and my legs grew woozy. Only Santou's steady gaze helped keep me standing. "But I was with him just last night."

Tolliver expertly moved in for the kill. "Yeah, you're a real good-luck charm, Porter. So far two of your contacts have died on you. But don't worry; you're about to get the chance to redeem yourself. You've been temporarily reassigned to work for the FBI. Think of it as your reward for worming your way in so tight with Galinov."

"What!" I sputtered, and turned to Hickok for help. "Can they do that?"

Charlie's hands balled into fists and he nodded.

"You bet your sweet ass we can," Tolliver fired back.

"Sorry, *chère*. But the FBI outranks Fish and Wildlife on these matters," Santou added consolingly.

"Butch and Sundance are right," Hickok seconded. "I just received orders from the head honchos at Fish and Wildlife that you're to cooperate with the FBI and do whatever they want."

Absolutely not!

A smug expression swam across Tolliver's mug, and I knew he planned to castrate my case. No way in hell would I let him do that.

"Fine," I acquiesced. "But I'll also continue to do my own work."

Tolliver pointed his finger at me like a gun. *"That's* where you're wrong. The only case you have is the one I tell you to work on."

I glanced at Charlie.

"Hickok can't gallop to your aid. Here's a little incoming grenade: for the time being, *I'm* your boss."

My face must have registered the way I felt.

"Hey, hotshot! Maybe you can get away with crap at a rinky-dink agency like Fish and Wildlife. But at the FBI, the game is played by different rules. Galinov has to be taken down before you trip up and make any mistakes—which means you're gonna get the information that we want pronto."

"So *that's* why I've been reassigned. Because I'm doing such a bad job," I scoffed.

But Tolliver refused to take the bait. "You're going to call Galinov right now and set up a meeting for tonight."

"What? You expect me to pull this off in one evening?" I asked incredulously.

Even Santou seemed surprised. "Wait a minute, Ed. I thought we were going to let this thing play out naturally."

"The plan's changed. If Galinov gets a whiff that something's going on, he'll immediately bolt. I haven't kowtowed to that bastard for this long just to let him slip away. Besides, Sergei thinks that Porter here is his little Russian Priscilla. She can play that angle to the hilt."

I was left with no choice but to agree. "What exactly is it that you want?"

"You're going to get him to tell you all about how the girls are smuggled over. I also want to know what brothels he's sold them to here in the States," Tolliver instructed.

"Santou and I can already give you some of that information," I volunteered.

"Yeah. But *you're* gonna provide us with rock-solid evidence that we can take to court," Mr. Clean said.

"And how do you expect me to do that?" I asked, immediately suspicious.

Tolliver played his last hand. "Because you'll be wearing a wire to capture each precious gem on tape."

So that was it. I was to be set up as bait. What bothered me even more was that Fish and Wildlife would so willingly roll over.

Santou sharply turned to Tolliver. "Hold on a second, bud. There was no mention of a wire. You know damn well Galinov always pats me down, what makes you think he won't do the same to her?"

"Because she's his 'hunka hunka burning love.' Ain't that right, Priscilla? He'd never imagine the girl of his dreams would turn out to be his devil in disguise," Tolliver jeered. "If that's a problem, I can take you off the case right now, Santou. I'm sure headquarters will understand. After all, she is your old girlfriend."

"Anyone ever tell you what a sonofabitch you are?" Jake angrily lashed out.

"All the time," Tolliver retorted, looking mighty pleased.

"Hey, *I'm* the one who hasn't yet agreed to this," I interrupted.

"Oh, but you will," Tolliver assured me. "You live for your work, Porter. Besides, don't think of it as a job for us. You're doing it for the greater good of the Sisterhood. Two million women and children are victimized by traffickers each year. Or don't you give a flying fuck about that?"

I cared more than he'd ever know. What I hated was having to obey Tolliver.

"Now make the call," he commanded.

A tape recorder was already attached to the phone.

I dialed Galinov's number. "Sergei? It's Rachel. I hope I didn't wake you."

"No, no my little Priscilla. In fact, I dreamed of nothing but you last night, and now here you are calling! I must apologize for what happened. Billy Paw can be totally useless—it's only my good nature that keeps him around. But I promise to make it up. When can I see you?"

"How about tonight? Perhaps we can pick up where we left off."

"What a wonderful idea! That will also keep you from going out on the river. You're far too precious a commodity to risk."

I imagined Woody floating facedown, being reeled in like a fish. I wondered if Galinov had given the order and who had carried it out.

"Why don't you come for dinner this evening around nine o'clock?"

"I'll be there." I hung up and turned to Tolliver. "It

seems you'll get one last shot to practice your meat loaf recipe."

Tolliver flashed a thin smile. "Wear pants tonight so that we can hide the wire, and leave your gun at home. It'll look like you trust him. Oh, and choose a top showing plenty of cleavage again."

"And whose entertainment would *that* be for? Yours or Galinov's?"

"Just be here at five o'clock sharp, so that we can wire you up and test the equipment. I can't be gone long or Galinov will wonder where I am."

"Yeah, I noticed you're kept on a short leash. I'll have to suggest he also get you a muzzle."

Tolliver grabbed my arm as I turned to leave. "By the way, you never thanked me for last night."

I pulled away, hating his touch. "What are you talking about?"

His laugh rang coarse in my ears. "Have you forgotten already? I saved your butt. If I hadn't dropped that teapot when I did, you'd have been the caviar on Galinov's toast."

I coldly stared at the man before taking my leave.

Twenty-three

I spent the day thinking about power and its games. It all came down to a matter of who had it and who did not. This time *I* was on the receiving end, being twisted. I didn't like the feeling at all. The phone rang and I answered to hear Jake's voice.

"Hey, chère. How you holding up?"

"Let's see. I've had my case sabotaged and am preparing to be sacrificed on the FBI's altar. How do you think I feel?"

"Listen, Rachel. I did what I could to keep you out of this. You wouldn't listen, and strings were pulled over which I had no control. But I'll be nearby. There's no way I'll let anything happen to you."

I could feel Santou's heat burning straight through the phone wire.

"I promise to keep you safe."

Silly me. I actually believed him. "I'll see you at five o'clock."

I picked my clothes as if choosing what to wear to my funeral. Black jeans seemed apropos. I added a black cashmere top with a plunging neckline, making me look like a black widow spider. Honey might be good for catching flies, but when it came to trapping men, underwire bras were better bait.

Then I headed to the Blue Mojo, hoping Boobie would cook me a mid-afternoon lunch.

Boobie issued a whistle as his eyes took in my outfit. "Good God, girl. That man of yours don't stand a chance tonight. What you tryin' to do? Get him rattled enough to marry you?"

"No. I have other plans for this evening. Any chance I can get some food first?"

Boobie warily nodded. "I'll heat a little something from lunch. But I ain't feedin' you too much; I don't want you poppin' outta that thing."

The "little something" consisted of chicken dumplings, candied yams, and buttered squash.

Boobie lit a cigarette as I finished eating and emitted a cloud of smoke. "You know, I been on this earth a long time, li'l girl, and I'm getting a feelin' you're about to place yourself in some real bad danger. That moon I tole you about last night? Well, my bones tell me this evening it'll be full and probably touching the ground. It's the type of night that breeds mischief and murder. I'd hate to think of that pretty face of yours all bruised and broken, lyin' somewhere waiting to be found."

I looked closely at the man and realized Boobie was older than I'd imagined. It was as if he willed me to see his age, allowing a road map of lines to spring out on his face.

"Why, Boobie. Are you trying to scare me?"

"Yes, I am. There's evil out there and you're too

damn cocky for your own good," he declared with a stubborn tilt of his chin. "You keep your rear end planted until I come back."

He headed into the kitchen, and returned a few moments later.

"Here. Hide this on you," he instructed, slapping a Ziploc baggie in my hand.

"What is it?" I asked, holding it up to the light.

"Voodoo powder to keep you safe."

The bag's contents were a reddish-orange color and as fine as grains of sand.

"Your voodoo powder looks like cayenne pepper." I chuckled.

"Listen here, li'l girl. The way you're dressed, you better hope it's voodoo powder. Any man puts his hands in the wrong place, you be sure and use that stuff."

"Thanks, Boobie." I gave him a peck on the cheek and headed out the door. It was almost five o'clock.

"You're late," Tolliver snapped as I walked into Fish and Wildlife's office. "I don't like to be kept waiting."

I figured as much. That's exactly why I did it.

Santou stood in a corner, his mood black enough to fill a Louisiana swamp, while Hickok sat behind a desk dotted with surgical tape, an Ace bandage, and a plastic spoon. Nearby lay a small transmitter out of which two thin wires sprouted. One had a miniature microphone attached to its end. My guess was the other line worked as an antenna.

"Galinov thinks I'm out buying groceries for tonight's dinner. That doesn't leave us much time," Tolliver chided. "Let's get down to work. Take off your pants."

"Excuse me?" I responded sharply. Who did this guy think he was? The Hugh Hefner of the FBI?

Tolliver emitted a bark of a laugh. "How else do you suppose we're going to wire you up?"

Santou pushed away from the wall with the fixed resolve of a bullet. "Okay, that's enough. Porter might feel more comfortable with some privacy and only one of us helping her."

Hickok planted his hands on the desk and stood up. "I agree with the coonass. Bronx don't need three of us here playing peek-a-boo just to tape a coupla damn wires on her."

Tolliver's eyes darted from Santou's face to my own, with the cunning of a weasel. "Well, well. Could it be that love springs eternal?" He slapped the transmitter into Santou's palm with the rap of a chastising ruler. "Hickok and I'll go out for a few minutes and get some coffee. Don't take too long; there's no time in the schedule for a quickie."

"Have you always been such an ass? Or is it your special FBI training?" I sweetly inquired as he and Hickok walked past.

"Just put the damn thing on!" He slammed the door behind them.

"Nice work, chère. I do believe you've made an enemy for life," Santou grinned and shook his head in amusement. "He had no idea what he was getting into when he took you on. Here, let's get started."

Santou's fingers smoothly unbuttoned my pants and released the zipper. He pulled the trousers down my hips, and they slid to the floor. That was all it took for my cheeks to begin to burn, inflamed by both desire and embarrassment. Santou's complexion equally deepened, followed by the quickening of his breath. I didn't hesitate, but stepped out of the trousers as if I were shedding a second skin. What had begun as an unpleasant task was turning into a surprisingly arousing session.

I stood before Santou, dressed only in a revealing sweater and a tiny pair of black bikini panties. We wordlessly looked at each other and his fingers reached out, gently cupping my rear end. Then he firmly pulled me toward him with one delicious, swift motion. But rather than making love, what followed was a much more subtle seduction.

Jake slid to his knees, his hair teasingly brushing my stomach, to place the transmitter against my calf. He snuggly covered it with the Ace bandage and used three strips of surgical tape to hold it in place. Then he sensuously snaked the two slender wires up my leg and under my panties, his fingers igniting brush fires wherever they touched my flesh.

"Lift your sweater," he instructed, his voice as rough as if he'd just chain-smoked two packs of Camels.

I exposed my bare stomach.

"Higher."

I raised the garment until nothing was hidden from his sight, only to gasp as Santou's lips brazenly kissed my breasts. Then he taped the wires against my flesh.

Finally, he broke the handle off the plastic spoon and placed the oval mouth over the microphone, taping that to my body as well.

"What's the spoon for?" I asked, trying to sound cool, calm, and collected as my pulse beat to a primal drum.

"It's so your sweater won't scratch against the mike and create any static."

I'd just begun to catch my breath when Santou's hand slid back inside my panties. His fingers lightly played with the wires as my heart thrummed in time with my pulse.

"I'm just checking to make sure there's enough slack for normal body movement." But his fingers did much more than that as his mouth brushed against my ear, heightening the sensation.

"Be careful tonight, chère. We've got a lot of lost time to make up." Then his lips pressed steadily against mine, claiming me as his own. "You'd better get dressed now. They could be back any minute."

I quickly lowered my sweater and pulled on my pants, flustered at the thought. Shortly afterward, Tolliver and Hickok entered the room.

"I trust she's wired up properly and there won't be any problems," Tolliver said with a suspicious glance.

"Let's test the equipment and find out," Santou proposed.

Tolliver produced a cassette recorder as I stepped into the hall and shut the door. Before I'd finished counting aloud to ten, Jake stuck his head outside.

"Okay. You can come back in."

I entered to find Tolliver already beginning his transformation back into Billy Paw.

"Here's the way it's gonna play out. I'll do my usual role. Meanwhile, you get Galinov to discuss everything that we talked about."

"What if something goes wrong?" I couldn't help but ask.

"Don't worry. Me and Santou'll be in a car down the road listening to your every word," Hickok promised. "Tell you what. Why don't we come up with a phrase you can use just in case things get hinky? How about, 'It's Mardi Gras time'?"

That made as much sense as anything else.

"Your job is on the line, Porter. So don't fuck up," Tolliver added, taking his leave.

Santou went with him, agreeing to hook up with Charlie later on.

Hickok waited until they'd walked out the door. "Screw that mother. Let's kick the tires and light the fire under old Sergei's ass. Get everything you can on his caviar ring while you're at it."

My skin tingled again, but now it was from anticipation of what might happen tonight.

Twenty-four

I scampered up Galinov's front steps at nine, my heart pounding like a Dixieland band out of control. Pressing the buzzer, I expected Billy Paw to appear and flash me a secret sign, as strains of "Love Me Tender" rang out to embrace the night.

But it was Sergei himself who answered the door, this time adorned in a royal-blue jumpsuit. Not only did its plunging neckline outdo my own, but Sergei even had decent cleavage! A wide belt valiantly cinched in his waist, looking as though it might pop open at any second.

Sergei's eyes devoured my own "come hither" attire. "Priscilla! You look good enough to eat!"

The next moment I was buried in rhinestones, synthetic fabric, and way too much flesh.

Oh my God! He'll feel the microphone on my stomach!

But my fears were allayed as I realized the mike was pressing against his heavily studded belt. A bullet couldn't have pierced the damn thing.

"Come! I have a surprise waiting inside."

I followed Sergei's bell bottoms, which hypnotically swished back and forth, each leg weighed down with sequins. Though I anxiously glanced around, Tolliver was nowhere in sight. Great. Wouldn't you know *this* was the night he'd decide to keep a low profile?

Sergei stopped at the Jungle Room and spread his arms wide in delight. "Is this not a setting fit for Elvis and his Priscilla?"

Talk about your mood lighting! Dozens of candles lit the space, each sculpted into a bust of Elvis. Their flames swayed to a silent Presley tune, casting shadows in every direction. Silhouettes of the King even danced on the green shag-carpeted ceiling.

Sergei led me into the room. "And look what the King has prepared for his Queen!"

A cut-glass bowl sat on the coffee table, its contents a shimmering heap of caviar. Next to it were oysters on the half shell, along with an icy bottle of Russian vodka. Galinov sank into the faux fur couch and pulled me down beside him.

Bending forward with a grunt, he spooned some caviar onto an oyster and held the concoction to my mouth. "How does it feel to eat the most expensive delicacy in the world?"

I swallowed, trying not to gag on the stuff. "Pure heaven."

"It is black magic on the tongue." Galinov agreed, shoveling some beluga into his own gullet. "I tell you for sure. I make more money in this business than anyone else."

I reached for the vodka and poured us both a glass. "That calls for a toast. Here's to the most brilliant businessman in Memphis."

Sergei downed his drink in one gulp, and I poured him another shot.

"I am more than just Memphis," Galinov bragged. "I am my own multinational corporation. The world is my oyster."

We clinked glasses. "Then here's to the King of the Caviar Trade." My guess was Sergei had been hitting the sauce long before I'd arrived.

He drained his glass once more. "I really am the best, aren't I? In many ways!" He leaned toward me, only to abruptly jump up.

"Dammit!"

Sergei's hand dove into his pocket, pulled out a set of keys, and threw them on the coffee table.

"There, that's more comfortable. Now, where did we leave off?"

Galinov's mouth attached itself to mine with all the finesse of a satellite making a crash landing. When he planted his hand on my breast, I instinctively jerked away.

Sergei's face instantly darkened. "What's wrong?"

"I think a mouse just ran by my feet," I hastily improvised.

Galinov looked dubious. "You're afraid of mice?"

"I know it sounds silly coming from a wildlife agent, but I can't stand the things. Maybe you should call Billy Paw and have him take a look around."

"Billy Paw isn't here. I gave him the night off so we wouldn't have any interruptions."

Damn the man! I knew it! Deep down, I'd suspected Tolliver thought of me as merely an expendable chess piece.

"This is a night for romance and I don't want you to feel inhibited," Sergei said huskily, and plied me with another oyster.

Oy vey.

"Then I should tell you that I'm probably a bit different from other women that you've known."

Galinov's eyes narrowed under their heavy lids. "In what way? Do you have something under your clothes that other women don't?"

Wrong thing to say! I didn't need him to start an exploratory journey.

I forced a flirtatious giggle. "No, I just like a little foreplay."

"Me, too," Sergei eagerly agreed with a lunge.

I raised my hands to fend him off. "I mean it excites me to know what a powerful man you are. I find it very arousing when you talk about your business."

Sergei's mouth slid into a roguish grin and his hand intimately rubbed my leg. "My perfect Priscilla! I'll tell you a little secret. That excites me, too. What should we discuss to heighten our pleasure?"

"Why don't you tell me about the Velvet Kitty?" I purred. "It seems like a very sexy place."

Sergei's lips began to explore my neck. "What do you want to know?"

"You must have, what? Twenty, maybe twenty-five girls working for you? That's a lot of women to pay. Is the club lucrative?"

Sergei broke into a hearty laugh. "The Velvet Kitty is a treasure chest! But then, I have a good deal. My girls are all from Russia and the Ukraine. They work for room and board, plus a little spending money. But they're happy, and it's far better than they could do back home."

"Still, I'm surprised they don't demand large salaries. Or worse yet, go to another club. Surely the girls do more than just lap dancing?"

I felt Sergei hesitate and immediately ran my fingers seductively down his chest.

"Personally, I think they *should* be happy working for you," I cooed.

Sergei relaxed, and his lips continued to glide along my throat. "Of course they do more than lap dance. It's all part of their job."

"But if you don't pay them much, why do they stay?" I persisted, my hand teasingly rubbing his thigh.

Galinov stared at me a moment, as if making up his mind. "Okay. I tell you the truth. These girls, they think they're coming over to be models, or big-time actresses. It's crazy, but they are from the countryside. Once they get here, they learn to deal with the situation. Besides, I tell them this is the way American girls break into show business. Since my partners in Russia front their travel expenses, I hold on to each girl's passport until we've been reimbursed."

I knew Galinov was lying about the details. He also seemed to sense I doubted him.

"Do you have a problem with that?" His voice held a menacing tone.

"Not at all. In fact, I just had a thought. If so many women are anxious to leave Russia, why not supply other clubs with their services?"

"You mean, sell these girls to them?" he asked carefully.

"I'm sure they can work out an agreeable arrangement with their new bosses," I responded, hoping to erase his doubts.

Sergei looked at me in amazement. "Now I know we truly are soul mates! I am already doing just that."

"That's incredible!" I marveled. "Tell me, how many women have you brought over so far?"

"Many!" Galinov boasted.

"*How* many?" I pursued, shivering under his touch.

Sergei took it as a sign of passion. "Well over a thousand women."

I was heating up, all right. Only it was due to the transmitter taped to my leg. Something had to be wrong; the damn thing was burning my skin. "Do you keep a list of the clubs that bought them?"

Galinov instantly froze. "Why do you ask?"

"So you can follow up and see if they want more women," I replied with a smile.

Sergei pulled me onto his lap and held me tightly in his arms. "Yes, I keep a list. But you are like a child who wants to know too much. You must learn to be patient. What I will tell you is that I plan to open an even bigger, better club in Mississippi with many more girls. Who knows? Maybe you can run it. We'll see how well you please me tonight."

I suddenly felt no different from Tatyana and the others, as Galinov's fingers began to slide down toward my breasts. The FBI could go to hell; Mata Hari was about to retire. My hand edged toward the heavy glass bowl with one thought in mind: I'd knock Galinov out, grab his keys, and quickly search his files. Sergei was saved from one hell of a nasty hangover by the piercing ring of his phone.

I remained pinned on his lap like a ventriloquist's dummy as he picked up the receiver. Galinov listened closely before uttering an abrupt response and pressing the hold button.

"I'm sorry, Priscilla, but this is an important overseas call which I must take upstairs. It should only last a half hour at most. So eat some caviar and enjoy yourself. I'll be back soon." Sergei kissed my hand. "Promise not to go anywhere?"

I batted my lashes as I imagined Priscilla might do. "I promise," I vowed, and meant it. There was no way I was about to leave with the golden opportunity I was being handed.

Sergei lumbered out of the room. My ears listened to his footsteps as they climbed the stairs. Then I glanced at my watch and noted the time. If Tolliver had wanted to rein me in, he should have found a way to remain on the job tonight. I planned to resume my own work.

The filing cabinets in Galinov's basement lured me like tantalizing sirens, seductively whispering they contained everything I wanted to know.

My fingers wrapped themselves tightly around Galinov's keys and I dashed to the cellar door, where I fumbled with the lock.

Come on! Let me find the right key! I prayed.

Somebody up there must have been listening. The door swung open; the light flicked on at my touch.

The stairs hummed beneath my feet, and my breath raced to keep pace with my heart. Four plastic buckets filled with roe sat cooling in an ice chest at the bottom of the steps. The eggs probably needed to reach a certain temperature before being frozen.

I headed straight to the filing cabinets, not wasting a moment. My hope was that they'd provide all the documentation I'd need to end Sergei's career forever.

I tugged at the top drawer to no avail. Galinov wisely kept his valuables under lock and key. I checked my watch. No need to rush. I guided key after key into the lock without any luck, until I thought I'd explode.

Get hold of yourself! Think of something soothing, like listening to the ocean, my inner voice helpfully suggested.

Yeah, right. I'd have rather had a stick of dynamite to play with. My eyes nervously glanced at my watch. Barely five minutes had passed. I tried the next few keys. Bingo!

I quickly rifled through the files, finding folders for airlines, cruise ships, and restaurants. Well, whadda ya know? Each was aware they'd been buying counterfeit caviar from Galinov. In exchange, they received a discount. Meanwhile, these chi-chi places unloaded the stuff as authentic beluga to their customers.

Another file listed Galinov's network of fishermen, noting their daily delivery of roe, and how many tons of paddlefish eggs were regularly sent out of the country. But it was the sight of a ledger that set my nerves thrumming. I opened it and scanned its contents.

Inside were copies of reports that Sergei had sent to

his Russian partners. They detailed the amount of roe processed per month, along with what had been sold. One look quickly revealed the figures didn't match up with what was in Galinov's other folders. That's when I knew I had Sergei by his sequins, spangles, and rhinestones.

Galinov's books were cooked. He was selling a hefty chunk of caviar and paddlefish here in the States, while reporting a far lower amount to his Russian comrades back home. Should his partners learn of this, Sergei's days would be numbered. He'd have no choice but to reveal the identity of his associates when confronted with this information.

I ripped the sheets out of the ledger and added them to the thin pile of papers on the floor. Then I checked my watch again to discover hardly any time had passed at all.

I moved to the second cabinet, exuberant at what I'd found. More locked files meant even more confidential information. I wasn't about to turn that down. I unlatched a drawer and quickly plunged my fingers in, only to have my flesh turn icy cold. It was as if I'd discovered a cache of ghostly spirits. Piled inside were hundreds of passports, each representing a life stolen for profit. The drawer was literally filled with them. I picked up a few and swiftly scanned their contents.

They held the smiling faces of women unaware of the nightmare realm they were about to enter. I imagined they now viewed the world through eyes that were empty, their mouths tightly grim, no longer wearing makeup to highlight their beauty, but to hide the bruises marring their skin.

Zap!

An electric jolt shot through my flesh. It was the transmitter! I lifted my pant leg and began to reposition the Ace bandage, when my eyes fell upon the papers I'd collected. Quickly removing the bandage, I held the transmitter in place and molded the thin stack of papers to my leg. Then I tightly rewrapped the elastic. Having finished, I stood up, only to again come face-to-face with those hundreds of passports. I had no choice but to leave them buried where they were for now.

I hastily moved on to the last drawer. When I jerked it open, my eyes fell upon a folder labeled *Livestock Sales*. I removed it and the taste of bile rose in my throat. In my hands was a list of every woman that Sergei and his partners had brought over and sold. *Livestock*. That said it all. The advertising slogan, "You've come a long way baby" could only have been written by a man. The majority of women in this world still had miles left to go.

I slipped the papers inside the back of my pants and pulled my sweater down low. Then I peered one last time at my watch. My stomach instantly hit the floor. It was exactly the same as when I'd looked before. No wonder thirty minutes had gone by so slowly—my watch had stopped. I had to leave *now*.

As if on cue, the door above creaked open, setting off a string of fireworks in my nerves. Sergei's foot hit the top step like a thunderous drumroll. Another clap

of thunder followed as Galinov came down the stairs.
The sequins on his pants cast a lethal array of shim-
mering light and shadows as foreboding as demonic
Tinker Bells.

I quickly scooted over to his collection of radio
equipment, knowing there was little time to lose.
Though I tried to appear utterly absorbed, I must not
have presented the picture of pristine innocence. Galinov stopped and stared as if measuring me for one of
his freezers.

"What are you doing down here?" his voice boomed.

"Don't be angry, Sergei. I became bored with waiting, and remembered you had all this interesting
equipment."

But Sergei wasn't appeased. "Give me the keys!"
he demanded.

I handed them over, turning into the little girl who
knew she deserved a scolding. "I'm sorry, I didn't
mean to do anything wrong. You will forgive me,
won't you?"

I did my best to melt Big Daddy by blinking back a
few tears. It wasn't that I was one hell of an actress;
I'd just learned to channel my fear.

"That's enough," Galinov gruffly relented. "But
don't do anything like that again."

I hung my head in shame, only to have Sergei lift
my chin and give me a kiss.

"Since you're so interested, I'll show you my
equipment."

Scratch the surface and Sergei was just like every
other man. Boys and their toys.

"I have an old radio that was owned by Elvis," he

bragged. "And of course, you know what *this* is." His hand came to rest on a police scanner. "I always like to hear what the boobs in blue are up to."

His finger flicked on the power switch, and it went in search of frequencies.

"Hey, Ralph. I'm heading over to Krispy Kreme," drawled a voice as Southern as fried chicken. "Want me to bring you anything?"

"How 'bout some glazed hot ones?" came the response.

"Will do. Over and out."

"I wish *I* could pay the cops off with donuts," Sergei jested. "Let's see what else we pick up."

The caviar and oysters churned uneasily in my stomach. "I've got a better idea. Why don't we go upstairs and get cozy again?" I'd found what I'd come for. Now I just wanted to get out of here.

"I first want to know what's happening tonight."

I was liking this less and less.

"Then I'll just use the bathroom." I didn't tell Sergei that I meant the one in my loft in Memphis.

"Go ahead," Sergei responded absently, having reverted to the techno-nerd from hell.

I was heading for the stairs when Tolliver's voice blared over the scanner. "Yeah. She's in Galinov's place right now. I thought she'd fucked up a minute ago, but things seem to be okay."

That damn idiot! He had to know better than to broadcast a sting operation in progress!

Unless Tolliver *wasn't* stupid, but looking to tack the murder of a federal agent onto Galinov's growing list of charges.

My feet moved fast, but not fast enough. Galinov grabbed my arm and spun me around to face him. The violence I'd sensed simmering beneath the surface now erupted in a raging inferno. His fingers plunged beneath my sweater and ripped the microphone off my skin, just as I yelled out, *"It's Mardi Gras time!"*

Twenty-five

"**H**ow *dare* you!" Galinov snarled. "Do you have any idea who you're dealing with? I'm not some local hick like those clowns Woody and Virgil. I'm part of a global operation that disposes of people like you as easily as swatting a fly. Whatever little game you and your wildlife friends are playing is over!"

"You don't want to hurt me, Sergei! Federal agents know I'm here and are already on their way."

Galinov regarded me with disdain. "How can you be so naïve? Do you really believe I don't have everything under control?"

The floor began to sway. Was Galinov saying *Tolliver* was in his pocket? I lowered my head and took a deep breath, listening for the front door to burst open. But all I heard was the pounding of my heart.

Sergei's playing with your mind. Santou and Hickok would never leave you hanging!

"I own you now, the same as all my other whores, and I will not be betrayed!"

I own you!

My wooziness grew worse—those were the exact words he'd used with Tatyana. Sergei must have believed I was about to faint, for his iron grip loosened. If

I ever hoped to escape, this was the moment. I lowered my head further, pretending I was about to throw up, and rammed it with all my might into Galinov's stomach. Sergei grunted and stumbled backward, caught off-guard. I immediately took off upstairs.

I'd only made it through the kitchen when Galinov began to close in; there was no way I could reach the front door. I veered into the Jungle Room and grabbed the caviar as Sergei's hands clasped my throat. Flinging the bowl backward, I nicked Sergei's head and he released me as a shower of roe flew through the air.

"You bitch! This carpet was made to match the one at Graceland! Now look what you've done!"

A sea of gray eggs lay buried in the carpet's pile, both overhead and underfoot. Galinov's hand flew to his bruised forehead as his other arm wrapped itself tightly around my chest, holding me in place.

Sliding my hip, I placed my leg behind Galinov's and broke his stance. Then I wrapped my hands under his knee and jerked his foot off the floor. Sergei went down like a toppled building. I turned to flee, only to have my own legs pulled out from under me. The next thing I knew, Sergei was back on his feet and dragging me out of the room.

Where the hell was my backup? Hadn't they heard my signal? Or worse, Tolliver might think his equipment was on the fritz, and refuse to blow the operation!

I tried grabbing hold of whatever I could, hoping to put the brakes on Galinov, but everything was jerked from my grip.

"I'm not going to kill you here and pay a fortune to

have the furnishings cleaned!" Sergei fumed. "Besides, I won't taint Elvis's memory with a murder."

Wasn't *that* a relief.

"We're going back to the basement, where Billy Paw can mop your blood off the floor."

We approached the stairs, and I had the sinking feeling Sergei planned to throw me down them. Instead, he pulled me to my feet.

"It's too difficult getting hair and clothing fibers off the steps," he grumbled.

"Cleaning up can be *such* a nuisance," I gasped.

"And this is going to cost me a fortune, just to shut everyone up," he complained.

"What do you care? You have plenty of money coming in from all the caviar in your freezers. It's just too bad you'll never get to enjoy it," I tormented him, laying the bait.

Galinov angrily pushed me forward. "Stop stalling!"

"Your friends aren't going to be happy when they learn you've been selling caviar without their knowledge, and keeping all the profits," I continued, giving the hook a strong jerk.

Galinov shoved me down the first step. "Not only are you stupid, you're also crazy. You don't know what the hell you're talking about."

"Then I guess there's no problem that the papers detailing your true business dealings are already winging their way to your associates in the motherland," I bluffed. "I'm sure they'll find it interesting reading, compared to the doctored reports they've been receiving."

I glanced back to see that Galinov's complexion was as gray as his freezers.

"What you're saying is not possible!"

"Why don't you check the files for yourself?" I retorted brazenly.

Galinov pulled me toward the cabinets, only to discover he needed both hands to open the drawer.

"Don't try anything funny," he warned. "Or I will make things even more unpleasant."

Like there was something worse than being offed?

"Where would I go that you couldn't catch me?" I docilely responded.

Galinov swiftly unlocked the file and began to thumb through the folders, his face growing more concerned with each passing moment. I inched my way closer to the freezers, stopping near the ice chest on the floor. I glanced around, but no weapons were in sight. Where was my knight in shining armor, damn him?

Galinov slammed the drawer and turned toward me with a cold expression.

"You're bullshitting me, Agent Porter. I don't appreciate that."

For once, I actually wished he'd called me Priscilla.

"Tonight was the only time you were down here alone, so the papers must still be somewhere on you. It seems we get to play our little seduction game after all." Galinov leered menacingly. "Since power is what turns you on, I'm sure you'll enjoy our interlude. I'm feeling particularly invincible."

Had I been James Bond, I'd have pulled out some super-cool, state-of-the-art weapon. Instead, I was an underfunded, overworked, not-so-well-equipped U.S. Fish and Wildlife agent.

I waited until Sergei was nearly upon me and then flung open a freezer door, slamming him soundly in the head. It not only put a temporary stop to his progress, but gave me enough time to overturn the ice chest and its valuable contents. A pile of caviar oozed across the floor, creating a slick and slippery puddle.

"What the hell are you doing?" Sergei angrily demanded and took a step.

Oh, oh, big mistake. He instantly lost his balance. I was feeling pretty smug until he reached up and pulled me down with him.

Though Sergei was bigger and stronger, he didn't have my wrestling moves. He crash-landed facedown in the roe, allowing me to scramble on top of him.

I quickly locked my right leg under his left, slipping my hands under his armpits and clasping them behind his neck. Damn! There was something I was forgetting! Sergei squirmed, which jogged my memory. I dug one knee into his back and rammed my chin between his shoulder blades to complete a full nelson.

"You really should have studied martial arts the way Elvis did," I chided as Galinov wriggled beneath me. "I also enjoy being in control, which is why I'm on top of things. But don't feel badly—you can always drown your sorrows in caviar."

I pressed hard, burying his face deep into the eggs, knowing I could end this situation here and now. There'd be no lawyers to contend with, no trial, no plea bargain, and no chance for injustice.

The faces of the women whose lives Galinov had destroyed flashed before me. I continued to bear down, only faintly aware of voices as two sets of arms worked hard to pry me off. I fought to stay on, but was pulled to my feet. My backup had finally arrived.

The blood pounded in my ears as I watched them roll Galinov over and establish that he was still alive. Only then did Hickok look at me, his face splitting into a grin.

"I think you just found yourself a new career, Bronx. If Fish and Wildlife gives you the boot, you can always open your own mud wrestling club. I never realized how much hellcat there is in you."

Neither had I. Now that I did, I was frightened. I jumped as Santou approached from behind, and whirled to face him. He tenderly wiped the roe off my face.

"Just my luck—you're probably spoiled for life. What can I offer a woman who bathes in caviar?"

Then he noticed the look in my eyes.

"Don't worry, chère. It happens to us all at some point. There's always the danger of snapping and losing control. The important thing is to stare the bastard down and don't let it get the better of you. Besides, if it's wrestling you want, I can help you channel that in a way we'll both enjoy."

Santou's roguish grin banished the fear, releasing my tension.

"The FBI will take charge of Galinov, but I'll break away as soon as I can. We're gonna spend some mighty fine quality time together."

It was no longer the transmitter that sent sparks

flying through my body, but Santou's suggestive touch.

Damn! I suddenly remembered the papers and pulled them from the back of my pants. "Here's a list of women that Sergei and his cronies smuggled in, along with the addresses of brothels which bought them. You'll find their passports in the top drawer of that cabinet."

Santou took the papers from my hand. "Maybe you should consider jumping ship and coming over to the FBI."

"Like hell she will!" Hickok roared. "I taught her everything she knows. This gal is mine!"

I knew that was Charlie's way of saying I'd done a good job.

Then I realized who was missing from the scene. "Where's Tolliver?"

"You mean Captain Queeg? We ended up pulling a mutiny." Hickok sniggered.

"I'll fill you in later," was all Jake would say. Then he handcuffed Galinov and led him up the stairs.

After they were gone Charlie opened each freezer and stared at their contents in disgust. "Well, I'm glad you helped solve the FBI's case. If you're lucky, maybe they'll give you a Twinkie. Meanwhile, we're left with nothing but this." He motioned to the gobs of trampled roe on the floor.

I began to lift my pant leg.

"Forget it, Bronx. A strip show ain't gonna make me feel any better."

That was a man for you. I unwrapped the bandage and removed the hidden treasure.

"If you don't want these, I'm sure someone else will."

Hickok snatched the papers from my hand and gave them a quick perusal. "Hell! This contains the whole ball of wax! Everything from Galinov's network of fishermen to his fancy-pants clientele."

Then he arrived at the sheets I'd ripped from Galinov's ledger.

"Holy crap—ol' Sergei just handed us his balls on a silver platter. By the time I'm through squeezing 'em, he'll not only give up the names of his partners, but everyone else involved in their caviar scam."

I chose not to burst Hickok's bubble by remarking that the FBI probably wouldn't share access to Galinov.

"Okay, Bronx. You can take the rest of the night off. But don't let this go to your head: I expect you in first thing tomorrow to start writing up your report. Then you can get back out in the field and check hunters' licenses."

Fat chance—there were still the murders of Mavis and Woody to unravel.

Charlie stayed to explore Sergei's basement as I dragged myself upstairs, leaving a trail of caviar in my wake.

Twenty-six

My loft had never felt so welcoming as when I arrived home. I emptied the contents of my pockets onto the kitchen counter, where I spied Terri's handwriting on a note.

We're back from our jaunt. Come meet us at the Blue Mojo this evening for a drink.

Love,
Terri & Vincent

They were now an official couple. While a drink at the Blue Mojo was tempting, the only thing I wanted to do was bathe, and then hit the sack.

I took a long, hot shower, then I crawled into bed with a glass of red wine, planning to watch a rerun of *The Sopranos*. The sudden ring of the phone took me by surprise, causing the wine to spill. I picked up the receiver to hear a near-hysterical Tatyana crying on the other end of the line. Her panic seeped under my skin as effectively as the bedsheets had soaked up the wine, her words an unintelligible stream of Russian.

"Tatyana, tell me where you are in English!" I sharply commanded.

"I'm at home! You must come right away!"

That was all the information I needed. I threw on some clothes and stuffed the items I'd tossed on the counter back into my pockets, grabbing my gun as well. Then I raced out.

My Ford tore through the night like a knife slashing in fright, not knowing what lay before or behind it. I flew down Highway 51 so fast that I must have left scorched rubber behind me. The nearby Mississippi's current easily kept pace, its sound a steady roar. Only when I arrived at Tatyana's house did I realize the bellowing river was the rush of my own blood.

I didn't knock. There was no reason to: the front door had been torn off its hinges. Inside, the place looked like a hurricane had hit it. But Tatyana seemed more broken than anything else, her face a canvas of inconsolable sorrow.

She wrung her hands as her anguished wails filled the room. A teenage girl stood helplessly by. A wet cloth was wrapped around the back of the girl's head, its white cotton stained with blood.

I stood in front of Tatyana, who didn't respond until I grabbed her shoulders and shook her.

"Tell me what happened!" I demanded in fear.

Tatyana's reddened gaze fixed on me as though she were a shipwrecked survivor and I, her only lifeboat.

"I called home from the club, as I always do, to check in with the baby-sitter and say good night to Galya. Only this time, there is no answer. I call again in five minutes. It keeps ringing and ringing. That's how I know something is wrong. My little girl, she always runs to pick up the phone and send me kisses. I immediately rushed home to find Irina unconscious on the floor. And my daughter?" Tatyana's lips quivered, barely able to form the words. "My *malenkaya* is gone!"

Her nails raked at her face, scoring red lines in her skin.

"It is my own fault! I should never have told you about Sergei and the *organizatsiya*. He warned me to talk to no one. Now *this* is my punishment. He has kidnapped my Galya!"

"Tatyana, listen! I've been with Sergei all night. He's now in the custody of federal agents. It couldn't have been him."

"Then tell me who took my child? Why have they done this to me?" Her voice cracked, hoarse with grief.

I turned to Irina, who looked away in embarrassment.

"What happened here tonight?"

The teenager wordlessly shuffled her feet.

"Tell me now, or I'll have no choice but to throw you in jail," I threatened.

Irina instantly burst into tears. "I don't know! I heard all the noise and I hid! Then somebody pulled me out from under the bed and there was a terrible pain on the back of my head."

"Was Galya with you?"

Irina nodded, her sobs growing louder.

"Show me where it happened," I insisted.

Tatyana led me down the dingy hall into a tiny

room decorated with posters of Britney Spears and 'N Sync. Bedsheets covered with fluffy lambs lay huddled in a pile on the floor. Getting down on my hands and knees I peered under the bed, where I spied Galya's little dog curled up and shaking with fear. I pushed the sheets away to reach for the pooch, and something fell from within their folds. A black wooden cross lay on the floor like the emblem of some chilling satanic ritual. Oh, dear God. It was Virgil Hardy who had taken the child. The question was why?

I thought back to when he'd trapped me in his shed. He'd made a remark about how I spent too much time with Sergei's hookers. Still, what would prompt him to kidnap Tatyana's little girl?

Oh, come on! Why not ask what made him toss a woman off a bridge, or feed Mavis to his hogs? Virgil Hardy's a certifiable lunatic!

Standing up, I ran out of the room and down the hall. Tatyana raced after me, catching up as I reached the front door.

"Where are you going?" she cried, grabbing my arm.

"To bring Galya back." I refused to consider the possibility that I might not be able to make good on my word.

I threw the Ford into gear and tore out, making tracks for Virgil's place. The only other cars on the road were cruising home from blues clubs, their drivers too mellow to get in my way. Those disappeared as I turned onto a country lane where the cotton fields lay still as graves. The few passing telephone poles were eerie reminders of Virgil's wooden cross, until even those dropped from sight. The gravel ended, turning to dirt beneath my tires, as I began my descent into Chickasaw Bluffs.

The kudzu cast shadows, playing tricks with my mind. The call of a night bird pierced the air. Off to my right lay a deep river ravine. I didn't even want to think of what could lay hidden in there. The bird's cry transformed into a child's laughter, and my stomach seized up in fear. The kudzu crept a little closer and I shut my windows tight, knowing the delta ghosts were out in full force tonight.

I felt sure I would find Virgil at home, but his trailer was dark and his car nowhere in sight. Even the hogs didn't make a sound, as if they were afraid of the night. Gathering every ounce of courage, I grabbed my flashlight and made my way to the shed with nightmare visions dancing in my head.

Though I stood and listened, there wasn't a peep. The structure was quiet as a tomb. The fact that no plank barred its entrance was all that indicated Virgil might be inside. Pulling my gun, I took a deep breath and flung the door open wide. I stared in horror as the cross above Virgil's altar seemingly sprang to life. A pair of ominous black wings raced toward me as if I were its chosen sacrifice. I quickly lifted the flashlight, and aimed my .38 directly into the demon's eyes. It wasn't until the very last second that I pulled back, causing my bullet to pierce the wall rather than shoot the owl that flew overhead in an exit worthy of Dracula.

My heart beat in syncopation with the flapping of its wings as I tried to catch my breath. The bullet's scream echoed loudly throughout Chickasaw Bluffs, blatantly announcing my presence. The hogs added to the ruckus with alarming squeals that could have wakened the dead. However, I was the only little piggy that might be going to market for losing the element of surprise. I waited for Hardy to come swooping out of his hiding place in a firestorm of rage, but all that bore heavy upon me was the silence of the night. Time was ticking by. I had to reach Galya soon if I had any hope of finding her alive.

Though the Sho Nuf Bar was the next logical place to go, gut instinct told they wouldn't be there. I was beginning to think this was a game of hide-and-seek in which Galya was the bait for much larger prey that Virgil was hunting. My paranoia linked arms with my determination to rescue and protect the child. Thoughts of Galya led to ruminations of Mavis, and I time-traveled back to her bedroom with those disturbing broken dolls. Something pricked at my psyche like an irritating splinter, forcing me to dig still deeper.

Closing my eyes, I once again felt Mavis's cushioned window seat creak as I'd realized it was a built-in chest. Inside had sat a blue cardboard box. The recollection stirred up a visual flood of images. I mentally dug through Mavis's collection of photos to uncover what I'd been searching for. The clue had been lurking in my subconscious all along—the black-and-white snapshot of Virgil standing at the fishing cabin that I'd passed just a few days ago. "Home Sweet Home on Black Bayou." I immediately knew that's where I had to go.

As I tore out of Chickasaw Bluffs, I spied something I hadn't noticed before: at the road's peak stood an old gravestone, its surface covered in kudzu's smothering embrace. The full moon hung so low that it came to rest on its top. But what chilled me to the bone was that tonight's crimson moon appeared to have burst, oozing blood throughout the sky. My premonition grew stronger than ever as I pressed down on the accelerator and flew toward my destination.

The bait shops were dark as I passed them. It was as though time itself had stopped, with the moon a beating heart, waiting to see how the night would unfold. I drove to where I'd parked when I'd come in search of Woody, setting his traps. Turning off the engine, I grabbed my flashlight and got out.

I started down the trail, the woods around me a sinister dead zone. Needles of terror pricked at my skin. Moonlight bleached the trees white as cadavers' bones, while dark shadows lurked like ghosts. An ominous stillness stalked through the night, devouring everything in its path with an insatiable appetite.

It felt like forever until the fishing cabin came into view. Virgil's car was parked nearby, and a kerosene light flickered inside the house, throbbing like an angry wound. I turned my flashlight off, and the night instantly drew suffocatingly close. I let my eyes adjust as I began my approach, my form melting into the darkness.

Then I heard a steady sound coming from the direction of the lake. It was the thrust and whoosh of metal rhythmically digging into dirt. My head told me to stay far away, but curiosity moved my feet closer. Virgil was working beneath a tree, silhouetted by a patch of moonlight. Clenched in his hand was a rusty shovel. My heart pounded as Hardy's foot drove the spade deep to scoop out the earth. Virgil was digging a grave.

My body froze; suddenly I could no longer breathe. I had to find Galya and leave.

Bending low, I hurried to the house, praying she hadn't been hurt. I'd kill Virgil if he'd harmed her in any way. I slid the gun into my pants and tiptoed up the wooden steps. Then I quickly slipped inside, afraid the light might escape and tip Virgil off.

Galya sat tied to a chair in the middle of the room, with a gag in her mouth. I placed a finger to my lips while I pulled a knife from my pocket.

"Galya, you remember me, don't you?" I whispered. "I gave you the little dog, Zouzou."

The child nodded, her eyes wide in a face drained of all color—except for a black-and-blue bruise the size of a plum on her temple. Her cheeks were wet with tears. I took a deep breath, careful to keep my emotions in check.

"Good. Then we're going to play a game. I'm going to get you loose, but you must remain quiet and hold my hand tight. Do you think you can do that?"

Galya bravely nodded yes.

I slit the rope that held her captive, along with those around her wrists, and finally removed the gag.

"Remember, not a word," I whispered. "The game is to be quiet as a mouse."

A jagged limb picked that moment to menacingly rake across the window, causing us both to jump. A squeal of terror slipped from Galya's lips and I swiftly covered her mouth.

"It's all right, sweetheart. That was just a branch. See?" The limb continued to scratch at the glass in taunting refrain.

Galya threw her arms around my waist. Her heart beat as fast as a hummingbird's wings. I held the child for a second and smoothed her hair, then broke the embrace.

"Let's get going."

Galya kept tight hold of my hand as we stepped outside, where we were swallowed up by the night—perhaps too well. Galya couldn't see and tripped down the stairs. At the noise, my heart zoomed into orbit, and I held my breath.

The hair rose off my scalp as I heard the sound of Hardy's shovel being thrown to the ground, followed by the clomp of heavy footsteps charging our way.

Quickly picking up the girl, I placed the flashlight and knife in her hands. "Galya, take these and run as fast as you can down the trail! You'll find my truck. Go there and hide!" If worse came to worst, she'd instinctively know what to do with the knife.

"But I'm afraid! Come with me, please!" Galya pleaded and started to cry.

"I'll meet you there soon, I promise! But I have to stop this bad man first. Now hurry, and go!" I ordered, pushing her in the vehicle's direction.

Galya's eyes brimmed with tears as she squeezed my hand and then ran without looking back.

I took off in the opposite direction, toward where I'd found Woody. I made sure Virgil followed by picking up a stone and throwing it at him.

"Get the hell away from us, you freak!" I yelled for

good measure. However, there was little question in my mind as to who he was after.

The trees closed in around me like a pack of hungry wolves, turning the woods into a childhood nightmare. Every twig crunched beneath my feet in a game of tattletale, as branches grabbed at my flesh. I knew the area was replete with cottonmouth snakes, and there was a real chance one of us would get bitten. All I wanted to do was draw Virgil far enough away from Galya before I took any action.

Then I stumbled over a gnarled root and twisted my ankle. Pain shot up my leg in an angry flame. My foot refused to take my full weight, letting me know the race was over. I had to come up with a plan, and quick. On the other hand, I could just shoot the bastard. That sounded like the best idea yet.

Maybe it was finding all those passports buried inside a drawer, and knowing that women's lives were considered nothing more than temporary sport, that fueled my rage. But I was damned if I'd ever become any man's victim. I pulled the gun from my pants and waited for Virgil to catch up. It didn't take long for Big Boy to come speeding around the curve.

"Hold it right there, Hardy!" I warned, my gun raised and ready. "Or I'll shoot your fucking brains out."

Hardy stopped dead in his tracks, the quills on his head vibrating in the ghostly moonlight, as if each hair had magically sprung to life.

"You've said that before. Whatcha gonna do, Porter? Kill me?" His voice was as smooth as a rattler sizing up its quarry.

"I just may, Virgil. It all depends on how you behave. Let's start with you telling me a few things first."

Hardy's lips twitched in macabre amusement. "Sure,
Porter. Whatcha wanna know?"

"Was it you who killed Woody?" The words stung
in my throat.

Hardy's pale eyes held my own, never blinking, until I nearly felt hypnotized. "I had to. You turned my
brother against me. We were blood. He should have
done what I told him."

"Which was?"

"To take you out on the water and kill you."

If Virgil could murder his own brother, there was
nothing he wasn't capable of doing.

"And Mavis?"

Laughter rose from the hellhole of his soul and
poured out of his mouth, polluting the air around me.

"Oh, come on, Porter. You already know what happened to her."

I could have sworn I heard the grunt of hogs fill the
air, followed by the crunch of bones.

"What about Tatyana's child? Why did you kidnap
her?" My finger itched to pull the trigger and be done
with it.

Hardy inexplicably appeared to grow larger, as if
Satan himself had slipped inside the man. I knew I
was staring straight into the face of evil.

"That was my way of inviting you to come out here
and join me."

His words slunk toward me like a beast crawling on
its belly, stealthily determining how to nab its prey.

"But how could you have been so sure I'd discover

you'd taken Galya, let alone know where to find you?"
I asked, beginning to feel confused.

Virgil smiled evilly, as if enjoying the game. " 'Cause
I know everything you do. I've been watching you."

A shiver tore through me. I'd sensed myself being
observed by a pair of unseen eyes all along.

"You see, Porter, I know you better than you know
yourself. Can't you feel it? I'm inside you already."

His words were like a worm eating away at my
brain, cunningly setting my nerves on edge. Hardy's
eyes then flickered to the ground, his pupils narrowing
as they followed something drawing near my feet.
Chills shot up my spine—it had to be a snake.

I quickly glanced down, when I heard the sound of
a child crying. The sob ripped at my heart and I had to
hold myself back from calling out Galya's name. Oh
dear God! Had she come back? And if so, where was
she hiding?

I frantically scanned the trees around Virgil, desperately hoping she wasn't within his reach, only to I realize the sound was coming from behind. I automatically
turned my head, needing to reassure myself the girl was
safe. That was all the time it took for Virgil to reach my
side. A searing pain tore through my wrist as the gun
was wrenched from my grip, then his hands were
around my throat.

"Like I told you before, Porter. You got some wantonness in you that needs to be ripped out, just the
same as that child and her whore of a mother. Admit
your sins and make your peace with God, girl, 'cause
you're about to die!"

I gasped for breath, but Hardy's hands were steadily

crushing my windpipe. My head pounded as if it were being whacked with a mallet. Even my eyeballs ached.

"Stop fighting, Porter, and release your soul!"

There was no way I was about to go down without one last fight. I leaned against a tree, which nipped at my back, and rammed a knee into Hardy's groin, but the giant didn't budge. Only someone like Vincent could take this guy on—or one of his wrestling techniques! I made a last-ditch try.

Quickly bringing my arms up between Hardy's, I clasped his left elbow in my hand and slammed my right forearm against his joint with all my might. His grip loosened enough to allow me to lurch away. But a moment later Virgil was back on the prowl, his breathing heavy with excitement.

"This is fun, Porter! I like a woman who puts up a good fight!"

Fury kept me moving, determined to find an escape though I knew I was trapped. My ankle throbbed as if jaws of steel bit into the bone; my throat was raw and chafed, with each gulp of air burning. I blindly forged ahead in the dark until my leg smacked something sharp and I tumbled to the ground. I cried out as my cheek scraped a metal object: Woody's Conibear trap.

It was then I remembered the one weapon I had left. I yanked Boobie's bag of voodoo powder from my pocket, knowing what had to be done.

Raising myself onto my knees, I waited for Hardy to approach, every muscle quivering in anticipation. A smile licked at Virgil's face as he saw where I knelt, and I knew he wanted me to beg for my life. I waited until I could feel the heat of his breath on my face and then threw the cayenne pepper into his eyes. Virgil roared in anger as he tried to wipe the powder away.

"Porter, your soul is going to hell when you die!"

Hardy reached down to make good on his word and I swiftly heaved the Conibear trap up, thrusting it forward so that his arms slipped inside. The steel tongs snapped closed, breaking Hardy's bones. Virgil's screams ruptured the night, laying to rest my delta ghosts.

Epilogue

A blistering guitar lick cleaved the air, igniting the audience as Gena glided on stage. She'd practiced her entrance well. Every move elicited a moan from the men, while her defiant look conjured women's approving roars. Her cornrows swayed to the rich gumbo of blues, each roll of her hips punctuated by a sultry chord. Caressing the microphone, she closed her eyes and sang about how a good man can't always make you happy, but a bad man keeps you awake the whole night long.

"Now *that's* blues at its best!" Boobie boasted, setting us up with another round.

I took a sip of my mojo special and succumbed to its magic. Terri sat next to me, dressed to the teeth. He was looking better than ever in his updated Sharon Stone do; his fashionable cream shirt and gray linen slacks ably displayed his newly toned physique.

"I'm telling you, this music has inspired me to create a whole new line in doggy yarmulkes. Not only that, but Sophie and Lucinda are ecstatic about designing apparel for wrestlers."

"Terri's taking me to Miami to meet them next week," Vincent added, with an uncharacteristic touch of shyness.

"Don't worry. You'll be a big hit," Terri assured him, then turned to me. "Speaking of hits, your cheek is looking less like puff pastry these days."

The sharp edge of Woody's trap had bruised my skin when I fell over it while trying to flee Virgil. A swollen cheek seemed a small price to pay, considering the contraption had saved my life.

"That's due to the good care you've given me." I planted a kiss on his cheek. It was true. He'd made herbal packs for my face, and insisted I place no weight on my foot for over a week. He and Vincent had pampered me every day, plying my ankle with cold soaks.

"Which reminds me. I think you should rearrange your work schedule with Fish and Wildlife," Terri added mysteriously.

"How so?"

"See if you can sell them on letting you spend six months in Memphis, and the rest of the year in Miami."

"And why would I want to do that?" I laughed, knowing this must be Terri's way of breaking good news.

"Because that's exactly what we're planning to do," Vincent revealed, placing his hand on Terri's. "Sophie and Lucinda think South Beach is the perfect place for a wrestling club."

"Did I hear somebody say wrestling? I believe you've got the female champ sitting right here."

Familiar arms wrapped themselves around me as Santou's lips brushed my ear. He'd taken care of me every night.

"What say we try out that ankle of yours and do a little slow dancing?"

"You keep her on her feet too long, and there'll be hell to pay," Terri threatened.

"I wouldn't dream of it."

I was becoming reacquainted with the man I'd loved for the past four years. I'd learned a lot about love and its risks, which was why I listened less to the music and more to Santou's heartbeat as we danced, letting go of a little more control.

I'd been given a few weeks of leave until the dust settled at work. A firestorm had erupted over why a Fish and Wildlife agent had become so entangled in an FBI case. Territories were being marked and lines drawn as to who deserved credit—along with who wasn't getting it.

The FBI had successfully forced Galinov into naming the ringleaders behind the white slave ring. The good news was he had agreed to help catch the men; the bad news was that he'd receive a minimal sentence in return. Meanwhile, Fish and Wildlife had drawn up indictments against a number of U.S. companies incriminated in the caviar scam. As a result, the pipeline was shut down for now, and all paddlefishing temporarily prohibited. The hope was that the species would be given enough time to rebound.

One person who wouldn't be getting any brownie points was Special Agent Ed Tolliver. It appeared my hunch had been correct. He'd demanded that Santou and Hickok hold off on coming to my aid, refusing to bring an end to the operation. Hickok had resolved the

problem by knocking Tolliver out, after which Santou
had handcuffed him to the car's steering wheel. It
seemed a safe bet that Tolliver's next assignment
would be in an even less desirable location than any of
my own had been.

As for Virgil, he was back in jail where he belonged, while evidence was gathered against him on
the two murder charges.

The Velvet Kitty had also been closed, and immi-
gration hearings were scheduled for the women who'd
been held there against their will. But hundreds more
were still lost in the netherworld of the underground
trade, their passports filed in a dusty drawer, their
shadow lives their own living death certificates. Fortunately, Tatyana and Galya weren't among them.

"Tatyana has the makings of a top-notch female
wrestler," Vincent had reported. "Not only is the
woman gorgeous, but she's strong as a bull. She's
been working at the gym and beating the hell out of
some of my students. A talent scout asked if he could
drop by and check her out. Personally, I think she's
going to be a big TV star."

Tatyana and Galya, along with Zouzou, had moved
into Vincent's building rent-free. The agreement was
that he would groom Tatyana for a shot at wrestling
stardom; in return, he would be her manager. Galya
was now in school, while Zouzou spent her days with
Terri and me.

"Just remember: your rear-end is mine in another
two weeks," Hickok had said when he'd last called.
"So don't get any funny ideas about leaving the Service."

There was little fear of that. I was addicted for life. Charlie had made sure I didn't lose my job by doing what he loved best—fighting the agency bureaucrats and telling them all to take a flying leap.

"You did the right thing, Bronx—rules or no rules. We did a number on Sergei's ass fair and square. What else do the head honchos want?"

I didn't know. But I felt sure I'd find out.

All thoughts of work dissolved as Santou pulled me closer.

"So what do you say, chère? Should we pick up where we left off?"

I closed my eyes and went with the flow. I knew Jake was questioning whether we should try living together again.

"Let's just take it day by day for now," I replied, already mentally rearranging my closets to accommodate the man.

It was as if Santou could read my mind. His hand caressed my back, sending ripples of delight through me as Gena ended her song.

A good man is handy during the day. But for rocking my nights, I'll take a bad man every time.

The last note of the blues guitar hung suspended in the air, its sting slowly blending into the delta night.

The Joanna Brady Mysteries by
New York Times Bestselling Author

An assassin's bullet shattered Joanna Brady's world, leaving her policeman husband to die in the Arizona desert. But the young widow fought back the only way she knew how: by bringing the killers to justice . . . and winning herself a job as Cochise County Sheriff.

DESERT HEAT
0-380-76545-4/$6.99 US/$9.99 Can

TOMBSTONE COURAGE
0-380-76546-2/$6.99 US/$9.99 Can

SHOOT/DON'T SHOOT
0-380-76548-9/$6.50 US/$8.50 Can

DEAD TO RIGHTS
0-380-72432-4/$6.99 US/$8.99 Can

SKELETON CANYON
0-380-72433-2/$6.99 US/$8.99 Can

RATTLESNAKE CROSSING
0-380-79247-8/$6.99 US/$8.99 Can

OUTLAW MOUNTAIN
0-380-79248-6/$6.99 US/$9.99 Can

And in Hardcover

DEVIL'S CLAW
0-380-97501-7/$24.00 US/$36.50 Can